I've travelled the world twice over,
Met the famous: saints and sinners,
Poets and artists, kings and queens,
Old stars and hopeful beginners,
I've been where no-one's been before,
Learned secrets from writers and cooks
All with one library ticket
To the wonderful world of books.

© Janice James.

The wisdom of the ages
Is there for you and me,
The wisdom of the ages,
In your local library

There's large print books
And talking books,
For those who cannot see,
The wisdom of the ages,
It's fantastic, and it's free.

Written by Sam Wood, aged 92

PINKMOUNT DRIVE

Twelve years ago, moving into the splendid new houses of Pinkmount Drive, they had thought the good times would go on forever. Then came the recession that would take its toll on all their lives. Jobless, devastated, Arthur Blaney left his wife and went in search of his first love; Mavis Higgison could not believe the days of lavish spending were over; Ginnie Carter brooded over a divorced husband who had put her off men. Meanwhile, the Macreevys coped with retirement, and the racy Radcots took one risk too many.

Books by Jan Webster
Published by The House of Ulverscroft:

COLLIERS ROW
SATURDAY CITY
BEGGARMAN'S COUNTRY
DUE SOUTH
MUCKLE ANNIE
ONE LITTLE ROOM
A DIFFERENT WOMAN
I ONLY CAN DANCE WITH YOU
BLUEBELL BLUE
ABERCOMBIE'S AUNT AND
OTHER STORIES
LOWLAND REELS
TALLIE'S WAR
MAKALIENSKI'S BONES

JAN WEBSTER

PINKMOUNT DRIVE

Complete and Unabridged

ULVERSCROFT
Leicester

First published in Great Britain in 1996 by
Robert Hale Limited
London

First Large Print Edition
published 1997
by arrangement with
Robet Hale Limited
London

British Library CIP Data

Webster, Jan, *1924 –*
Pinkmount Drive.—Large print ed.—
Ulverscroft large print series: general fiction
1. English fiction—20th century
2. Large type books
I. Title
823.9′14 [F]

ISBN 0–7089–3729–2

Published by
F. A. Thorpe (Publishing) Ltd.
Anstey, Leicestershire
Set by Words & Graphics Ltd.
Anstey, Leicestershire
Printed and bound in Great Britain by
T. J. Press (Padstow) Ltd., Padstow, Cornwall

This book is printed on acid-free paper

1

SOME of the neighbours in Pinkmount Drive saw or heard Arthur Blaney come home that day. Ginnie Carter thought his face looked uncommonly haggard and remarked as much to her mother and Nipper, their Jack Russell terrier. As her mother, Gracie, blanketed in her chair by the fire, was in the Land of Nod, where she spent most of her time nowadays, Ginnie directed most of her speech towards Nipper, who was himself very old and barely able to steer himself on stiff, arthritic legs. He was, however, incurably nosy and dragged himself to the picture window to gaze out as his mistress was doing.

"Something's up," said Ginnie. "He's never home this early." Nipper yapped in agreement. Gracie, grasping at a dream in which her own mother was alive, stirred and made small questioning noises. Her old hands moved restlessly and knocked the local paper from her lap. Ginnie picked it up and tsk-ed. She was often very impatient these days. Since losing the shop.

★ ★ ★

Bernard and Mavis Higgison were tackling the pyracantha along their front wall. A shame to cut it while its berries were so bright but shrubs getting out of hand worried them. Anything getting out of hand. The sound of Mavis's high, almost childish voice niggling at her husband to take off a bit more, yes, more *here*, and here, reached Arthur as he closed the garage door. Mavis waved to him but he didn't respond.

"What's up with him?" Mavis asked Bernard.

"Moody bugger," he responded, savaging a woody branch. It was surprising how often Bernard felt aggressive. It stemmed from being so much with Mavis. You didn't need to be a Dr Anthony Clare to see that. Cheek by jowl they'd been, since The Closure. Mavis pointed out reasonably enough that she wasn't responsible for the fact that the

2

nuclear plant was finished (for better or for worse) but there was always the merest tantalizing hint that somehow *he* was. Better to bite his tongue. Otherwise Mavis had the modern equivalent of the vapours, ranging from no feelings in her fingers to noises in her ears. Bernard had come to know the game wasn't worth the candle.

★ ★ ★

Helen Macreevy heard the familiar car engine and door-closing. She was trying not to eat between meals. She took a bite out of a chocolate mallow. After that she finished it and ate another. To wash away the taste of chocolate she made a cup of tea.

★ ★ ★

Judy Radcot was trying to get her husband to go to bed with her in the middle of the afternoon. As she drew the bedroom curtains she saw Mavis wave and Arthur ignore her. Judy gave a little smile. In her heyday, there had been no

3

stopping Mavis. She'd patronized Judy and Frank, the newcomers — no doubt as she saw them, the *nouveau riche* — like mad. Wait till she heard she and Frank were going to Florida soon to buy a second home there. Frank didn't know this yet. It was the purpose of getting him to bed now. Meantime, serve old Mavis right . . .

* * *

In the bungalow, Dougie Walker spoke to the wife who was no longer there. All outside noises came to him like reverberations from outer space.

* * *

At first Arthur Blaney reflected it had been like having the top of your head taken off and your stomach stirred with a red-hot poker. Now it was duller. It was remembering every single time his father had told him he was useless. That thin street back in Lanarkshire. His mother cutting his hair. His socks that never fitted at the heel. Running messages to get enough for the pictures. But for his grannie, the only one with a soft knee and a listening ear. She'd dipped into her purse for him, told him he'd make it if he tried hard enough.

Sylvia said, "I won't like being poor."

"My grannie was poor all her days. It didn't stop her having dignity."

"What has your grannie got to do with it? What if we lose the house?"

He looked at her dully.

"It'll not come to that." But he knew it might. And she'd furnished it, bit by bit in her immaculate, tasteful way, putting heart and soul into the choice of the spare room wallpaper; knowing where to go for the different, the classy, the remarkable. She'd educated him in the finer points of domestic life and by God, he'd needed it.

When she began to weep in a careless, silent way, he went out. Tears never had any effect on him. He'd seen enough women's tears, growing up with a father like his.

★ ★ ★

On the golf course the mist had come down suddenly and the old geezers who had nothing better to do than punt a ball about loomed through the white blur like Leviathans. Bertie Macreevy pushed his trolley in front of him and gave the younger man a sympathetic look.

"It were always on the cards. Plenty's been laid off round here. Tha' must ha' known."

"Doesn't make it any easier."

"Tha'll get a fair sum in redundancy."

He couldn't satisfy his old friend's curiosity about how much. But they'd all be able to make a fair guess. It would be all round the club. It was less than they would think it was and it would soon go. There were the payments on Sylvia's car, the new carpets, the club fees. He felt unutterably tired, beyond speech.

"There was this chap in the *Daily Telegraph*, said unemployment is hitting hardest at the middle class. Structural unemployment, that's what they call it. Downwardly mobile is what the middle class is, them days. You got architects," Bertie droned on, "doing filing clerk's

6

work and barristers and the like doing the telephone selling. This chap was saying, the more qualifications you have these days the harder it is to find a job. Not that I'm trying to depress you, old son. You'll think of something."

★ ★ ★

Arthur didn't want to think of something. He wanted back to the womb that was the firm, where he'd gone as a shaver and stayed till now, and he'd thought that was it. He'd been good at his job, had a natural feel for machine tools and engineering, had brought in millions of orders in his time. He hadn't let them down. They'd let him down. At least the government had. The manufacturing base on which the country's wealth depended had shrunk and shrunk like Alice on the bottle. He could hear old Bertie going on about members of social class A driving London taxis, doing 'the knowledge'. The old boy mercifully disappeared behind a tree to relieve himself and Arthur didn't wait for him, walked on into the mist, past the club house, his clubs thumping his legs. Redundant was something that happened to somebody else. Oh, Christ, save me. Tell me who I am without a job.

What if he ended up like the old tramp who haunted the bus station? He was glad of the autumn mist. A good metaphor for his mood. He hadn't even known the word metaphor till he met Sylvia. What if he ended up in a model lodging-house, as his dad had after his mother threw him out? Sylvia wouldn't let that happen, would she? But her sense of what was right, what to say, what to wear, how to live so that you impressed the rest, would be of no use to them in the new situation. He'd always provided the wherewithal, the dosh. She'd done the rest and he'd loved her for it. Loved his cocoon. Heard ancestral voices praising him for getting there, for presiding over the Rotary away from the morass of parish handouts, livid drinking bouts, scornful faces.

There were beggars on the streets again, all right, but he had thought Pinkmount Drive was well away from all that. Yet as he came round the corner

8

from the golf course and the sun came out, chasing away the mist, dismissing it as early and irrelevant, he saw the street where he lived, hypnagogically, curving up that green hillside, as though it was somehow hanging on. Here and there gardens unattended, lawns uncut, that shaggy look houses got as well as people when things weren't going quite right. The recession look. He staggered a little, not just from the weight of his clubs.

They had all been at the peak of their earning powers when they'd moved in twelve years ago. Able to enjoy flash cars, good clothes, meals out and the holidays and hobbies of their choice.

They were not a million miles from either Manchester or Liverpool but went there more and more rarely. Sylvia said the culture there was gross, nothing but brutal plays about the disaffected and piles of bricks or driftwood masquerading as art. If she saw another TV play or film drama about a cute and doughty Scouse housewife she would consider emigration, Sylvia said.

The women of Pinkmount Drive preferred to shop in the boutiques of nearby Wilhowbry where there were also superstores with chill cabinets which met their every food need and then it was back to the Drive which swooped and soared in the low hills outside the town. Thus had the middle class laid down the pattern of stability and habit which gave cohesion to the nation and something for the lower classes to aspire to and Thatcher's Children did for the twentieth century what the cotton and railway barons had done for the nineteenth. Only now it was fresh Cheshire brick, Palladian columns, the South Fork ranch look; Cheshire flash some called it, instead of the plonking great villas erected by the Victorians.

He didn't want it to end. He didn't want to retrain, start his own little business or drive a taxi. He wanted it all exactly as it had been since he'd married Sylvia and life had taken on its comfortable rhythms, golf and tennis in the summer, dinner parties, charity balls, whist drives and language classes in the winter. Houses painted every four years, lawns fed and cut, flowers and shrubs tended and you gave what you could — well, maybe a little less than that, but something — to the orphans in Romania, in Rwanda, in Cambodia.

I am not a hard-hearted man, he told himself, but now he thought he might have been and that he might have done more, felt more. If he'd had the time.

He let himself in at the tradesman's entrance, not knowing why he did this yet feeling this new, sapping lack of self worth. Who was that cartoon character he kept seeing on the telly, a little stick man in free fall? Him, wasn't it?

2

GRACIE knocked the custard off her lap tray and her slippered feet puddled in the yellow goo. Ginnie Carter cleaned up the mess. First the carpet, then her mother. She wondered what would happen to her if she struck Gracie. Or shook her. But she tidied up the inglorious stickiness and then walked out of the back door, leaving it open, and through the little picket gate at the end of the garden and into the wood. What had happened to her? She had meant to get a life. She'd told Gracie she wouldn't put her into a home. It was partly selfish, for she feared being on her own. Had she really owned one of the smartest dress shops in Wilhowbry, the cubicles scented with Chanel No. 5, the Porsches dropping showbiz and the crude fruits of entrepreneurial efforts at her door? But that sound? Was it her own sobbing? And she'd come out with her pinny on. She retraced her steps, back through the gate, back through the door. Her mother had tried to get up and had fallen. Nipper was licking her face. Ginnie lifted the frail but surprisingly heavy old body and put it back on the chair by the fire. Gracie moaned.

"It's all right, Ma." But it wasn't. Any longer. She couldn't go on with this, forever changing, washing, trying to keep the smell of bodily functions at bay. Aching. Angry. Gracie gave her a look that was suddenly fully aware and conveyed some kind of appalled pity at her daughter's plight as opposed to her own. Ginnie phoned the social worker. Then she switched on the television and made some tea and waited, thinking she could never be forgiven.

The first week the old lady went into The Chase, Ginnie luxuriated in scented baths, phoned her friends to justify her actions. "You've been a saint" they told her. "Nobody could have done more." Gracie had a high bed and a special friend in the communal day-room. But Ginnie knew the indignities, the nurses who heaved her mother out of her wet nightgowns less than ceremoniously, speaking to her as if she had left the species. But then so had she. As though the only option to a brute response was an exaggerated show of scrupulous practicality and silly baby-talk.

After the first couple of weeks, she stopped meeting her friends for coffee. Stopped the extravagances of new clothes and make-up, reverting to the dun skirts and jumpers she'd worn when caring for her mother and impatient for her visits to The Chase.

★ ★ ★

When Sylvia Blaney came to her door, bearing a pot plant for her to take to Gracie, she was abashed. But Sylvia's pale look and hesitant demeanour jerked her out of self-absorption.

As neighbours, they had always got on rather well in an arm's-length kind of way. Now, to cover up for Ginnie's discomfiture at the untidiness of her sitting-room, Sylvia launched into confidential mode.

"I don't know what to do with Arthur."

14

"I like Arthur. Arthur's lovely. He always managed to give Mother a wave. More than some."

"But Ginnie, he's shattered. Up the creek without a paddle. He wants to go back to Scotland to see his grannie's grave. He never went to see her when she was alive!"

"At least you've got him. Got somebody."

"I know. 'For better or for worse'. But I didn't expect to have him for lunch as well. He wants me to give everything up, change my schedule, my dramatic society, my poetry class, my French. You know he would never let me have a proper job, just the temping to keep my hand in. He needed a lot of backing up when he was working. Everything had to be right for Arthur. Meals. House. Car. I gave in to him all along the line."

She felt about a bit uselessly for a hankie. Ginnie handed her a paper one and said, "I know in a way how he's feeling. Probably very lost."

"How is going to Scotland going to help him? He knows I won't live there. Our life is here. He could turn out the shed. Tidy the garage." She smiled

15

faintly through her tears, knowing how absurd it really sounded. "He's got to face up to things."

"These are hard times," said Ginnie, delicately trying to bring the conversation round to include her own situation.

Sylvia wasn't listening. She pulled at strands of her hair, plucked at her skirt. "Look at me. I'm going to the dogs."

"You've got great legs," said Ginnie upbraidingly. "You could wear short skirts. You don't know how lucky you are. With your skin you could take beige, biscuit, cream. With soft pastel accessories." She laughed ruefully. "I still run a fashion shop. Up here." She pointed to her head.

"Couldn't you start again?"

"After going bankrupt?"

"Your mother asked a lot of you, Ginnie. Even when she was well."

Sylvia was right, of course. Mummy had asked a lot of her. She had started to think of her as Mummy again, not Mother, now she no longer had to get out of bed half a dozen times a night or go round the sitting-room with an aerosol. Mummy hadn't wanted her to marry Sydney and it had been crucial when he'd taken off for London and she had decided not to follow immediately, because Mummy had not long lost Daddy and Evelyn her younger sister had just flown the nest. "Don't let her catch you up in her web," Evelyn had pleaded, but Ginnie had never seen it like that. She'd quite enjoyed being the praised and dutiful daughter, flaunted around the summer resorts and the winter bridge sessions and supported through the acrimonious divorce when Sydney had found that doe-eyed bimbo in Finchley. Model, indeed! But now she had time to think she saw part of her had not really been very grown-up. Not really. She had not liked Sydney's enthusiastic attitude to sex but when he'd gone she'd hankered wanly after someone who would be kind and undemanding and sheltering. Why had she been like that? Unable to stand up for herself? That little voice you couldn't hear behind a bus ticket? Why had she not put her hand up at school when she knew the answers as much as the next one? 'Diffident,' her mother had said, shaking her head. "Don't be so diffident, darling." What was she going to do now? Failed marriage, failed business, her mother cared for by strangers. She got out old silk trimmings and obsessively made them over into roses, harebells, buttercups to applique on to dresses when she reopened some new mythical dress shop. Isn't that what women had done in the villages round here in the old days? Made garters and buttons and flowers? She ate some cornflakes for her lunch and washed the grapes to take in to Mummy.

Nipper went into the bathroom to look for Gracie. There were towels there that bore her scent. Ginnie went off somewhere each day without him and he was sure it was to see his mistress for when she returned there was the old smell and sometimes he got quite excited.

He slept a lot, chasing rabbits in his dreams, but when it came to eating, the same old tinned stuff he'd always liked, he couldn't get up the energy. He drank a little, mainly to please Ginnie and panted a lot. She took him again to the vet and he felt something, down there, and said the old boy wouldn't stand the operation, did Ginnie not think it was time for — you know? Nipper didn't know why she got so sad and quiet in the car afterwards. He licked her hand, flicking his tail, almost a wag. "You miss Mummy, don't you?" Ginnie said. He showed the white of his eyes. His breath was rancorous. "Poor old boy."

* * *

"She looks distraught," said Dougie Walker to his late wife's photograph. "Do you think I should go and talk to her, Connie? She's just standing by the gate. I don't think she's combed her hair."

The thing about Connie's picture was that it always acquiesced in anything he suggested. He went out, pulling on his pullover, thinking it was a good job his ex-pupils didn't know how careless he'd become about his personal appearance and diffidently approached Ginnie.

"Something up, my dear? Can I help?"

She gestured towards the house, opening the gate for him. In the kitchen, in his basket, lay the little dog, stiff as a board.

"I don't know what to do with him. How shall I tell Mummy? She won't take it in."

"He was very old."

"The vet told me he'd go in his sleep. He wouldn't eat, you know."

He knew he had to calm her down. He took her by the hands and led her to a chair. "I'll put the kettle on, eh?"

She said to the back of his head, "How did you cope?"

"Still coping." He didn't turn round. "Where's the tea?" She pointed. "Day at a time," he said. "All you can do. Tell me where your spade is. I'll bury him."

He was beginning to take in that she hadn't cleaned the stove and dishes were piling up by the sink side. The floor looked dingy (how Connie would have tut-tutted) and a grubby dish-cloth hung limply from a plastic arm.

He felt the wish to get involved stir briefly in him then subside. His legs felt boneless and weak, like after a fever.

"How do you clean windows?" he demanded. "I've been meaning to do

20

mine. Connie used to buy stuff."

She felt in a cupboard, brought out a spray bottle, handed it to him. He turned it over between his hands. "Are you going to be OK now?"

"When will you do it? Bury him?"

"After lunch. Just show me where you want it."

"Thanks. Thanks for coming."

"Try not to cry."

3

THE train.
He'd intended taking the BMW but Sylvia had argued her Astra needed the clutch fixed. Arthur knew she wanted to use the big car to put a face on things. They'd argued in a cold, passionless way and he'd given in. It was a long time since he'd travelled by train. The youth opposite was squirming about in time to his Walkman. Did he know how stupid he looked?

He just hadn't listened to her. What he'd been, what he'd done for the last fifteen years or so just didn't seem relevant any more. Relevant was Scotland. Relevant was his roots. Visiting his grandmother's grave. He hadn't been able to go to the funeral, four months ago, he'd been in Honkers. She hadn't gone up. She was in denial about all that side of the family. He didn't know about Sylvia, he really didn't know at all. For fifteen years he'd approved of

22

everything about her, her elegance, her laugh, her dinners. He'd been able to take her anywhere, bring anybody home, he'd shown her off, never minded when those wonderful legs of hers were admired, she was his, wasn't she, and the knowledge had sent a shiver of delicious comforting smugness along his veins. Now? Now it was a bit like looking in a great sweetie shop window with nothing when you went inside. The sex grudging. The face oddly passive. Everything presented from her point of view, what she would have to give up. Resentment because she hadn't had the guts to stand up for a career of her own. She'd wanted to be an actress: taken courses. He wouldn't be blamed. Not now. Not now when everything was so grey and indeterminate. She could have come with him. Shown willing. "Why do you have to go? Why now?" He didn't know. He wanted some place where he could feel secure, at home, belong. "Home was the place that when you went there, they had to let you in." She could have humoured him.

He wasn't easy about going away but there was a sense of compulsion behind it. Once or twice she'd looked like the vulnerable easily moved girl he had married. As though he'd taken away some kind of treat. "Look at you. I don't like you in a track suit. You look like somebody off a picket-line." Was she hinting he'd reverted to working class? That was well below the belt. "What should I make you think of?" "Business. I like you in a dark suit."

Way to look at it, he was entitled to a break. It was no good constantly trying to see some way forward when answer came there none. That was what was driving him half-insane, getting him up in the morning before the birds, making him shout at her. He didn't like to see her quiver. He couldn't bear to let her down. So. The train shook over the points, the Sony Walkman next to him crackled faintly, a child opposite gave him a sickly grin, its mouth smeared with chocolate from a bun.

★ ★ ★

Wee grey town. What had he thought it would offer up? At least it had one or two

24

hotels now, catering for reps and the odd returning son like himself. In the main street the butcher still sold big steak pies in ashets, the baker had snowballs, pineapple cakes. Returnees took them like trophies back over the border.

Elmlea Private Hotel had a blue carpet in a restrained pattern, glittering ornaments and shiny bannisters but stingy with the soap and towels. He thought they probably measured the meal portions with a ruler. From the landlady's tight shoulders he guessed that times were hard here too. He didn't want to hang around indoors anyhow. He saw his grandmother's grave alongside the older ones of his parents. *Agnes Mary Harding, aged 87. 'Til the day break and the shadows flee.'* Aye, what then?

He sat on the iron bench with its blistered green paint and the old woman reiterated in his mind what she had brought him here for: go and see Ida. *What for?* he argued back. *What for?* She answered *You know*. And as he'd done as a child he replied *No, I don't* and it didn't sound convincing now either.

Jesus, he was down to the nitty-gritty

now. Supposing she'd had the bairn? No, she'd told him she was getting rid of it but supposing . . . Women changed their minds. He might be a daddy. Sylvia had not been able to have a child. That had been that. But supposing he were a daddy. The kid would be sixteen, no, seventeen now. Ida would have married, in any case. Moved away. They had been two raw bairns. He had never meant . . . It had been his gormlessness that had enraged Ida's mother, made her refuse to negotiate with him. That, and the fact that he was 'off the Blaneys', with a father like his, not that Ida's family were saints.

The wind whipped papers and cans at a fast clip along the street in the housing estate. The Grove. There was more than irony there, a bitter jibing edge that was pure Billy Connolly. An ice-cream van jangled a worn-out tune and irrepressible black and tan mongrels waited for toddlers to show a moment's disregard so they could snatch their cornets.

"The Grants?" The woman in the paper shop was writing numbers on the evening papers. "The old woman's dead these past four years. Oh, aye, Ida's still there. Ida and Tracy-Lee."

"How old is Tracy-Lee?"

"She would be about seventeen I would say."

Heart — stop.

★ ★ ★

He didn't have the bottle after all. Not to go and ring the doorbell. After two whiskies he retired to his bedroom in Elmlea. Looked at himself in the mirror with the pink and blue plaster flower frame. This very honest-looking face gazing back at him. Sylvia always said he had a look of total integrity; that's what had made him a good salesman. The eyes were very blue and steady. A man whose word you could trust. But he'd dived out of responsibility all those years ago, hadn't he? Left that poor lassie. Well, he was going to dive out of it again.

A last stroll along The Grove, half-trembling from a new, jarring consciousness of what he was about. All these years, working like a Trojan, but at base nothing but a welsher and his mother had been right, he'd turned out like his dad, he let people down.

"You all right?"

He hadn't been looking where he was going and had bumped into the young woman, the only other person in the street. These housing scheme streets were like deserts. No one around.

"So sorry, sorry," he apologized.

"It's all right. I get lost in a dream myself sometimes." She was laughing, fair, full-bosomed. Nice. Blue-eyed. God, the face was as familiar as his own. It *was* his own.

"You're Tracy-Lee, aren't you?"

"How would you know my name?"

He looked down. He couldn't explain. He was having difficulty breathing, thinking, functioning. His legs actually shook.

"I'm a friend of your mother's," he said. "Could you take me to her?"

★ ★ ★

The doorbell went in Pinkmount Drive as Sylvia was finishing her morning coffee.

He was six foot, smiling, slender. Trainers and a bomber jacket. Shock of dark, untidy hair. She knew him. Just. Bernard and Mavis's maverick son, the one who'd gone to university and done well there but so far hadn't made his pile. He gave her a sheepish, apologetic smile.

"Have they left a key with you? They did know I was coming, but not exactly when."

"They always go to Sainsbury's on a Thursday. For the weekly shop."

"Oh, sure. *Do* you have their key?"

"I'm sorry." Pause. "But come in. Have a coffee. They shouldn't be long."

Bouncing in on his long, ever-so-slightly bowed legs. Full of nervous energy. The smile flashing. The eyes taking everything in. He was some kind of journalist and freelance film-maker. His dad had wanted him to follow him into finance. No way. She warmed to him. They were two of a kind. Creative sorts. Well, she wanted to be creative but hadn't yet found her metier. With Arthur away, out of her life for the first time in nearly fifteen years she had been thinking about her spiritual core. Reading poetry. Why not?

"You haven't seen your parents for a while?" Mavis had been evasive. Once Conrad had been her sole topic of conversation.

"No. Well, you know how it is."

"Do I?" she challenged, offering him a *café noir* biscuit. "I don't have offspring."

"What do you do with yourself?"

"I keep busy."

"Looking after your husband? How is the man himself?"

"Out of work."

"Another?" He gave her a look of concentrated concern. The rest had been banter. "You do know we're in the middle of a bigger revolution than the industrial one? You do know there are going to be millions who won't work, in the sense they have always known it, ever again? You do know the rug's been pulled from under us? By us, I mean my parents, me, the middle managers, the professionals?"

"Maybe it's for a reason. That we can learn to be like the lilies. Spinning not."

"What does your husband think?"

"He's gone back to Scotland to touch base. I don't know why. I don't understand. But that's what he's done."

"Left you to sort yourself out?"

"I could have gone with him."

"But you chose not to? That's quite brave."

"We're not joined at the hip."

"No. But to see when another person needs space . . . that's something. My last attachment couldn't see that. That's why we split up."

"I'm sorry."

"Don't be." He gave her a grateful look. "You're easier to talk to than my mother."

Just then, Mavis and Bernard returned laden with their shopping from Sainsbury's. They could see them through the trees, taking the plastic carrier bags from the boot of the car in orderly fashion.

Conrad sighed and rose. Sylvia thought she saw a kind of filial terror on his face. "Best be going," he said.

4

"SO it must have been a great shock, to you and your wife both ... when you got made redundant."

Arthur couldn't believe it was happening. That he was sitting here, in the living-room of Ida's house in The Grove, talking to her so easily. Feeling comfortable — no, more than that, alive, accepted, himself, for the first time since Andrew Carpenter had called him into the boardroom and polished him off with the anguished phrase he kept hearing in his dreams — "It's over."

"Well, you know, I guess we had a kind of charmed life, to be honest. Maybe we had too much. But it's a hard thing to live with, everything turned upside down and not knowing where to turn next. I'm not saying that in the general scheme of things we haven't been lucky. Just that it's still hard to deal with not being wanted any more.

32

On the scrapheap. *Finito.*" He could feel the tears rise up behind his throat and he hadn't shed one single tear up till now. The girl they called Tracy-Lee was watching him carefully from the settee she shared with her mother. He addressed her ruefully. "You must think me a bit of a right wally," he said, blowing his nose. Ida said easily, "Greet if you want to." (When had he heard that last? 'Greet' for 'cry'. So much more expressive somehow.)

She'd known him at once and he her. She had grown chunky, in the way Scotswomen often did, but she was smart enough in dark leggings and a coral-coloured tunic. Hoop ear-rings (pity, that) and a short, shaggy haircut that gave her face a merry, schoolgirl look. She'd been a daft sort, always ready for any piece of mischief at school. Dipping the end of the single plait of the solemn Mary MacGurtie in the inkwell. Putting a Swizzle sweetie in the test-tube of the irascible Mr French.

He was full of admiration for the way she dealt with his blundering re-entry into her life. First she had paled. Yes, she'd certainly paled. Then she had brought him in — dragged him in really — and sat him down in the tidy, scuffed room. Ineffably cheap prints on the walls. A fan from Spain. Then she'd said to Tracy-Lee, "Look at his face. You know who he is, don't you?" And Tracy-Lee had said, sounding almost unconcerned, "Yes. It's my dad," and then there had been a flurry of tea-making and questioning. Yes, Ida's mother had died four years ago. No, she had not married anyone. Yes, there was somebody. Just somebody. Yes, she had a job. In a do-it-yourself place. Not bad pay. She'd been twice made redundant herself. And Tracy-Lee was looking for something at the moment. So yes, they had come round to Tracy-Lee. He could not keep his eyes off her. Her accent was very broad. He would have made sure she had more schooling, maybe elocution. She had her mother's wayward thick hair, but it was the same colour as his and the eyes, they were the giveaway, like the pink complexion, the straight nose. Pure Blaney. Pure him.

"You see" — he spread his hands

towards the girl — "I didn't even know if your mother had had you. A big iron curtain came down between the two mothers — you'll agree, Ida, they were a pair of tough cookies, to say the least — and Ida, here, your mother, just disappeared from sight."

"I stayed with my Auntie Maggie in Ayr."

"So where did *you* go, then?" There it was, the first note of truculent hurt.

"I was *persona non grata* around the place. I just headed south. It was a toss-up between Manchester and London and Manchester was nearer."

"Is she nice?" demanded Ida. "I've often thought about you and who you would eventually marry."

"She's a very competent woman."

"That's not very complimentary," said Tracy-Lee unexpectedly.

"Why not? Competent means she's a good housekeeper, an excellent cook, a good dresser."

"But — "

"But what?" Ida interrupted her daughter sharply. "What's turned you into the Grand Inquisitor?"

"I'm only asking."

"She's entitled to," he said.

"Have you any children?"

"No. It never happened."

"So I'm your only child?"

"Yup."

"There's no denying her," said Ida, looking from one face to the other.

"I would never do that," he said softly.

★ ★ ★

"When are you coming back?" Sylvia demanded.

"In a day or two. The weather's nice. I thought I would take a run down to the West Coast. Largs maybe. Are you all right?"

"Of course I'm all right."

"Having the neighbours in for coffee? If you get lonesome."

"Don't be wet. We've got the Alan Ayckbourn coming up at the Amdram. They're casting Friday."

"You want to keep it up?"

"Arthur," she said patiently, "it's more important than ever to have our interests.

Our separate interests."

"Right," he said, on a harder note. "I'll ring you again, Friday. Keep you in the picture."

★ ★ ★

What he hadn't said, what he couldn't say, was that Ida and Tracy-Lee were going to accompany him. Ida had said she had a few days' holiday leave due her, she might as well take it and Tracy-Lee had not had any kind of break this year, she hadn't been able to afford it. This was on him, he'd said, and Ida had said No. They'd book into a decent small place, with a double room for Ida and the girl. He and Ida were desperate to rationalize it, the first opportunity they had had to be on their own, while Tracy-Lee went for a boat trip.

"I don't see why I should have any hard feelings," said Ida, tucking into a sundae in the resplendent Largs cafeteria. "You were as much hard done by as I was. Our mothers thought they had the power of life and death over us and certainly in my case the power to decide who I would marry. They never let us grow up, Arthur."

He said, with a painful access of conscience, "You brought her up on your own."

"Well, my mother helped. She was an easy child. No trouble. Wouldn't work hard enough at school, but she's clever — she can knit anything, my mother taught her Fair Isle, all that, and she makes her own clothes."

"What has she worked at?"

"This and that. Hairdressing. Florist. Shelf-filling. I wish she'd had more training, but she couldn't wait to leave school. She sees the error of it now."

"Has she got a boy-friend?"

"She's flirted around. Nothing serious. She doesn't meet the right sort. I've tended to hem her in. I'm scared for her — drugs and all that."

"And you?"

Ida suddenly became animated, her face lighting up. She reached for the small metal case in which she kept the few cigarettes she was trying not to smoke and extracted one with a shaky sort of pleasure.

"I'm happy to tell you I've found him. The right man. His name is Norman. No, really. We've been going around for the past six years." She looked at him, almost as though she expected him to protest, almost as though he had prior claim to her and he did feel it, a stab of jealousy, none the less sharp for being irrelevant.

"What does he do?"

"He's an airline steward, Arthur. He wants me to go and live in Miami with him." She gave him a penetrating look and again said, "No, really."

"Do you want to go?"

"Do birds want to fly!"

"But?"

"But there's Tracy-Lee."

"I can take some responsibility for her now. I want to help her."

"You can't just land a full-grown daughter on your wife. I know I wouldn't go for it if I was in her shoes."

"I could say she was my niece." Where had that piece of chicanery come from?

"Are you saying that she could come and live with you? Oh, no, Arthur, I don't want to break up your marriage at this stage."

"Well, I could keep an eye on her."

Ida gave him that direct, straightforward look that had always endeared her to him. That still endeared her to him. He hadn't been wrong about her all those years ago.

"She and I have been close, you see. Because of the way things were. So I don't know if I can go away and leave her. And she says she'll not come with us."

"I admire her for that. She knows life is about standing on your own two feet, Ida."

"Maybe." Regretfully she exhaled her last puff of cigarette smoke. "If only life was always what it's supposed to be. Still, it's funny you turning up at this very moment."

★ ★ ★

The girl with his face was touching his arm, at first it seemed accidentally and then she put her hand through the loop of elbow and hung on to him. They

40

faced the Largs wind and rain on the Esplanade, Ida back in the hotel with a magazine and a pot of tea.

"I'm not going to let you go. Not now we've found each other. Don't get that look on your face. I don't think what you did was bad. Even if it was, I would forgive you, because you're my dad. You can't believe how great it is to be able to say that."

How did she get to be such a nice normal kid? No axes to grind.

"Did you think about what I might be like, sometimes?"

"My mum's got this one photo of you. You're wearing loons and your hair's long. You can't tell very much from it but I used to stare and stare at it, trying to make you come alive."

"I'll try and make things up to you somehow, Tracy-Lee."

"You don't need to try. Just be."

5

PINKMOUNT DRIVE was hazed in the gold of autumn sunlight. It was a spectacular late October, the trees every shade from crimson to a translucent pale yellow. A stranger passing might have been lured into the conviction that all was fine with these well-set-up domiciles, that here the complexities of modern life had been sorted out and dealt with in a satisfactory manner.

The heavy glass door of the Higgison residence opened and then closed with a resounding thud and Conrad Higgison walked off down the cobbled drive with an expression that was far from in keeping with the sunny demeanour of the day.

At the white gates he stood undecided then did a quick right turn and walked up the drive of the Blaney house. Sylvia answered his impatient ring and drew him inside.

"Not more trouble at t'mill?"

He came into the spectacular sitting-room with the air of a man who knew his way about — which chair to choose, which question to answer. Sylvia brought him a cup of coffee from the kitchen. Her own face was brooding and her eyes shadowed, but like the room her presentation was faultless. Beautiful repro prints on the stippled walls, perfect eye make-up on the well-moisturized skin. Harmony between the soft blue carpet and the gold and peachy suite and curtains; harmony between her well-cut plaza pants and exquisite crocheted top in a bud-soft green.

"We got in an argument about modern art. I shouldn't rise to the bait, but I do. See, they just shut their minds to it. I wouldn't mind their objections if they were based on anything but ignorance. He thinks men who put dead sheep up for public scrutiny should be flogged; she thinks you should go for photographic accuracy." He gave her a smile of half-humorous resignation. "I was trying to tell them I thought Matisse was the next greatly gifted human being after Shakespeare. They look at me and wonder how they could have produced me, where they went wrong. I'll have to go, Sylvia, before we send each other stark, staring bonkers."

"Come on, it's not as bad as that."

"Oh, believe me, it is. It's worse. They don't think art has any validity at all. They think music stops at Richard Strauss and books should be about mountaineering and how to grow a better begonia."

She began to laugh, his face was so woebegone.

"I'm just thinking: Fate can certainly throw some wobblies. Here's you, a mover and shaker if ever I saw one and the practical, down-to-earth Bernard and Mavis have to cope with you. How did they have you in the first place?"

"Dunno. Must be a changeling. I do have one aunt on my mother's side who plays the cello. Why can't Mavis be more like you? I knew whenever I saw you that you were like me. The way you comport yourself, the way you express yourself — "

"I should have been an actress. But I came up against the same kind of constrictions and limitations that you have, people saying 'Who do you think you are?' 'What makes you think you can do it?' It wears you down in the end!"

She was passing his chair to twitch a curtain, awkward and embarrassed somehow that they should be talking about her, about a part of her she seldom revealed to anyone and he caught her hand impulsively, held it, looked up at her in an eloquent, enquiring way. She seemed to freeze, he could feel it, could feel her stubborn, conventional reaction, what he might have expected, but he hung on to her hand, turning it over palm upwards and making a game of it, saying, "What do I see in your hand? Desdemona at the RSC? Ophelia? Lady Macbeth?"

She laughed, relaxing at last. "Bit part in our new local production, more like. Was a time when I could have taken on *Hedda Gabler*. Left it too late to slam that doll's house door, though, didn't I?" She tugged her hand, releasing it and sat down suddenly by the window, as though looking for someone to arrive, her posture strained, her expression almost tearful.

"What's up?" he asked quietly.

"Nothing's up. And if there was, my dear child, why should I tell you?"

"No reason," he admitted. "Except that I'm here, full of goodwill and with time on my hands."

"Shouldn't you be writing? Working on a script or something? Or do you just say that to make yourself appear less idle?"

"Don't you start! My mother is much better at that sort of thing than you. I'm waiting till they go out. I can't work when they're there, somehow."

"More excuses!"

He went silent on her, his dark, good-looking face clouded by introspection.

At last he burst out, "But you've just characterized me as a mover and shaker. I can't be both, mover and idler."

"I meant you were a dreamer. You know the lines, don't you — "'We are the music makers, We are the dreamers of dreams, We are the movers and shakers, Of the world forever it seems.' I don't regard dreaming as unimportant. I don't mistake it for idling. The dreaming has to come before the reality, before the action."

She had grown pink-faced and defensive and he found himself smiling at her in spite of his lingering sense of grievance.

"OK. OK," he conceded. "You get off the hook this time. Just remember." Artists united. "Otherwise we drown in the seas of the petit bourgeoisie." He half got up to go but then said, presenting it as a sort of after-thought, "But you could tell me what's bothering you, if you like."

"Rather not." She sniffed.

"To do with hubby, is it? Being up there in Scotland?"

"Partly."

"After being so brave and letting him go off on his peculiar odyssey?"

"Not brave at all." At last the stiff upper lip gave way. "Worried," she confessed.

"M'mmm?"

"I think he might look up a girl he was in love with before he met me."

"Did he say as much?"

"No. *Of course* not."

"What makes you think it then?"

She walked about the room, working her hands together.

"I just sort of — divined it. You do, when you've been with someone a long time. There was unfinished business, you see — "

"What sort of unfinished business?"

"He'd got her pregnant. She was spirited away and was supposed to have had a termination. I'm not sure he's ever believed that."

"I don't think," he said heavily, "he would do that to you. He'd be a cad and a bounder if he did. Without your consent."

"He's not a cad. He's not a bounder. He's a man who's lost his way since he lost his job."

"You do love him, then?" he demanded, almost in surprise.

"Of course," she said, the tears starting. "Of course I love him." She let out a cry that was more like a moan. "Ahhh — what am I going to do?"

He put his arms about her and offered her his clean top-pocket hankie. He patted her back. Feeling its thinness. "Sylvia, stop it," he commanded. "Come on, dry up. Artists take their suffering and use it, don't they? You've heard of

48

the wound and the bow?"

A half-smile glimmered at him. "Stuff the wound and the bow."

"Nonetheless, you have to be a big brave girl and put these silly fancies from you. He'll be back before you can say Jack Robinson. Things'll knit together. You'll see."

★ ★ ★

"She's a pretentious bitch," said Mavis Higgison "And I'd rather you saw a bit less of her, Con."

"Who else is there to talk to round here? At least she's literate At least she's read a book."

"Books no one else has ever heard of. She's not read Susan Howatch. She's not read any Cookson. Hers have to be translations from the French and out of the last century. *Madame Bovary* she says. Makes modern writers look anaemic It's swank, that's all it is. She talks like that to impress you and the vicar."

"Come on, Mum. Don't put people down. Look how much you know about the garden. The proper Latin names. I think it's phenomenal. Your bit of swank, isn't it?"

"Not in my case!" answered Mavis furiously. "In my case it's totally practical. Gardens matter."

"To you."

"They should to everyone. No, don't turn your back on me like that, when I'm talking to you. Leave Sylvia Blaney alone. I'm sure everyone's talking about the pair of you already. You're round there more than you are in your own home. I won't have it, Conrad. The Higgison reputation has always been smirchless. When your daddy gets round to starting up his new financial consultancy, we don't want gossip tarnishing the gold letters on his door. Hear me?"

He heard. Of course, he heard. It just made him more self-conscious about visiting Sylvia, but in his present limbo, when inspiration was as scarce as hen's teeth, he wasn't going to stop seeing the one person he could talk to about the things that mattered to him.

She let him fly his kites. She didn't think it impossible that one day he would sell an idea for a full-length feature film.

She knew the difference between an art-house movie and a commercial one. She respected a man's integrity.

Also she had a beautiful and mysterious female body, the perfume and aura of maturity about her. Experience and wisdom in her judgements. She'd got there, where younger women he knew were still searching. He liked the feeling of her hand in his. It was warm and crisp. He liked her quick, disarming smile, evanescent as the flash of kingfisher. He liked the way her hair was always soft and fluffed about her face, never lank or dispirited and how she didn't trump him in debate, but listened to him. Really listened.

Jesu, he said, into the darkness of his room at night. I wish I were lying next to her, listening to her breathing, my hands where they never should be.

6

DOUGIE WALKER'S bungalow was, to be honest, a bit of an anachronism in Pinkmount Drive. Its walls were pebble-dash, its garage added on somewhat carelessly at the side and made of something cheap and nasty for economy's sake. Skewed and rakish, like a dowager's hat. One foolish owner in the late seventies had added a porch and truncated Palladian columns. But in actual fact the Drive had been built around it: it had been there before all the rest, built in the thirties and the owner before Dougie Walker had made a small fortune selling off his considerable garden for building plots. Dougie had no time for the petty snobberies of home buying; he had merely seen the view, rolling away across the golf course and Connie had fallen for the apple trees. They'd taken the despised and derided dilapidated bungalow off the estate agent's hands, put their rackety old Triumph in the falling-down garage, ignoring the grander vehicles in other drives, bought chickens and cabbages, and been happy as pigs in muck.

Now he stood looking at the windows he had been trying to clean. From top to bottom they were a smeary mess. So much for the cleaning liquid Ginnie had given him. She came up the cracked asphalt path now, on her way back from The Chase, clucking like one of his Redincote hens.

"Strewth, Dougie, did you make that mess all by yourself or did somebody come in to help you?"

They surveyed the swirling milky whorls, halfway between laughter and disgust. "You should never clean windows with the sun on them," Ginnie admonished. "Here, give it me." She took the liquid and soft cloth and with neat, expert strokes cleaned the lower half of one set of windows. A trim little creature, he thought. A bit like a sparrow. "Don't use too much stuff and finish one pane before you go on to the next," she stipulated. "Go and put the kettle on and I'll do all I can reach."

He brought out folding garden chairs and they sat in the autumn sunshine drinking Dougie's strong brew out of man-size mugs.

"Want a Penguin?" he offered companionably.

She shook her head, looking abstracted.

"How's your mother?"

"She doesn't know me, Dougie." That soft voice. Disappearing like an echo.

"You can't be sure of that. At some level, maybe she does."

She gave him a sceptical look. "She's physically quite strong, they say. I don't know how much longer I can go on, visiting and getting no response."

He said adroitly, knowing more was to come; how she missed Nipper, how sharp and responsive he had been, nearly human; knowing there would be tears and he never could stand them, never knew what to say: "I've got another job I want you to help me with indoors."

"What is it?" Nervously. "I haven't got the time, Dougie — "

"Yes, you have." Gently. "You'll have the time for this. I'm collecting stuff to send out to Croatia. With the winter coming on. Clothes for the refugee camps mainly. I'm helping out at the school. They've got enough on their plates there." He wouldn't go into his first visit back. They'd been pretty decent, the harassed young women teachers and the men, like himself till Connie died, coping with scheduling, extra-mural activities, sexual precocity, drugs, government upbraiding (never mind teaching). Half of them would have liked the luxury of not-exactly-a-breakdown, a turning-away, a declaration of 'Enough', a hiatus. It was the half-ashamed acknowledgement of this that had made him volunteer to more or less take over the Croatia project.

"Oh my God!" Ginnie ran an aghast eye round Dougie's sitting-room. It was crammed with cardboard boxes, plastic carrier bags, bin liners, all spilling out children's clothes and toys. The damp, fusty smell of jumble assailed her nostrils. "What do you want done with that lot?"

"Most of it's washed, clean, but some mums haven't bothered. Some will have to be junked. Then it wants sorting into rough sort of age groups." He pointed to a pile of flattened boxes. "These are new. We set them up, put in clothes, a blanket or other cover, some groceries that won't perish, cutlery, a few sweets. Then there's soap, toothbrushes, shampoo. The usual."

"Do they still need all this?"

"Our place does. We've taken on the responsibility for it. Our school runs fairs, sponsored walks and swims, you name it. We hope to equip a gymnasium and a clinic. It's good for cossetted middle-class children to see they have moral obligations and to be fair, most of them are only too ready to help."

"I'll have to wash and press some of these." She was holding up jumpers, jackets, the kind of little clown-like dungarees toddlers wore. "Even if they're not new, they should look like new. They're good expensive clothes, mainly. People round here don't stint on their kids!"

"Don't try and do it all. I've got others who'll do some of it."

"Let's get stuck in then. Do a bit of sorting before tea."

He turned so she would not see his

smirk of satisfaction. No more talk of not having the time, then. And mercifully, no more reminiscences about the almost supernatural power and prescience of Nipper.

★ ★ ★

Ginnie phoned her sister Evelyn and said, "I won't be able to get in to see Mother so often."

The statement hung, undigested, in the air but the airwaves rippled with Evelyn's unspoken disapproval.

"Won't Mother miss you?"

"If you think that, maybe you should get down to see her more often."

"You know how difficult it is for me. With children."

"They can look after themselves, surely. For a day or two?"

"You don't know teenagers, Ginnie, do you? What they get up to?"

"I'm helping Doug. My neighbour."

"Doug Walker?" Evelyn's voice sharpened. "Whatever with?"

"A project. For Croatia."

"Don't get in too deep."

57

"How deep in I get is my affair. I'm going now, Evelyn. Try to get down. It might not be long, you know."

Helen Macreevy brought round a mound of jumpers that she thought her departed brood would not want again, all carefully washed and pressed.

"Marvellous," Ginnie gloated. "Dougie will be pleased."

"Been good for both of you." Helen was laconic. "You're looking brighter."

"How's the diet?" asked Ginnie. Deflecting.

"Do you mean the no-fat or the bananas and milk?"

"Whatever."

"I've given up on both. I will never be one of Pharoah's lean cattle."

"So you think Dougie's looking better?" Ginnie wanted to hear Helen say it. She had been making an evening meal for both of them. She thought herself he was losing at last that gaunt, haunted look. She had even done some shirts for him — where was the effort when she was laundering other things at the same time? Nonetheless she didn't want anybody thinking there was anything between herself and Dougie. Evelyn's silence on the phone had niggled at her. What had she been thinking? And if so, how dare she? But it would be nice to think her intervention had pulled Dougie up a bit. She looked at Helen hopefully.

"I think he is," said Helen, consideringly. "He and Connie were so close, weren't they? And men are so lost when they are left on their own."

"M'mm." She was furious with herself for colouring up and knew Helen had probably noticed. Even when Helen had gone, the discomfited feeling remained. Well, of all the stupid things, she told herself. He's at least ten years older than you. Look how grey his hair is! And you like men who are fussy about their appearance. He goes about in old cords and frayed pullies. (But he could be tidied. Connie had done it when the occasion demanded and he had then looked, well, distinguished was the only word for it.) He's an interest, Ginnie told herself at last. I need things other than Mother to think about, other than the compulsion to open yet another shop that will just go down the drain like the one before. Having come to this conclusion, she immediately felt better. What did she want with men, after all? They only wanted one thing.

It took them the better part of two weeks. In the end, it seemed to Ginnie she was packing boxes in her sleep. She dreamt about pinafore dresses and duffle coats, Pepsodent and canned stew, her reveries interrupted by flashes of the photographs she had seen of those without warmth, without food, in a cold winter. It made her appreciate what she had, the house at least: enough to keep things going. Though the house was Mother's really and if anything happened to her it would have to be sold and half would go to Evelyn.

"What's up?" Dougie had rung her doorbell with a kind of ferocity that made her jump.

"Problems." He came in nippily, smartly, not the slow-moving man he had been. "We've got the van all right. The crew, no. He's broken a leg and she's had to go and see a daughter who's having a difficult pregnancy."

"All those boxes!" They were encroaching on her space now too.

"I'm going to take it." He gave her a defiant kind of grin. "I've made up my mind. I've driven on the Continent before."

"Not in Croatia. Not a pantechnicon. Not in winter."

"Same difference. I've discussed it with Connie — in my mind."

"Dougie — "

"I know, my darling has gone, but I still talk to her in my mind. She would want me to go."

She walked through the pile of boxes, thinking of her mother in the pink bed at The Chase, remembering the times she had danced to the old lady's bidding. You don't know me any more, Mother. Tell me I'm free to go.

Dougie went on, "I'll try to get one of the younger teachers to come with me. There's a chap called Martin, volunteers for that sort of thing. We can't let people down."

"Why can't I go?" said Ginnie.

Dougie spun round on his heel, his face a picture of bewilderment.

61

"You can't go because — " He looked at her. You're too small, he thought, too frail. You're too much under that old lady's thumb. Even now. I can't see you up in a great van wearing four jerseys under a Barbour. Yet he'd grown fond of a kind of doggedness in her, that had kept her working all hours to get the boxes filled and although her conversation ran mainly to the inconsequential, she wasn't without a certain blithe sense of humour that sometimes took him by surprise. "It's not going to be a picnic," he warned her.

He saw her fists were clenched. "I feel I want to get away, Dougie," she said desperately. "Evelyn will have to visit Mother. She can do it if she has to and it's time I took a stand."

He said, suddenly decisive. "OK. OK. I'll get on with the necessary paperwork."

She was quiet for the rest of the morning and he wondered whether at some point she would go back on her decision. Despite the fact they had been neighbours for twelve years he did not feel he knew Ginnie all that well. But Connie had always been fond of her.

He let his eyes slide away from his late wife's photograph. He wasn't at all sure what she might think of this latest proposition.

★ ★ ★

Judy Radcot brought round armfuls of clothes redolent of her Estée Lauder perfume plus a plastic bag crammed with toiletries.

"Did I tell you? Frank and I are house-hunting in Florida? We fly out next week."

Despite everything Ginnie found Judy hard to dislike. For one thing she had a great respect for clothes and wore an Armani suit even for this piece of charity-tripping. In her evening gowns she looked like Meryl Streep with attitude. She was vulgar, but open-handed. She set such store by material things but Ginnie knew very well that Frank, of the paunchy stomach and ribald jokes, would one day step over a certain line, the one that separated the legit from the fraudulent. And everything, the houses, the fast cars, the expensive cruises, the Armani suits, would go, leaving not a rack behind. Poor Judy then: when the shop had gone, Ginnie had tasted something of the much greater ignominy Judy would surely know. Ginnie sensed this in her bones, in her water and so thanked Judy most profusely for her offerings, even giving her a kiss on the cheek.

7

WHEN Mavis awoke that morning — the morning the van drove away from Dougie Walker's front door, on its way to Croatia with Ginnie propped up there beside him like a little puppet doll (and with just as much expression); the morning Frank and Judy flew off to the sun with a new set of Louis Vuitton luggage — Mavis had an additional sense of unease on top of the vague, cloudy anxiety that had plagued her ever since Bernard's job had folded.

She felt cautiously around in her mind to try to pin it down. Was it because Bernard was being so tentative about setting up on his own? Goodness knows, they'd talked it through often enough and everybody thought he could make a go of it, but there had been a sapping of confidence, in addition to frequent silences and taciturnity that made Mavis fear he was keeping something from her. She hoped he wasn't going to do a Dougie Walker on her, turn New Age and woolly-pullovered. They had standards to keep up. They'd been the first in Pinkmount Drive to have their drive cobbled, they'd put up the stone pineapples on either side of the black wrought-iron gates; they'd had Sky, a Merc and a splendid conservatory added before anyone else.

Just the same . . . Mavis looked at her partner's sleeping form and was not without compassion. She hated to see him down. They chimed in agreement over most things — from choice of newspaper to what they ate. Their grumbles matched. Conrad was an unsettling influence. She had had to talk Bernard out of giving the boy some of his redundancy money. For something as frivolous as setting up a film production company! Over her dead body! She wasn't sure whether Conrad would have taken it or not. He said not, but what was he hanging about at home for? He might have been persuaded, especially if they'd cloaked the deal as a loan.

And then there was the question of

Conrad and Sylvia next door. He hadn't gone round there for a couple of days so that was something. Why the niggle, then, at the far corner of her mind? Was it that she hadn't seen Sylvia in all that time? Not once. Not going out in the BMW, not pruning anything in the front garden, not wandering down the garden at the back. Had she gone off somewhere? Was she well, was she all right? Funny Arthur taking off like that . . .

"Have you seen anything of Sylvia?" she asked her son casually at breakfast.

"You know I haven't." Like his father he was always grumpy in the morning, his face stuck in the *Guardian* while Bernard devoured the *Telegraph*.

"I haven't seen her."

"Not at all?"

"Come to think of it, was her light on last night?"

"Dunno. Didn't notice."

"Maybe you'd better pop round."

"But I thought — "

"I don't want her thinking I think anything is going on between you."

"Nothing *is* going on."

67

"Take her round a book or something. But don't stay for coffee."

"For God's sake!" Conrad glared at her and even Bernard looked up and shook his head minimally. But later Conrad did go round. He was aware that his heart was pounding and that if she was in she would probably be a little distant with him again, when he had worked so hard at trying to get close to her. But even so, he felt better. He saw the gloss on the yellow and bronze fallen leaves, he heard late birds rejoicing, he felt youthful and free and buoyant. Ready, even, to put behind him the fact that his latest script, which last week had looked like being taken up, this week was not so promising.

He knew she was in there. She was just taking an unconscionable time to answer his ring. Through the rippled glass of the door he thought he saw a hazy shape cross the hallway and go into the kitchen, turning a white glimmer of face towards the front door as if to identify who was there. Wasn't she going to answer, then? He felt a spasm of anxious rage, then fear and on an impulse went round the back of the house where he could see clear into the kitchen. She was sitting there with her head on her hands, frail wrists sticking out of a pale-blue dressing-gown, mules on her feet. He rapped peremptorily on the window but she did not raise her head. He knocked again, gesticulating in an urgent fashion that she should come and unlock the back door. Eventually, sluggishly, she did, going back into the kitchen and resuming her old head-holding position as if she had never been interrupted.

"For God's sake, Sylvia, what's up? Tell me."

The mouth, turning down. The awful pathos of that pale, unlipsticked mouth before it opened in a fearful cry, a hoarse, unguarded, uncivilized cry. "He's gone away. He's left me. He's not coming back."

How to touch her, quieten her? He knelt in front of her, taking her unresisting hand, talking as if to a child or a frightened animal. "There, we'll talk about it. I'll put the kettle on, shall I? Tea is good." He rose to his feet and pressed her tousled head into his chest, feeling his heart thump, feeling the soft, taunting scent of her shampoo rise to his nostrils. Holding her and patting. Soothing. Rocking. Waiting.

"I told you, he was going to see her. The girl, Ida. And she did have the baby, she did have a daughter and he has met her and he wants to bring her back here." She turned her face into his fogeyish green pullover, then finally raised her eyes to his, the tide of grief finally going out, ebbing, the hunched shoulders sagging. "No way," she said. "No way."

He put her tea into a proper cup and his into a big mug she kept for the gardener. Absently, he cracked his teeth down on a ginger biscuit.

"He phoned?"

She nodded. "I've never heard him like it. His voice was like a boy's, animated, babbling. He couldn't stop. She was his spitting image, he said. He met her in the street and he knew right away who she was. I know now he went back to Scotland thinking that was what he'd find, something to give him hope again, something to hang on to, because when he lost that job, the light went out for him, I wasn't there for him, he couldn't look me in the face."

"Well," he said consideringly, "he probably felt he'd let you down. From what I've heard he wanted to do the best for you, give you nice things and suddenly it was all wrenched away from him, he couldn't do it any more."

She nodded. "Oh, yes, that part's true. But I'm not just a kept woman, Conrad. I could have scaled down, been happy with a lot less. If he'd just let me find my own answers. But it was as though to counteract his own sense of failure, if you like, he had to chip away at me, restrict me — "

"God, for an outsider looking in, marriage seems impossible. Always has. You can't, you shouldn't ever, relinquish the things that are important to you."

"He wanted to stop my acting, my classes. I couldn't even have people in for a meal. He just wanted to sit and go over the reasons for the crash, how it could have been averted if they'd listened to him. I may have been impatient with him, Conrad, but I thought I would go

71

mad if he didn't stop — "

"Half a mo". You said (a) he'd left you and (b) he wanted to bring this — this young girl back here. Which is it?"

"Well, if I won't agree to it he won't come back, I suppose. Same thing. He's already left me in spirit."

"What about the Ida person?"

"Oh, I don't think she counts, from the sound of it. Anyhow, she's got somebody. No, his infatuation is with the idea of having a daughter. He had the nerve to tell me I would learn to love this girl. With the improbable name of Tracy-Lee." She stopped and drew in a deep breath. He saw the vestige, the very ghost of a smile however, and then he was in there, snatching at the chance of an upturn in her mood.

"Suppose you go up and dress? Suppose we bugger off and have a pub lunch somewhere, somewhere up in th' hills." At her hesitancy he said, shaking his head, "No, I'm not leaving you here to brood on your own the way you've done the past two days. Even Mater noticed. It was she who sent me round to see how you were."

"Not your own idea?"

"No," he said honestly. "I was trying my best to keep away."

★ ★ ★

The lunch had been the perfunctory sort, watery soup and a toasted sandwich, hard round the edges. The pub brasses had not been polished that day and there was a strong draught coming in the half-open door. They got into the BMW with mutual relief and he suggested driving to the mere: there they could watch the ducks.

Of course she drove: it was her car. The ducks came up out of the water, looking for food, making it difficult to park without squashing one. And then it was warm, the sun came out again picking out the beautiful turquoise on the mallards' necks, and they watched while two swans conducted a love affair, winding their long necks around each other, tranquil and exquisite, a tableau, a picture.

"They're faithful, aren't they?" she said sadly. "All of their lives together."

"M'mmm. Think what they miss." But he said it not altogether jokily, his voice ringing with disillusionment.

"I like the idea of fidelity," she said. "Of not letting each other down. It's just — sometimes you can't do anything to help the other person. Sometimes you are shut out. And when one area breaks down, so do the rest."

"You mean sex."

"That. Yes. The whole of loving goes."

He put his head on her shoulder. "Sylvia, what would you say if *I* told you I love you?"

"Tell you it's not love. It's born of your present boredom."

"But you like me too. You trust me."

"I like listening to your airy schemes, your storylines, I don't even mind helping you build your castles in the air."

He lifted his head and looked at her mouth so longingly she moved towards him and they kissed. It went on for some time and when they broke apart the swans had sailed right in front of them and were stretching their necks, croaking for titbits. Two geese skimmed the lake, honking.

"There's a lot of it going on," he said bleakly, watching two mallard ducks clash beaks, engage in battle and then sail off together. "I wonder at the profit in it."

"Please," she said. "Don't you be down. One of us is plenty."

He began to quote, while she started up the engine:

"'I met a lady in the meads,
Full beautiful, a faery's child;
Her hair was long, her foot was
    light,
And her eyes were wild.
She found me roots of relish sweet
And honey wild and manna-dew,
And sure in language strange she
    said
'I love thee true'."

"I do love Keats," she said.
"What about me?"
"Let's leave it at the poet."

8

"YOU'RE lucky," said Mavis Higgison to Helen Macreevy. "Your kids don't land in on you for weeks on end when their money runs out, eating you out of cornflakes and caramel wafers and watching The Late Show when you've gone to bed. You should see the way he piles on the Three-Fruit marmalade, that one. And he somehow manages to patronize me at the same time, wrong-footing me at every turn."

"I don't feel lucky," said Helen. "Tell the truth, Mavis, I feel the way poor Arthur Blaney must feel, *and* your Bernard and, to a certain extent, even Ginnie Carter without her dress shop — I feel redundant. I only ever was a mother. No career. I was supermum with knobs on — home-made soup, hand-knitted jumpers, always there behind the door to receive the satchels and the overcoats."

"You did a good job. Look how well

yours have done for themselves."

"And look how far away they all live! I see my grandchildren once a year if I'm lucky. Not that I'm really complaining. I want them to live their lives. But I am bloody redundant and nobody ever thinks about the likes of me, what I'm going to do with myself, with leftover life to kill."

Mavis looked at her neighbour, her face puckering sympathetically. "A job?" she suggested.

"Probably not up to it," Helen admitted. "And I couldn't stand. If it was a job that involved standing. Not with my back."

Mavis moved the conversation swiftly away from Helen's preoccupation and back to her own. She hadn't asked Helen in for coffee just to provide a listening ear. Rather the reverse. Helen was the only one to whom she could confide her own worries, because Helen never blabbed or gossiped. There was a kind of innocence and probity in her neighbour which Mavis recognized and admired even though she did not aspire to it in her own affairs. Helen could be trusted not to pass on a confidence. Mavis supposed of all her friends and neighbours she was really fondest of Helen, though often exasperated by her. Although fifteen years younger than Bertie, her husband, she had always acted as if she was the same age, getting into flatties, letting her figure go, generally behaving as if she too, were retired and drawing her pension. Showed one the futility of putting all your eggs in one basket. Bertie thought his wife was blissfully happy, but it seemed even Helen was afflicted with this new *dolour* that had overcome Pinkmount Drive like a flu epidemic. Even poor Helen was feeling redundant.

"Look, *café noir*," said Mavis, handing Helen the plate of iced biscuits, knowing this would cheer her up. Her own face became more intense. "Helen, I know this won't go outside these four walls, but I'm worried about Conrad. He's getting too close to Sylvia."

"I don't think you need worry," said Helen carefully. "Sylvia has always had her admirers, with those legs of hers. But she and Arthur are a pair, aren't they? I don't see them splitting up, ever. She's put too much into that beautiful home of theirs."

"Which he's chosen to forsake. Conrad knows the reason but I can't get it out of him. Secretive, little beast. He's always been like that. Lived a life of his own. Why couldn't I have had a nice, uncomplicated accountant for a son? Someone like my Bernard?"

"What does Conrad *do*, exactly, Mavis?"

"The difference is," said Mavis, "the difference between Conrad and say, your Peter and Eric, is, Conrad trades in words and ideas and your Peter in leather handbags and your Eric in cement. That's what it comes down to. He writes book reviews, but they're for literary magazines that don't pay very much. Same with films. And he puts up ideas for films and for television series. He's done a film-making course. He's half-finished a novel. He skates from one project to another. It's not that I don't have faith in him, Helen. It's just that I see his friends and they're mostly the same as him and some make it and some don't." Suddenly Mavis buried her head in somewhat theatrical fashion in her hands. "And what worries me is Sylvia next door is just the same kind of fly-by-night. He gives her books and she lends him hers and they chomp them up like feeding-time at the zoo." Helen thought for a moment, and unworthily, that Mavis looked almost comical in her genuine bewilderment. "But Helen," said Mavis, "you know the truth of this as well as I do: high-falutin notions butter no parsnips. You don't learn about real life from books."

"Maybe you do," said Helen mildly.

"Such as?" demanded Mavis offendedly.

"Well, what to expect. Love and romance. I liked *Jane Eyre* at school. And *Black Beauty* — "

"Phooey," said Mavis, expelling an outraged breath. "Helen, be sensible. The country's in an awful state and Bernard says we've got to adapt to information technology and Internet and all that and you want love and romance!"

"Well, not just. But you can't live by bread alone. Even the Bible says that, Mavis dear."

Mavis scarcely heard her, her exasperation at fever pitch.

"The chattering classes — oh, I'll admit my son belongs therewith, yes, I'll have to admit it — they'll do us all down." She turned once again to Helen, who saw to her dismay that she was close to tears. "And how do I get him away from her, with her acting, and her good taste, so-called, and those legs? I feel I'm losing my son, Mavis. We used to have nice, sensible chats, reasonable chats — "

"We all have to loosen the apron strings."

"Spare me the clichés."

"Don't take on," said Helen. "Can I have this last *café noir*?"

★ ★ ★

Bertie Macreevy had been knocked off his perch somewhat by Dougie Walker's departure. It seemed like too much of an adventurous project for someone he'd always regarded as a bit wet. You couldn't say Dougie Walker was a man's man. When the jokes got a bit blue at the clubhouse, or someone even unconsciously displayed a racist tinge, or there were ribald remarks about a passing female superstructure, Dougie looked like your vinegary maiden aunt. Yet here he was, setting off for an unknown country and the winds were already indicating Europe could be in for early snow.

Ignoring his partner's protests about protocol, Bertie took first swipe at the ball at the fourteenth tee. What did it matter who had won the last hole? This Johnnie-come-lately had had the nerve to criticize his swing. They all thought because you were retired you couldn't hit a bloody ball any more. He'd hit the drive of his life but ended up in the bunker. He pretended not to hear his partner's ongoing protests about the rules being there to be followed.

Normally Bertie was a stickler. It dawned on him he had better make his peace with his opponent. "That were a fine putt," he conceded.

The younger man, on leave from his desk in an insurance office, narrowed his eyes. What was bothering the old boy? Bertie began a diatribe about the uselessness of people trying to help the likes of the former Yugoslavia. Drink and drugs were what they were up against, he insisted. The soldiers there were out of their trees.

Still, volunteered the young insurance specialist, you had to admire those who went out there to try and lend a hand. Such as Dougie Walker, who had so recently lost a wife.

"Had me down his school, before he resigned," said Bertie. "Talked me into giving a talk about t'war. Torpedoed twice, me. You go to Russia now you get welcomed for your money, right? *We* sailed into Murmansk we got the bum's rush. Hostile faces. Down in t'bloody water thought we'd never see land again. Cold froze our bloody hair and the water in our eyes. That was being bloody useful, in t'war. But you don't get no credit now, lad. Not now you don't. It's all bloody Yugoslavia, or Rwanda."

For some reason he was remembering the boy in the front row, when he'd given his talk. He'd fidgeted through most of it then ended up drawing the pupils of his close-set eyes together and sticking his tongue under his upper lip so that his face took on a look of simian lunacy.

Sod off, you old tosspot, he had been saying, you bore the life out of me. Yet he, Bertie, had been not much older than that bum-faced little Caliban when the Germans dragged him out of the water and into prison-camp.

"They forget," he said now, and felt such an uprush of anger and protest he knew his blood pressure was going right off the Richter scale.

"War was a long time ago."

"Aye, I were right. They do forget."

★ ★ ★

Helen always watched her husband pull the golf trolley up the hill with a little pang she could not articulate. He put everything he knew into the game, his loyalty to it even on filthy days nothing short of heroic.

Yet she knew it was no substitute for the days when he ran his warehouse business, when he was so busy providing for her and the children, determined she could have the fur coat she wanted (fur coats were acceptable then) and that they should go to the best schools. Rough diamond, she thought affectionately. Sharp as a tack yet, according to their younger daughter Jane, wouldn't know what to do with a decent broadsheet newspaper but wrap his chips in it. So what was wrong with a little lad from the wrong side of the tracks making it to a nice house in Pinkmount Drive? They took his attainments so lightly. But she never would. She made him chips if he wanted them; steaks too. Knitted his socks for he said shop-bought were rubbish by comparison. He was still her buccaneer, even if his snoring had got heavy and his temper testy. She'd been a plainish, lumpy lass, a little bit higher up the social scale than him, (they said pardon in her house) but not a lot and he had seen something in her no one else had.

She didn't mention missing the kids too much for it set him off about ingratitude and serpent's teeth. They had each other, after all. Along with the arthritis, the high blood pressure, the problems with weight. What was it the man said on the telly? Old age isn't for cissies. And she did not like the fact that Bertie was further down that road than she; as Janie the family cynic said, she only *looked* old because she wouldn't truck with slimming and fashion though she really should do something about the former. Maybe.

Helen stared at the contents of the cake box. A tired-looking Eccles cake. The remainder of some ginger parkin. She tried to keep her eyes away from the new packet of chocolate marshmallows. What she really fancied was a slice of chocolate cake, the death by chocolate sort, that she used to make for the school fêtes. The sort that gunged up your cavities and arteries, layered with frosted icing, pitted with kirsch cherries.

Think of your extra weight in terms of packets of sugar, the experts said. Helen's mind boggled. She found she was unwrapping the chocolate mallows, anyhow. Once unwrapped, she might as well eat one. It was quite small. So small really, that she felt she might as well have another.

9

ARTHUR BLANEY took his time climbing from the bottom of Pinkmount Drive to his house at the top. Partly out of cowardice and partly because it was good to be back where streets were quiet and private and that impression of hassle, conniving, desperation in the towns was missing. *Sale. Clearance. Half-price. All stocks must go.* And the dayglow lettering. The dire punctuation and weird spelling. He was hot on spelling and punctuation, the one area in which, because of his Scottish schooling, he felt superior to Sylvia. And that was all down to Miss Jessie MacColl, spinster and despot, who'd hammered 'I done it' and 'accommodation' out of him in Grade Four in that greystone institution, Bessell Street Public School, (sic) which in Scotland really was for the public. And why was he diverting himself with such irrelevancies? Because of the fear, oh yes, certainly because he was afraid. He'd just booked Tracy-Lee into the Green Man Hotel in Wilhowbry and told her to wait there until. Until when? Until what? He did not know. But certainly hanging about in Scotland had had to come to an end.

Latterly Sylvia had been really strange during their telephone exchanges. First not answering his direct questions. Then saying she did not know. She did not know if they could go on together if he brought his daughter back, even just for a visit. She did not know if she wanted to sell the house for something smaller (and she had been the first to suggest this). She did not know how she felt, what the neighbours thought, whether she might still love him, what bills were outstanding. It seemed to him she scarcely knew the day of the week or what time it was.

He had begun to miss her, the sensation like a gnawing toothache that never subsided. Desperately fond and taken up with his 'new' daughter as he was, he had still begun to think that perhaps he should never have embarked on the Scottish venture. Seeing quite a lot of

Ida, he had even begun to have delusions of somehow going back to her, of being a family, a Scottish family, with her and Tracy-Lee and that certainly wasn't on for Ida wanted her air steward and his prospects in Miami. When once he'd got slightly sentimental with Ida, she had laughed till, it seemed, her stomach ached. She wasn't careful of him, of his feelings. She made him realize he had no call on her. Now Sylvia was never harsh, as such. He had begun to see her thoughtful eyes, her somehow wistful look, more and more in his mind's eye. What a team they had been, eh, what? Him in his hand-tailored suits, those striped shirts she insisted he suited best, the shoes he bought in Italy. Her in that pink suit with the little squared pockets outlined in navy blue, or the cream dress so artfully draped about her figure, and her legs in those impeccable, unsnagged tights and the immaculate plain court shoes. Tracy-Lee wore trainers a great deal of the time. Trainers and her hair in a raggedy-Anne topknot. He wasn't just afraid now: he was positively panicking.

The thing was, when he went in to his

own house and found Sylvia in the big sitting-room, the son, Conrad, was there from next door and gave no indication of shifting himself. The suggestion had to come from Arthur himself and he didn't care tuppence if it sounded a bit peremptory.

"Do you mind, lad? I want to talk to my wife in private."

The oik had given Sylvia a long, considering look, as though he had been half thinking, half having the bloody nerve to remain, to pick up some thread of conversation, broken by Arthur's arrival. But Sylvia had nodded at him and falling over his big size tens he had gone.

"What does he want?" Arthur demanded. The thought crossed his mind that Conrad might have a fancy for his wife, but young men often did fancy her, there was nothing new in it. They strutted their stuff in front of her, telling her of amazing air journeys they'd made, financial coups they had brought off, new-tech cars they had purchased, speed limits they had exceeded, films they had seen, impressing her with arcane information about nano-bites, Greek civilization, deep-sea diving techniques in the Maldives, you name it. She had a way of listening, interjecting, responding that sent the testosterone level soaring into the stratosphere. So, Conrad-blooming-Higgison had better watch out or he'd get eaten for breakfast.

Hadn't he?

Sylvia gave him a look that jerked Arthur from the plane of imagined catastrophe into the present, an altogether more soiled and adulterated present, which he had brought about by leaving her. He began to see, with a pulsing kind of terror, what he had done to her. He had desolated her. He had deserted her. His mind began to make scrabbling motions of restitution, apology, cringe, but nothing came forth in words. Her look was stripping him of words, insisting he saw the reality then. A look which said she had felt closer to Conrad Higgison now than she did to him. A look that said he was a stranger in his own home. He wished wildly he had never come back. If only Ida . . . But he was back and he had to say something. He said, "I've brought Tracy-Lee back with me. She's an amazing girl. I've left her at the

Green Man. Till we decide what to do about her."

* * *

"It's dead nice here," said Tracy-Lee, when he went to pick her up. But her face was pale with apprehension.

"It's all right," he reassured her.

"Does Sylvia say I can come up to the house?"

"I've told her I'm bringing you."

"That's not the same thing."

"Well, we're going to front it out, Trace," he said grimly. "I think you should fasten your seat belt, it might be a bumpy ride."

He eased her into the car. As her elbow clumsily jabbed him, she apologized. "Sorry." She ran her hands over the fascia and the leather on the seats. "There's posh," she said. Suddenly the imposing neighbourhood was registering with her and she burst out, "Dad, I'm nothing. I've done nothing. I've been nowhere. 'Cept the Costa del Sol. I don't even talk right, do I? You'd have thought I needed an interpreter when I asked for coffee back at the hotel."

He stopped the car, drawing into the kerb under an imposing chestnut tree.

"I don't want any more of that. No more working-class cringe, do you hear? You're as good as anyone — "

"But I wasted my time at school. I did, Dad. I never saw the point of applying myself. Now I do. Now I wish I had."

"Well," he said slowly, "I'll see you get a chance to learn. It's not too late to take some O or A levels — "

"Not them!" she cried in horror. "I couldn't go back to school with a load of kids. But I'll read books. Maybe you could tell me the ones. I'll watch my accent, I'll talk nice — "

"Nicely," he corrected automatically. "Just be yourself. I know how it feels, not being very sure of yourself, but you'll pick things up, you'll be fine. Don't let material things over-impress you. It's what folk are inside that matters."

If that's the case, he thought hollowly, why do I still feel put down by big houses and public-school tones? You can take the boy out of the working class but you can't take the working class out of the boy. Or girl. It had only started to matter to him again after losing his job, but he could see the terrible constraints and worries that were Tracy-Lee's and he thought he would not allow anyone to put her down; he knew ways now of getting back, Sylvia had taught him composure and hauteur. If he could only get her on Tracy-Lee's side. That was all he was asking.

She had still been protesting it wasn't right, not to bring the girl back like that when their own situation was so far from clear and when he had asked her what she meant, she had burst out that she didn't even know whether they should stay together, he had imposed so much misery on her by his underhandedness that she began to feel she would never trust him again.

One word had certainly borrowed another, till he had heard himself casting up Conrad Higgison, anything for return fire, not that he had been taking him seriously. And then she'd said, as a matter of fact Conrad had asked her to go on the recce with him for his next film; it was in London, and she did not see why she shouldn't go; she had always wanted to know more about how films were made and Conrad felt she had the right *aperçus*, not that Arthur would know an *aperçu* if it rose up and smote him but she didn't care, she was past caring, for as he had shown so little consideration for her feelings why should she go out of her way to please him?

"I'm bringing her back," he had kept reiterating and she had retorted he could do what he liked, she was going away, she would not be around to be imposed upon.

She was still there when he shepherded Tracy-Lee through the front door so she and Wilhowbry's answer to Steven Spielberg had not begun their London odyssey yet. She even came forward and shook hands with Tracy-Lee and distantly he admired her class.

"So you're going to stay with your father for a while?" Sylvia asked.

"If that's all right." Tracy-Lee sat down on one of the well-upholstered chairs, her spine very straight. "All right by you, I mean."

"Well, I will be going away," said

Sylvia evenly. "I don't know when I'll be back." She glanced almost idly at Arthur. "If ever."

"You two shouldn't fall out," Tracy-Lee protested. "I'll go away again if it means you two will fall out."

"Well, it isn't your affair," said Sylvia, adding more kindly, "You can't help what has happened. What are you going to do while you're here?"

"Get to know Dad. I would really like to get a job. Be independent."

"What can you do?"

"Sorry. Not much." Tracy-Lee looked down at her lap. "A bit of hairdressing. I could work in a dress shop. I can do alterations."

"Can you type? What about computers?"

"Sorry."

"She can't type, she doesn't know about computers but it doesn't mean she can't learn," Arthur interposed. "Give the girl a chance to settle in."

"Just tidy up in the kitchen as you go along," said Sylvia, ignoring Arthur and addressing Tracy-Lee directly. "He tends to let things clutter, especially when he's depressed. Don't touch my things in my bathroom, please. Or my bedroom."

Tracy-Lee looked mortified, but said nothing. In a little Sylvia left the room and they could hear her moving about in the room overhead. "She's packing," said Arthur disbelievingly. The phone extension tinkled so she was obviously contacting someone. After a time she came down to the hall carrying a suitcase and smaller bag, dressed in a suit and Dannimac, ready for travel and at the same time the doorbell went and a taxi-driver sketched a salute from the doorway.

"*No*," said Arthur, barring her way.

"I'm meeting him at the station. He'll pick me up there. No point in filling the gossips' mouths." She gave him a wry little look. "It'll be work, you know."

"Does *he* know?"

She looked beyond him to Tracy-Lee's dismayed face. "Enjoy your stay," she said. "And take one piece of advice from me, Tracy-Lee. Stop saying you're sorry, sorry for this, sorry for that. OK?"

"OK," said Tracy-Lee. "Sorry."

10

"I REMEMBER Pinkmount Drive when we first went there," said Ginnie, peering ahead into the Austrian gloom for signs of the other vehicles they should be joining. Nothing yet. It was important in this welter of uncertainty to touch base, to remember where you came from. Dougie was crouched over the steering wheel, his eyelids drooping with fatigue but still steadfastly refusing to let her take over till they joined the bigger convoy. She talked at random, anything to keep him alert. Her feet were so cold they no longer belonged to her and she was having visions of hamburgers, big fat chips, the kind of junk food she never ate unless ravenous.

"Quite a place," said Dougie. "Connie and I were never part of it, never part of that onward-and-upward philosophy, but I saw the attraction. Conspicuous consumption. Bigger, better, greener, fatter."

"We've had to trim our sails now," said Ginnie. "But I remember the thousand-guinea suits and hats that would have kept a refugee going for a year. I have to say it, Dougie: I think a kind of sickly greed got hold; enough was never enough."

"Fun though, wasn't it?" he said surprisingly, bending his neck to relieve the stiffness. "Remember your dad's pale-blue Daimler, the stir it caused at the golf club, and your mother's outfit the day she went to the Palace garden party? Vanity Fair — but the carousel music made a lovely sound."

"You and Connie never judged anybody harshly," said Ginnie. "That's why everybody liked you."

"I don't think she missed out," he said, but his voice had dropped. "Tell me, do you think she did, Ginnie? I'm haunted by the feeling that I didn't give her all I could have given her. And I asked so much of her. In my mind's eye I see her endlessly pricking out seedlings, just to please me, satisfy this implacable whim of mine we should be self-sufficient. I made her get up early to feed the birds — "

"You didn't make. She did it gladly."

"What option had she? I was taken up with school affairs — "

A horn sounded out of the dark and lights from the main convoy they were to join raked the Stygian sky at last. About thirty vehicles in all. The British lorries tacked on at the end and Ginnie insisted now, brooking no argument, that she should take over some driving. "All I do is follow the tail-light in front," she said. He scrambled into the passenger seat, crumpling gratefully and immediately into an attitude of relaxation. "Be ready," he said. "Be ready for brake stops." Within five minutes he was asleep.

How different he was, Ginnie reflected, from Sydney, her ex-husband. Sydney had been bright, flash, amusing. A lovely dancer, she remembered, a little wistfully. But cruel and cutting of tongue and ungenerous in his summing-up of other people, going unfailingly for their weak spots. Where did people like Dougie learn to be kind, to make everybody feel they mattered? She decided it was a kind of gift, like the ability to play the piano or to write a story. Being in their company was like sitting in a sunny spot in the garden. You got warmed. Even frozen as she was now, you got warmed.

The swaying vehicle in front came to a sudden, crunching halt and Ginnie slammed on the brakes. Beyond the windscreen she could see the start of snow, flakes slanting across the glass. Business-like flakes. A man muffled in a padded anorak and woollen scarves got out of the van ahead and walked back towards her. "Hold-up," he mouthed, pointing ahead. "Been a pile-up at the crossroads. Done this kind of thing before?"

Ginnie blew warm breath into her big gloves. "Nope."

"Worth it." He was a big, bluff-faced chap, the sort who wouldn't know the answers in a pub quiz but would be there with a shoulder when anything needed shifting or anyone needed comforting. She could tell by the eyes, the hurt and innocent eyes. "Be prepared," he advised her. "Be prepared for the kids who've lost limbs, the babies with shell-shock. Couldn't tell the missus back home, she'd have cried her eyes out."

"My name's Ginnie," she said. "Ginnie Carter."

"Frank. Frank O'Connor." There was a movement ahead. "Wagons roll!" He ran back to his vehicle, giving her the thumbs-up sign as he went. She let in the clutch.

She wasn't prepared for the strange, eerie beauty of the deserted villages they drove through. The handsome, even beautiful houses. What if it had all happened in Pinkmount Drive? How would Mavis and Bernard, Helen and Bertie, Judy and Frank feel if they had to give up their comforts, their fat sofas, tellies, wonder ovens, for a refugee camp? How would *she* feel?

She only knew how she felt as of the moment: like someone in a fairytale, under a spell which insisted she go on, that she should look, see and not turn away. For that way lay some kind of salvation.

"Any coffee left?"

Ginnie shook the outsize thermos. "Might be a smidgeon." She poured what there was for him and he grimaced as he drank: it was going cold and rank. "What about you?" She shook her head. She was past wanting to eat or drink: she just wanted them to get there, the camp, wherever it was and for the endless bumping motion to cease. He had taken over the driving again but she couldn't catnap as he had done. She felt her eyes were stuck open for good: embedded in concrete, like her joints.

"Shall we sing?"

"Don't know any songs."

"Sing something. Anything."

Not knowing where it came from, what source of memory, she began 'Smoke gets in your eyes'. "That was nice," he congratulated her. "More." She came up with 'My bonnie lies over the ocean'. It had been a good idea, they were making better progress, or at least it felt like it. He promised her they were nearly there.

Frank O'Connor's vehicle ahead came to a sudden, juddering stop and only by a miraculously swift response on his own brakes did Dougie avoid going into him. The van behind tipped their rear bumper. When the motor engines quietened, a staccato, chilling sound reached their ears: gunfire. Dougie put a hand out to calm Ginnie, who had jumped like a flea. "Snipers," he said. "Trying their scare tactics. Soon be over. Keep down."

She huddled into her padded coat, hauling her woollen hat further down over her ears, absurdly reminded of Guy Fawkes' Night when she was a child. She hadn't liked it much then either. Dougie's forecast that it would soon be over hadn't been all that accurate. Whether she liked it or not she was witness to a gun battle between villagers on either side of the highway, using the convoy as a kind of baffle wall between them. She heard cries and shouts and saw a man stagger off into some undergrowth holding his arm. "Keep down," Dougie repeated. She sank down but only a fraction of an inch, unable to tear her gaze away from the scene.

"No!" she heard Dougie shout and following his gaze saw Frank O'Connor alight from his cab and dash into the dark ahead. He came back half-carrying, half-dragging a slight body, somebody young, whom he tried to lift into his cab. Before she could protest Dougie was down and out of his seat and giving Frank O'Connor what help he could. There was another burst of gunfire and to Ginnie's horror Frank slumped in an almost obscene, jelly-like fashion all over Dougie and the casualty. Ginnie could hear her own scream flare out like a ribbon into the dark and then she was down and running, her cap falling over her eyes, her feet stumbling from cold and terror.

Dougie had turned Frank over by the time she got there. There was just sufficient light for her to see those innocent, hurt eyes she had noted opened wide in a kind of accepting surprise. "He's bought it," said Dougie unnecessarily. "The bastards." He was pulling and tugging to get the other figure into the cab, as Frank had intended and then by mutual consent he and Ginnie struggled and finally got Frank's body on board too. Ginnie tidied his clothes and his hair, sobbing. "This one's a girl," said Dougie. From the pale glimmer of skin and the swell under her coat, Ginnie had already noted this. Blood ran from the young woman's mouth.

Unbelievably, the convoy in front had already started moving again, agonizingly slow, but moving.

"I'll drive this. Can you go back and take ours? Not far now," he said calmly.

She nodded, the spittle drying up. *Alistair Maclean*, she thought, running. *Jack Higgins*. They write about this, don't they? War. Gunfire. I'm in it. I'm in the middle of hell. Mother.

As suddenly as it had started the gunfire subsided. She remembered as she drove — they were driving along so effortlessly now, the lot of them, as though some clot had been released from an artery — the short story Douglas Hurd the Foreign Secretary had written for a newspaper about old neighbours in the former Yugoslavia falling out. People who'd never had a cross word till their country broke up.

It had stuck in her mind. Now, bloody murder. There had been blood all over Dougie's hands. Her own shook relentlessly on the wheel. What were they doing here, in a place that had no relevance to their own lives? Everybody had assured her the convoys were pretty safe.

They got to the refugee camp as dawn was breaking, big streaks of sickened yellow showing through palest grey and the refugees crowded round the van Dougie had driven, crying, horror-stricken. The girl was Croatian, known to them, she had been out getting milk from a farm for her child, nothing to do with the snipers who everybody said were wild young men high on drugs and alcohol. "What about him?" said Dougie, pointing to Frank O'Connor. "He had no quarrel with anybody." They could not look at him, Ginnie decided, they were too ashamed of what was happening in their country. They took the girl away and they heard later she was recovering, her wound with any luck would not be fatal.

"He couldn't get a job," said Frank's oppo, a postman on leave, when they met him later. "He felt all his self-respect had been taken away from him, but working for the refugees helped. He was the kind of bloke who would do anything for anyone." He could not stop crying. The tears streamed but he ignored them. "We've got to take him back home. I'm not leaving him here." And he looked round the desolate, mountainous area with hatred. "I shall never come back. This was my fourth mission. Now, I shall leave them to it."

Dougie and Ginnie went to see Nana, the girl who had been wounded, in the marquee that passed for a hospital. Afterwards they helped to organize the medicines and equipment in a new, bare hut and as they established some kind of order Ginnie began to feel the first stirrings of satisfaction, reward for what they were doing. She turned to say as much to Dougie but he had disappeared and she found him eventually back in their van, curled up against the cold, his eyes red.

"It brings back Connie," he said, as she climbed up beside him. "All the suffering, the days when I couldn't do anything for her and she would look at me. So beseechingly. They do that here, too, the sick ones." He began to pound the fascia with his fists, his misery so inchoate he could not articulate it. She did not even think about it, she simply put her arms round him and held him, rocking him like a child.

11

THEY read about their neighbours — '*Heroic Twosome Save Young Mother*,' '*We Tried to Save Man on a Mission*', '*Light in a Dark Corner*' — over breakfast in a clean but shabby Hackney B. and B. There were pictures of a much younger Ginnie and of Dougie setting out with school kids on a foreign trip some time ago. Conrad gave a whistle of disbelief. "Wouldn't have thought old Dougie had the stamina to put up a chicken coop, never mind drive a truck through a war zone." "What about Ginnie?" said Sylvia, "with *her* delicate constitution?" "Ginnie delicate?" "Her mother told me they had to feed her cod liver oil when she was little. All that stuff." They sat back, bemused, what they were doing, the recce, the interviews, somehow diminished, less relevant.

"Got to get going," said Conrad resolutely. She was looking uncertain again, despite his having rehearsed her carefully about the questions she must ask at the women's hostel, how she must go in without attitude, neutral, a sponge for their stories. He was going to Wapping: he wanted his drama-doc about the extremes of society, the City rich and the submerged tenth, the flotsam and jetsam, to have a Dickensian feeling to it, and he wanted to suss out the riverside. Later they would meet up at The Grapes at Limehouse. "Come on," he said, just a shade irritably. "It's all about brio, going in there." "You mean — 'Get a life'" — she mimed a pencil-chewing, hard-nosed interviewer with some skill and he laughed; she could be irresistible, he wished he could get beyond first base but so far there was no succumbing on her part.

She walked into the women's hostel acting the part of the researcher. She did not feel like a real researcher. She had once worked as a junior in a weekly newspaper office but in those days had lacked 'front' — that was something she had learned after marrying Arthur and having the money to dress to impress. People thought Arthur had married up but her parents had never had one bean to rub with another; her father had been charming but shiftless, mostly unemployed. She had learned early to pretend to be other than she was, to be educated, middle class, refined, but the education had been of the self-help sort; she had read assiduously and the rest, the taste, the ability to tell good from bad was a gift, possibly from her mother's family trailing as they did residual elements of 'class' from some earlier ancestry in the shires. It was why she empathized with Conrad; she was a dreamer of the first water, you had to be when actuality let you down and it was why she had always been a bit of an actress. She had played the rich bitch to the hilt and Arthur in his unsophisticated way had encouraged her, trusting her implicitly as arbiter and trend-setter.

She was shaken by what she found in the hostel: wretched women with discoloured eyes and bruises fading on cheekbones, trying to keep order among unruly small children, with hectic cheeks and runny noses, hostile towards her at first but then opening up and telling horrifying tales of abuse and torment with an almost defiant relish.

Over lunch at The Grapes afterwards she described the pathetic rooms, the frantically anxious children, the smell of poverty that had never become unfamiliar to her (from the shops and classrooms of her childhood) and together they thought they saw how the projected film might go, how it might marry in with Conrad's stuff about greed, near-corruption in the very rich, his vision of how the great writers from Dickens to Dostoevsky had got it right; there were always the exploiters and the exploited, the Fate-favoured and the congenitally damned.

"I want this to rise above politics, above economics, sociology. I want to say, look, the poor are always with us, but for God's sake let us all display a little more charity in our dealings with each other. Do you know what I mean?"

Of course she knew what he meant. She always did, her quick, sharp mind picked up every nuance and emotionally they were open maps, each read the other's heart. He tried to explain to her what would happen next, his angling for a cameraman he respected, his determination to get the right presenter and the right film editor. He was going to direct the thing himself but she should be his PA, his personal assistant, she would put more into it than anyone would know; she already had. Did she think he was too proselytizing? Of course she didn't, she assured him, the facts would speak for themselves. He must stick to his vision of how he wanted to present them: he would do it, she was very sure he was capable of it.

Before they finished the meal she fished in her neat Chanel handbag and brought out something hand-written, giving it to him. It read *All good things come by grace and grace by art and art is very hard.* "I wish I knew who wrote it," she said. "Do you?" He shook his head. He said, his voice gravelly, "Come out in the car."

They drove down to the Island Gardens on the Isle of Dogs, looking across to Greenwich and the view Canaletto bequeathed to the world.

"I wish you'd think of leaving him," he said.

He took her into his arms and kissed her carefully. Their cheeks touched, their hair intermingled, their hands clutched. She felt she was surrendering more and more of herself, that the moment would inevitably come when she would give in to his pleading. Yet at this point, panic usually invaded her. Was she really ready to leave Arthur for good, to give up Pinkmount Drive and all it had meant in the past? She acknowledged the shadowy figure of Tracy-Lee in the back of her mind, but contrary to expectations the girl had not antagonized her, but had instead touched some weird vein of compassion, of recognition. Maybe she saw an image of her own teenage insecurity. She knew this was curious, that she had expected fury and a sensation of usurpation, but it had not happened.

She said with a flash of bitter, sudden anger, "It is what he deserves. He just turned his back on me, you know, when it happened. When he lost his job. He simply went away in his mind where I couldn't reach him. After fifteen years of marriage. It was as though he was reaching back into the past for comfort, as though there was nothing in our house, our home, any more, that meant anything to him." Carefully, she was mopping tears.

"Do you not think," he argued, "that marriage is too constraining? Maybe he felt he couldn't develop, couldn't change, yet circumstances were forcing change on him."

"I know I want to change," she said, gulping. "I want to do real things instead of little practice runs. I want to go up for roles on TV. Get myself an agent. At the expense of failing. Conrad," she appealed to him, "do you think I could do it? Do you think I should try?"

"You said it yourself," he reminded her. "Art is hard. You'd have to be prepared for setbacks. I'll help you all I can — I have a friend who is a good agent — but cash and security don't come into it. And you're used to that."

"You're right to use the past tense. I *was* used to it. It subverted me in some way."

"But Arthur himself," he pursued,

"what about Arthur himself? I think your feelings for him are dead — "

"No," she said quickly. "All over the place, because of him going off the way he did, but it was hard to leave him, I did it to pull him up — "

"And what about me?" He gripped her wrist, so hard that it hurt and she twisted her arm away from him. "Don't do that," she warned. "I could do a lot worse." His voice thickened. "You won't so much as say how you feel about me and I'm bloody obsessed by you. You're not being fair to me, Sylvia."

She pushed the hair from his eyes and kissed his forehead. "We did come down here to work, you know. That was the package. As for how I feel about you, I should think it was obvious, you're my kind of person, we're soul-mates — "

"You'll always be there for me, di-da, di-da." He turned again in his seat, so that he was almost falling on her. He was kissing her passionately and his hands were everywhere.

"No!" she said forcefully. "Conrad, no." She pushed him away with all her strength.

"You frigid bitch!"

"No, I'm not that," she said, steadily.

"Sorry," he said. "Sorry."

"Conrad," she said, "how do I face your father and mother when I go back if I've been sleeping with their son?"

"Why go back at all? We could find some place here."

"Using what for money?"

"I'll keep you."

"Don't be silly. I pay my way."

"It always comes down to money. Money doesn't matter. It's not important."

"It is when you don't have any."

There was a silence while they watched a patchy old drifter sail down the river. Its drunken skewed insouciance somehow cheered them both a little, but she did have one final say about their situation: "Tacky, isn't it? What we're doing."

With a kind of resignation they went into each other's arms murmuring reassurances. He drove her back to the hotel and went off to see a commissioning editor at Channel Four. She lay in her room reading a Joanna Trollope. And thinking of how much of her consciousness had been formed by books.

Not real life. Thinking of her husband, how different he was from Conrad. The latter so intense, responsive, nervy; Arthur her husband so clean-fair, with his blond stubble, his sturdy physique. She was remembering how hooked she had been on his physical presence, the ache of wanting and wanting him that had thrown all other reservations out of the window. Not having children had been more of a hurt to him than to her: after her noisy, semi-deprived childhood with too many siblings, she had found childless adulthood curiously satisfying, as though the young one in her now had time to expand and grow.

He was a man's man, though, finding his satisfactions in playing games, in joining clubs and institutions. Inevitably there had been great shaded areas of her life he had known nothing of: her intellectual and artistic explorations left him cold if impressed. They had had a good life in the main till he was made redundant. He'd gone down like a tree under the woodman's axe and there had been no reviving him. She saw how things, habit, usage, work, lifestyles had been pushing them away from each other, when they had thought these things were the glue that held them together. How mistaken could you be?

She closed her Trollope thinking that the best thing was for her to stick to her freshly declared ambition: to find work where she could express herself. Be as arty as she liked.

After a bit she found she was waiting for Conrad's knock on her door.

12

ARTHUR BLANEY and his daughter gazed at each other across the breakfast table and then looked away again.

"What would you like to do with yourself today?" he asked, in what he thought was an encouraging tone. Tracy-Lee fastidiously buttered her toast. "Maybe get a job?" she suggested. Arthur said nothing. Getting a job suggested permanence and despite his determination to make his daughter part of his life from now on, he was beginning to think the pieces would not fit together. For a start, Sylvia might never come back to him. He had lain awake with that possibility tormenting him for most of the night and the dawning realization that he had treated her less than fairly when he went off to Scotland. At the time it had seemed so clear-cut, the only possible course open to him. But then he hadn't been seeing straight. He had simply been all hurt and terror, terror that he could no longer hack it, that it would all go, the house, the cars, the lifestyle. It hadn't been rational, the National Grid that was his mind had closed down, he had been in breakdown.

The letter coming yesterday had jerked him back to a more normal plane, offering him the chance of joining Grant and Pershor Associates, a young firm that had set up in the teeth of the recession and with whom he had been doing business before his own firm closed down.

We were very sorry to hear of the closure of Claverton's. There is a vacancy in our Sales Department which will entail some travel in the EU and we are prepared to interview you if you are interested in applying, it read.

Certainly it had been a shot in the arm. So somebody actually still thought something of him. He wasn't rubbish for the dump. He wasn't totally written off. The relief was so total it was painful. When he thought of Grant and Pershor Associates he remembered how people had drawn in their breath at their insouciance, had predicted disaster for them, starting off when they did, but they had a young team who had ridden the wind, cut out fancy cars and office lunches, went about in windcheaters and jeans rather than expensive suits and refused to take no for an answer. Did they see him as fitting in, then? Had he just enough of his original rough edge left to appeal to them? It was weird; he would never have believed it could happen, but ever since reading the letter he had felt the old competitive zest come back, invading his body like a shot of something powerful. He wanted back in there. If he got the job it would all slot back into place . . . or would it? He wanted Sylvia back but perhaps it would be best to wait till he saw how things went.

"Dad," said Tracy-Lee, somewhat forcefully, "if you get a new job, I want one too. I want my own money."

"What about taking some courses at college?"

The corners of her mouth went down. "I'm not a scholar. Maybe later. First I want a job."

He sighed. Talk about rough edges!

His child had swamped the bathroom floor by leaving the bath-water running, turned his underwear pink by putting one of her T-shirts in with it in the wash, chipped the spout of an expensive teapot and brought mud in where mud had never been seen before. Even allowing for the strangeness of her situation, she was proving awkward and unpredictable. But she gave him one of her uncertain smiles now and his doubts, as ever, were vanquished. She was just *there*, by some miracle, as though she had always been there and it was passing wonderful to have her, a late stripe he had neither earned nor deserved.

"What do you have in mind?"

"Hairdresser. They're advertising for a junior in that place next to the Green Man."

Even in the first week after she had landed the job he could see the difference. Out went the trainers and she borrowed from him for platform shoes and black opaque tights. She ran up a small pelmet of a skirt on Sylvia's sewing machine, had her hair lightened and crimped, placed rouge high on her cheeks to make them look thinner. She looked, in other words, like the other trendy youngsters who cut, dyed, shampooed, swept up and sang along to Radio Two in the defensive ears of older customers and when she got her pay and share of tips was blissful. Debs and Sue and Allie became like sisters, the quoted arbiters on everything from what to wear to how to lose weight. "Dad, I'm dropping the Lee," she informed Arthur. "From now on, I'm just Tracy. Deb'n Sue'n Allie think the Lee is too Hollywood." She even had a new little high-pitched giggle which was obviously borrowed from one or other of her fellow-workers.

He took his time over phoning Gordon Pershor. Two days. Two days to plan what to say, what to wear to the interview. In the mirror, it was a hollow-cheeked version of his former self who looked back at him and when he tried on his best suit the jacket hung loosely on him, as did the trousers, but that spacy look was in, Tracy assured him. Record company executives wore it. So that was all right, then.

She hugged him before he set off.

"Don't worry, Dad," she assured him.

"If you don't get the job, I'll keep you in your old age." Her cheek put a half-smile on his face, taking away some of that intolerably strained expression. Gordon Pershor had made up his mind to have him. The salary was a lot less than his old one, but the prospects were wide open. He drove home as though he were just getting over an illness: weak and on the verge of trembling, but seeing the outside world again in its true colours, a place where people lived and worked and spoke to each other, not a kind of shadow-play.

Tracy had made a prolonged and thoughtful visit to the chilled cabinet at M and S and brought home a feast of spare ribs, won ton and egg fried rice, followed by apricot yogurt. Buoyed up by her thrilled reaction to his appointment, he showed her how to open a wine bottle and make coffee in a cafetière. She regaled him with the tale of a dowager's head dyed green by Debs' errant hand and of coffee spilled down an outsize bosom because Allie laughed so much.

It was only later that Sylvia's presence

seemed palpable in the room and the funny thing was it was like she had been when he first knew her, a slightly chubby-faced girl with a shy smile and a way of talking he had never encountered in anyone before, bookish and eloquent and imaginative. Who else would have praised his cuddly, ursine body, the gold hairs covering his arms and torso? Or used a word like ursine? She had a soft down, too, on her forearms and on the gentle swell of her lower belly — "Down, down all over her, Hey nonny nonny no," she had quoted gaily at him, adding, "but more all over *him*." He had this vivid image of them stroking each other that was almost more erotic than the thought of the act itself — and he had been thinking a lot about the act recently.

Now he had a job lined up again, there was no reason why they shouldn't take up the old tenor of their ways. Except that she might bang on more about her interests and be less ready to bend her life round his. He knew this for an emotional impasse: something in him did not want to give her her freedom (as she put it); wanted to control and have the final say in what she did. Wanted to be responsible for her. It was because he knew how attractive she was, how other men were intrigued by her poise. Even her voice, low and musical with a hint of teasing, was an unconscious come-on. He felt something struggle wildly in him, always, when he reached this point in his deliberations. He simply didn't want to argue. He wanted to assert his needs. When she had been her warm and amusing self, before the catastrophe of the job-loss, she had said ruefully he was an unreconstructed cave-man, a Pict and a savage, but the savage and the sophisticate had somehow struck a balance. Which was surely what most marriages were about.

But the way she had gone off with that young shyster from next door . . . He had not really thought that Sylvia was having an affair with Conrad Higgison, more that she was flirting again with her old dream of independence, doing what she liked. Not being beholden to him. Now, like a creeping paralysis, the fear took hold . . . maybe Higgison had some secret appeal, maybe the whole trip was a cover for his wife's infidelity. It was as though now the work thing had been solved this other matter had been waiting in his mind to clout him. He had pretended that while he was workless there was no point in worrying about anything else. He should never have gone off to Scotland as he had done and then to bring Tracy back . . . But he couldn't regret that. Tracy was in the picture. Whatever Sylvia had in mind, Tracy was in the frame.

It took a lot to go round to the Higgisons' front door but fortified by the wine he had drunk with the Chinese meal, he did so. It was a pale-faced Mavis who answered and grudgingly gave him the London phone number Conrad had left her.

"Didn't Sylvia give you it?"

"I must have mislaid it."

"You got someone staying? A youngster?"

"A young relative." He stared her out.

"I won't ask you in. We're about to eat."

"I didn't intend to come in." The door closed swiftly in his face.

It was Higgison who answered the London number, but he wasted no time on preliminaries. "I want to speak to my wife."

"Arthur?" The brown sugar voice.

"I've got a job. Thought you'd want to know."

A silence. Then, "What sort of job?"

"Much like the old one. Lower salary. Good prospects, though."

"Is your daughter still with you?"

"Her name is Tracy. Yes, she's here."

"Keeping her side of the bargain? Keeping the kitchen tidy?"

"Not bad. She cooked tonight," he lied. "When are you coming back?"

"I don't know. I can't be exact."

"Roughly."

"Can't say."

"We can't leave things up in the air."

"You should have thought of that. Before you took off for Scotland."

Afterwards he was shaken by how much he wanted her. She had not sounded too hard when they'd spoken about Tracy.

Before dark, in the evenings that followed, he saw the boy going round in circles on his bike just outside the gate and peering up the drive towards the house. He wore his hair combed over one eye in the current fashion, a baseball cap back to front, a plaid shirt with the tail hanging out, skinny jeans and the ubiquitous trainers. There seemed quite a lot of him folded over the handlebars: gangly would be the word. Yearning.

He tackled Tracy about him.

"Who is he?"

"Just Gary somebody."

"What's he hanging round here for?"

"How should I know?"

"Did you encourage him?"

"No, of course not." Bright red now. Giggling. "He's in a band."

"Whose band? What band? What does he play?"

"His, actually. It's called Kick the Moon. He plays guitar."

He softened slightly, thinking, who hasn't once been in somebody's band with a stupid name, in somebody's garage or somebody's attic and who hasn't played guitar? Somewhere in the back of his mind he strummed the riff for 'I Want To Hold Your Hand'.

"Tell him to lay off."

"Oh, Dad!"

He identified the strange feeling inside him as paternal jealously. If he ever hurts her, he thought, I'd want to kill him.

Was this how fathers felt and did it make him a real one, a proper one?

He went out to the front porch and gave the boy an upbraiding glare.

The initiator of Kick the Moon answered with a friendly wave.

13

WHEN Sylvia Blaney and Conrad Higgison wanted to talk they had to go to each other's rooms in the Hackney B. and B. for the Cypriot establishment boasted no sitting-room. East End London was a disgusting old harridan, Sylvia thought, seedy, dissolute, dirty, hard. Sometimes she yearned for northern ways, shop assistants who smiled, window cleaners who whistled, what her father would have called a little humanity. But in the likes of Kensington or Whitehall there was also an ambitious throb — fashion, colour, cameos, strangers — that could be enthralling, even if it quickly tired you out. She didn't want to leave it all yet, but Arthur's phone call had unsettled her, was pulling her away from these new diversions. She even found herself thinking what it would be like to have a daughter in the house, the house she had put together so carefully. A daughter going in and out of the front door, up and down the drive, running the kitchen taps. How could it be that she did not totally preclude this idea of a daughter, she who had not particularly wanted a child of her own flesh? Was it because as you got older and your biological clock ran out, some old maternal chime was rung, willy-nilly? She had posited that there might even be something maternal in what she felt for Conrad but he wouldn't have any of it; he said Freud was discredited, there was nothing at all maternal about her, not with those legs. Mavis, now she was maternal, the full whack, Oedipus-schmoedipus, he'd had to cut himself free from her restricting arms and once was enough.

The trouble was, the trouble had been, he had looked so much in need of care and protection when she first met him, protection from the hard-nosed trade and industry-based bourgeoisie who sneered at anything aspirational, who put down 'arty talk' as pretentious, she had just wanted to dash in and rescue him, shake him down and lend him a listening ear. The occasion had been a party in his parents' house and it had been Christmas. Golfing pullovers much to the fore. Sports, holidays, children's school fees the big topics. In the middle of it all he had quoted the Christmas Betjeman and been rewarded by hostile, alarmed stares, then roasted in a rather nasty, philistine way that hadn't let up. "Do they let you drink *Real Beer* in the south, Conrad?" with references to the softness of poets, the absurdity of modern art, the now past necessity to read books when the Internet beckoned and on Conrad's harmless head it had all been heaped, because he was, whisper, an intellectual, he wrote boo-yiks, he made films, he'd be telling them next he ate quiches.

She was in his room now, to talk about Arthur's phone call and she knew there was nothing soft-bellied about him, he could work with a fierce untiring concentration once a project was under way, he was even harrying her to get her latest notes typed up on his lap-top computer for they were rapidly approaching the yea/nay stage for more money.

He might be a dreamer but he was

also a man who knew his craft and she had learned a lot from him. But after Arthur's phone call she knew she had to think about going back. If she was going back. She put her notes to one side and said, "Conrad, we have to talk about what I'm going to do."

"Can't we get on?" he said testily.

"Maybe I should go back. That's what I'm thinking."

"Can't spare you yet." His head was down, he was turning pages, stroking out, pencilling in.

She was silent, letting him get on with it. Automatically she tidied and folded clothes he had left strewn about on chairs. Her mind raced in all directions and the silent tension between them seemed to mount till he threw his manuscript to one side and said with angry fury, "I thought you had decided. I thought you wanted your freedom."

"Can one change the habits of a lifetime?"

"I thought you wanted to act?"

"How do I know I can?"

He caught her by the wrist, so roughly she grimaced. "By giving it a try. I've got you an audition. I was saving it for supper. They're looking for new faces for an afternoon serial. You'd be up for a part not dissimilar to your own real-life situation. A woman breaking away. I met my old pal Ernie Frank. He's willing to test you on my recommendation."

She sat down on the bed, her face colourless.

"When?"

"Tomorrow."

She *should* be an actress, he thought detachedly. That face shows so much. There was a kind of leaping excitement, there was reluctance, there was guilt, too.

"I am letting him down," she said. "Arthur."

"No more than he did when he went off as he did. Go back and you know how it will be again. Arthur's adjunct. Doing things his way. Go back this time and you know you'll not have the strength to break away, ever again."

"Where do you come into the question?" She put the question to the world at large.

"You *know*," he said. "I am waiting

for you to acknowledge that you know. I can't change the way I feel about you."

"Have you been trying?"

He ducked his head in acknowledgement. "Preparing for the worst. The indications have not been promising."

"You might take me over too."

"No. I only want you to be happy."

The last exchange was different from the previous part of the conversation, suffused with something tender, exploratory, loving. She said, "I have been thinking a lot of when we first met, at that awful Christmas party and how I knew how you felt. I have been thinking a lot of things."

"Such as?"

"How wonderful it would be if I landed this acting part."

"Don't," he warned her, "put too much into it. There'll be others, just as keen as you."

"And with more experience! Do you honestly, God's honour honestly, think that I'm in there with a chance?"

"I think you've got great presence — "

She was suddenly quite still, as though steadying herself for what was ahead. "I think I've got the gumption. I am going up for it." She held her arms out to him. "Oh, come and hold me. I need to be held."

He needed no second bidding, holding her against him, if a little self-consciously. She looked up at him and gave a brief laugh. "In for a penny," she said. "If I stay — and I'm going to stay — I stay with you."

"What do you mean?" Slowly.

"I think I've decided. It's you."

He gave his work no more than a backward glance. Unresisting, she allowed him to undress her and then for the first time she saw him naked too and realized how young he was, strong and muscled and long of body. Even as they touched, she was acknowledging her arbitrary impulse, the way the two were intertwined, her ambition and her libido and how even then they warred with something else, something too complicated and long-standing to define.

Their love-making was wild and tender, broken off while they questioned each other, renewed each time with an ever-greater depth of feeling, till both knew every affirmation had been made, every doubt relinquished. "Mine," he said. "Mine." When they were both exhausted they lay flattened against each other, knowing a kind of peace that painted a vulnerable look of utter tranquillity on their faces. He could not forbear from touching her hair, kissing her shoulder, sighing over her. She ran her fingers over him as though to memorize every plane, every pore. "Have we been wicked?" she asked, against his cheek. "No. You know it had to happen," he answered.

Afterwards, when he was dressing, she said, "I don't care." She repeated it. "I don't care." What or whom she did not care about was not spelled out. She held on to the back of the bed as though she were on a storm-tossed boat in a heaving sea. "I don't feel like the wicked temptress. I feel new. Sixteen. Me."

His head came up through his pullover and he gave her his attentive, tender-gazed scrutiny, saying nothing. She had the fleeting illusion that he was, indeed, older than she was; wiser. And that she was in his keeping. It was not how it was meant to be, but it was how it felt.

As she sat up in the bed, her sweater wound about her for warmth, she made him think of a light-weight boxer, shoulders scrunched, fists balled, ready to fight off all doubters and challengers.

★ ★ ★

The rehearsal room was somewhere behind Kennington Oval. Dusty. Redolent of stress and sweat. Although she was still warm from Conrad's loving, warm and rejuvenated, something else was there, a ghost that dodged behind the people she spoke to, one with a burry Scots accent, raising an admonitory finger and saying, "You loved me too. *And* it was good." What did people do with former husbands, former lovers, she wondered? How did they accommodate their memories of them? Arthur had behaved with hideous insensitivity towards her, but now it was only what was worthy about him she recollected. How he brought up hot tea with honey to her in bed. How he could lift and carry her when

141

the notion took him. How hard he could laugh when his funny bone was tickled. Laugh till the tears ran out from those honest blue eyes. She glared at this ghost — how dared he, after all the hurt, the pain he had caused her? — and a woman with a straight-haired bob, straight as March rain, interposed herself between Sylvia and the misty protagonist. "I'm Jane Banks. Ernie can't make it. I've to do the necessary."

The script shook in Sylvia's hand and the young director — as Sylvia heard her described by a previous contender for the part of Louise Albury — gave a sympathetic laugh. "Don't worry. It happens to all," and began briskly to put her through her paces. "*Stand here. Raise your head. Stop! She's loved this man, you know, now she's leaving him. Stop! Too many gestures. The small screen will exaggerate. Do it subtly. The eyes have it. Again. Yes, just this bit, again.*"

She was wringing, tearful, walking on legs that had no substance, when Jane Banks peremptorily called a halt.

"Ernie will want to see it," she said.

"How was it?" Sylvia demanded.

142

Jane Banks did not answer her. Merely smiled her infuriating smile. But even then Sylvia knew she had landed it. She hadn't acted the part, she had inhabited it and she knew from the abashed smiles of the others in the big room that she had hit home, moved them. A sense of exhilaration entered her, a knowledge and certainty of who she was and what she was capable of accomplishing. Conrad had come to pick her up and she saw him smiling at her from behind the glass exit doors.

14

BERNARD HIGGISON came into the large, immaculately planned kitchen where he and his wife breakfasted and stopped in the doorway, aware something was wrong. It was his wife's back. It was a back that was very still. And hunched. A back that spoke such volumes he could feel all sorts of nameless fears rise from stomach to gullet. What would it be? The tachycardia or the recollection of how her mother had always favoured the others? He tiptoed in. "Mavis?" he queried.

"You'll have to go round there." The face pale above the green dressing-gown, big brown gouges under the eyes. "Get Arthur Blaney to bring his wife home. They're having an affair, Sylvia Blaney and our Conrad — "

"That's not what Conrad said," he interrupted. "She's helping with his work."

"Believe that, you'll believe anything,"

said Mavis savagely. "Look. When you were out at the golf club meeting last night, I phoned Conrad at that London place, that Hackney set-up. I just felt like a chat. The telephonist said I'll put you through to their room. Then she corrected herself. I asked him straight, was she there and he didn't answer me directly, just went on about how well things were going. I couldn't pin him down about anything."

"Well, he's not answerable to you any more."

"I've known. Ever since they went off."

"Well, even if it is the case, there's nothing we can do about it."

"I'm the one who has to go into shops, face people. It'll soon be common knowledge. To think of the advantages we gave that boy — "

"Get it through your head. He isn't a boy any longer."

They glared at each other. "You should have been tougher on him," she said.

"And if you fussed less he'd confide more."

He had to go into the new office,

where he sat waiting for business to come in, playing about with figures in front of him to convince himself this new venture would not also go to the wall, like the nuclear plant. What had happened since the eighties, when people were willing and able to have a go? Now it was all caution, caution. Cutting your cloth. Cutting back. Nearly as bad as the war. He could just about remember his mother saving string, margarine paper, unravelling jumpers, scolding you for not eating up the fat on your plate. "Waste not, want not." So we were back to that, were we?

Mavis showered and dressed when he'd gone, fastidiously using the remains of the expensive unguents Bernard had bought her when things had been better. She knew the suit she wore had a dated look, the trousers not quite the right cut, the blazer top with too many gilt buttons but at least it had a good label and she made sure it showed when she took the jacket off in the cafeteria in the middle of her shopping. Discontent was fizzing in her, especially after she caught sight of her dark roots in a shop mirror and then met a friend on her way to an expensive gym. Almost outside her own volition she found herself in her favourite boutique, trying on outfit after outfit and finally buying a flamboyant royal-blue dress and jacket that would scream top-price range to the Wilhowbry fashion cognoscenti. She rationalized it on the grounds that now Bernard was in business again she had to fly the flag.

She bought some Dior perfume and some new shoes, then not content with that, an Oriental rug for the hall that she had been coveting for some weeks. Painless enough with her credit card. At the end of the spree she was shaking from forbidden pleasures, prepared to go off to her mother's if Bernard's protests went over the top.

In the same way that she had gone into the boutique almost in spite of herself she found herself walking up the Blaneys' drive once she had put the car and the shopping away. She didn't know what she was going to say. She only knew that Arthur Blaney took it in turns to come home at lunch-time to feed and exercise the old dog, Sinbad, and as his car was at the front door it was obviously his turn.

He was eating a ragged sandwich at the breakfast bar but hospitably offered her coffee.

"I'm worried."

Sylvia had always maintained that that was Mavis's life vocation. Worrying.

"Uh-huh? What about?"

"Sylvia and Conrad. Why don't you just get her home, Arthur?"

"Well, first of all, I'm not the boss of her. And secondly, what are you trying to say, Mavis?"

"You know."

"I think you're wrong. My wife wants some kind of career, it seems, and she doesn't know many people who can help her. Conrad is one of them."

She gave him an old-fashioned look and he coloured up, his blue eyes sparking resistance. "You've no right to suggest anything else, Mavis. Sylvia and I have had our troubles but our marriage isn't over. I feel if I give her some leeway she'll get her head straight. I've certainly tried her patience — "

"Well, now she's going to try yours,"

she said in sepulchral tones. "I know my son, I don't need things spelled out for me." She was shoving tears away, gulping as she tried one last plea: "Get her home, Arthur. Before things get out of hand."

★ ★ ★

"I'll take care of you," said Tracy. "We don't need her back here. I can do it all, make the food, do the shopping, et cetera, et cetera."

She was wearing big shoes, like she'd walked on something, and a tight, short, stretchy dress that revealed her bosom and, practically, her crotch. He remembered Sylvia's beautifully cooked dinners, (plaice with grapes!), and sighed at the thought of sharing yet another Macdonald's with Big Fries. His stomach was permanently sour. But she tried. The marks hadn't come out of the carpet where she'd spilled the Chinese sweet and sour. The kitchen resounded to the crash of glass and china and a month's ironing fell out when you opened the airing cupboard. He worried about the boy on the bike, who now came to the back door and had a daytime occupation — student of computer studies. But she kept up his morale with her chirpy comments on her new life and her loyalty to him was like a big warm scarf, like the hand-knitted one his grannie used to toast at the fire before he went out on frosty mornings, along with his gloves. She was family, all he had, and precious to him.

"I don't want you to have to run a big house. You should be having fun. Enjoying yourself. Sylvia had it down to a fine art, we could entertain — "

"Oh, have her back then, for all I care," said Tracy, clamping arms across her bosom. "I can take a hint." Sulking.

"You quite like her. You told me so."

"She could be worse."

"If she came back, it would take a weight off you, wouldn't it? You wouldn't have to make shopping lists or run home to see if old Sinbad's bladder is bursting. She'd get somebody in for the ironing and the kitchen floor and put flowers in the vases — "

"I do flowers."

He could not say they were not the

same. The child tried. She wasn't useless. Just young. Sylvia could oil the wheels and for all three of them. Providing she didn't go off and act or get involved with other work outside the house. He couldn't change his deeply held view that women were best employed in the nurturing role. Like his grannie. He saw it as the best thing a woman might aspire to, never demeaning.

The girls in his old office had teased him about it, calling him Unreconstructed Man. But he wasn't the only one. And there were still enough Unreconstructed Women about, too, women who liked men to be the bread-winners, to decide the family lifestyle. Who was to say who was right and who was wrong?

He picked up the phone and put it down again a couple of times before he finally did ring the London number. He had been angered and upset by Mavis's visit, knowing her for someone who always saw things slightly skewed by her own neuroticism. Not that he trusted Conrad Higgison. The moody-browed aesthete was so different from most of the men he knew he simply couldn't read him. He was the kind of man Sylvia attracted to her but she had always been able to cope with them. She wouldn't really have an affair with him, would she? Someone twelve years younger? He began to feel a curious squirming sensation in the pit of his stomach. His wife capable of infidelity? It didn't happen to the likes of them. He knew Sylvia's moral stances as well as he knew his own. But then look how he had felt when he saw Ida again. He hadn't been prepared for how easy it might have been to retrieve old feelings if she had shown the slightest interest in him. Worst of all, surging through him all afternoon had been the recollection of how Sylvia had been when things had been good between them, him earning big money, her contented with her interests and the sex good and golden on summer afternoons and holiday islands. He was gripped by a pole-axing sexual angst seeing how crazy he had been to think he could just get back with her when it suited him. But then he had been crazy, more than a little off his trolley, out of his tree, when the job had packed up.

They liked to call it depression but crazy — daft — was a better description. Now that things were part restored he at least had his daughter, but what of his wife?

"Is that Conrad Higgison? Arthur Blaney. I want to speak to Sylvia."

"Yeah. It's Conrad. I'll get her. I think she has something to tell you." The voice was uncompromising. "I hope you'll listen."

"Just get her."

"Arthur?" After a minute her breathy tones. "How are you? I am coming up to see you. I have something I want to tell you."

"What is it?"

"I'd rather wait till I see you. Face to face."

The receiver had obviously been snatched from her for next it was Conrad's voice. "It might not be altogether a surprise to you, old man, but Sylvia and I see our way ahead together. She wants to be with me. Not you."

"Put her back on. I don't want to speak to you. I want to speak to my wife. She is my wife. You understand that, you damned greasy punk, you. Come up here with her and I'll knock your bloody block off. Savvy? Do I make myself clear?"

"Arthur? Wait. Please listen. I have landed an acting job down here. It is going to keep me busy for quite a long time, if it all works out. I'm not coming back north. It's nothing to do with Tracy, tell her, it's just I'm doing what I've always wanted to do. I'm sorry, Arthur, but it's all over between us." She was crying, her voice high and strained with the effort to keep contact. "No hard feelings in the end, Arthur. It's just better for all of us that things should be this way."

"Put him on to me again."

"No point, Arthur. I'm so sorry. Truly I am."

"I want to speak to him."

"Sorry. Speak soon. Take care." Conrad had seized the telephone. It made a clattering sound then hummed in Arthur's ear. "Naw," he said, in broad Scots. "Naw. Na-a-a-w."

15

THEY hadn't been able to leave the refugee camp as soon as they'd intended. Because of renewed fighting they would have to take a longer, less straightforward route back to the Austrian border and news kept reaching them of heavy snowfalls and impassable roads. Food was short and the people they had come to help infinitely in more need of it than they were. Ginnie was glad of her small appetite but worried about Dougie.

The British contingent had been shocked and angered by Frank O'Connor's death, but as they took in the desperate needs of the refugees, compassion returned. In the so-called baby unit there were big, dark-eyed orphans with missing limbs and even shell-shock. Ginnie watched Dougie shake himself out of self-pity and into a vigorous kind of insistence on doing what he could. While she fed and nursed babies, he put his skilful amateur carpentry and plumbing to good use. People who had been examples of man's inhumanity to man became friends, took on the individual characteristics that endeared, irritated or humbled. Ginnie began to feel she had lived forever in this great, dark, seething compound. But at last the weather was letting up, there was talk of getting out. They went around shaking hands, hugging children, giving the assurance they would raise more help back home.

When the big van rumbled into life, with a full tank of black-market petrol, Ginnie began to imagine she could already feel the scents and hear the sounds of home. Fresh-baked bread, the faint hum of the central-heating boiler, the radio blaring out the fatuities of Desert Island Discs. She said this to Dougie and he gave her a complicit smile. "Me, too. I want a bath with a whole packet of Radox in it."

Knowing what they'd left behind, these indulgent thoughts made them guilty and then quiet. The roads were demanding of Dougie's full attention, in any case.

They were skiddy with impacted snow, then, as the thaw advanced, dotted with pot-holes and lined at narrow points with ditches easier to get into than out of without assistance. But at last they were on a proper highway and moving, gliding almost, as effortlessly as images in a motion picture. Dougie whistled tunelessly. Ginnie felt warmth creep back into her fingers as the tension eased and went.

"You've been a total brick," he said. "Seeing you with those babies, you're a natural."

"I didn't know I liked babies," Ginnie confessed, "but they get to you."

"It's brought us close, hasn't it, all this?" Studiedly he kept his eyes on the road. "When we get back, I want to take you out to dinner. I want you to put on your big best shoes, as the song says, and come out with me. I never thought I would say these words to any woman. Not after Connie." Now he trusted himself with a quick glance. "What do you think, Ginnie? Shall we give the neighbours something to talk about?"

"I don't mind," she said easily. "Where shall we go?"

"Some place that does good soups with bottomless nourishment."

"I shall start with something prawny."

"Then I'll have a steak bigger than my plate, with a wine and cream and mushroomy sauce."

"I think I'll have chicken. I like Thai cooking. Something spicy and delicate."

"And a pudding smothered in golden syrup, light-as-air sponge. And custard."

"Greedy pig!" she laughed. They were both aware there had not been much laughter around in the camp and that their near-exultation was there nevertheless. Ginnie sat quietly then, trying to sort out her emotions, her memories and above all, now that there was time to think about it, what there was between her and Dougie. The closeness he had just referred to and whether it was going to survive. For, face it, things would be very different when they were back in their separate homes. Old habits would reclaim them. She would be back to visiting Mother and he to the sideboard that, with its photographs, had become a shrine to Connie.

That night. That night she'd gone to find him and ran him to earth in the driving cabin. Nothing, no nothing had been the same since then, since holding him, rocking him, cuddling him and in the end putting her lips to his and kissing him. Pity sliding over into something else. Ever since, in her moments of rest, thinking of him, fantasizing about making love to him, about him making love to her, making him say the things she wanted him to say. "It's brought us close, hasn't it?" She wanted him to add 'darling'. She wanted to say 'darling' back. But it was all too precipitate and it might be totally false, once they were away from this No Man's Land. After Sydney, she had been pretty certain men were no longer for her.

But that night. To get back to that night. His jacket and shirt-neck had been open and she had seen the dark hair growing high on his chest. She had stroked his hands and felt the hair on the back of his hands. The masculinity. The thrill of otherness.

159

Just recently, she had pondered a good deal about her sexuality. How wrong she had been for Sydney and how that had somehow denigrated her in her own eyes and she suspected, her mother's and sister's. But now she allowed herself to think that if Sydney had been less of a bully she might have made a good wife. He had displayed no patience and no sensitivity. Their first night together had been more like rape, she saw now, and maybe she had never really got over that. She could still feel that same sense of cowering, back in her mind. But equally she could remember the first springs of carnality, going on a picnic in the woods with school friends of both sexes, playing hide and seek, and the first flash, the touch of immortality she had felt, when the boy she liked best caught her hand. Maybe men were for her, after all. Certainly, desire chased helter-skelter down her imagination, trying to focus on what it would be like to be in bed with Dougie. His compact body next to her in the cabin was a source of both embarrassment and pleasure. How did he feel? She looked to see and caught an expression on his face, a warm and connecting Dougie-look and she felt a new, slightly dislocating sense of wonder, sheer astonishment, that just maybe she had been responsible for putting it there.

"Shall we sing?" he asked.

"If you like. What shall we sing?"

"Anything you like." She could trust herself to sing, he thought. Ginnie's singing voice had a richness and depth denied her diffident speech pattern.

She had sung it to the babies back at the refugee camp. The little ones who would eventually die of Aids. The dark-eyed repositories of a country's pain:

"Jesus bids us shine
With a pure clear light
Like a little candle
Burning in the night.
In this world is darkness
So we must shine
You in your small corner
And I in mine."

They came then, the tears she had not been able to shed till now, for everything they had seen, for the certainty that it would all go on, that the world wasn't finished yet with its darkness. Dougie put out a hand and held hers, momentarily, in a vice-like grip. They rode over the border in chilling rain.

★ ★ ★

Evelyn had that hard and piggy look in her eyes that Ginnie remembered from their childhood, when she thought Ginnie had got a bigger piece of apple pie or better skipping ropes.

"So you've been in all the papers," she said.

"Not intentionally." *How was Dougie making out? Ginnie was wondering. Had he eaten yet? Had he got something for his cough?* It was strange, them being in separate houses again, next to each other. She would get him some Vick or Olbas Oil —

"We knew, didn't we, when you put her in the home? How quickly the money would go? We'll have no option but to sell the house, the fees are exorbitant. It was so much better all round when she was at home."

"For you, Evelyn. Not for me."

Ginnie was adamant that she would not apologize. Neither would she try to explain to her sister that the action of putting her mother in a home had been a last-ditch one for her. Explaining to Evelyn never had any effect. She had known she could not go on, without doing some violence to either her mother or herself. Thank God she'd had just enough native wit left to know when breaking-point had been reached. It was all very well to talk sentimentally of 'carers', for the government to issue specious assurances that they would be helped, backed up. It had not been her experience. Her experience was that no one took a blind bit of notice, till perhaps some similar calamity entered their own lives. She knew she had loved her mother, given her all the affection and support she was capable of and in the beginning it had not been too hard — if there had been a light at the end of the tunnel, but there was none. She had known her own mind was beginning to splinter, her own personality go under and Dougie had saved her sanity by getting her involved in the Croatian project. Now she knew that although her mother's plight was grievous, it was not singular and knew, too, that if it came to selling the house to provide for the old lady's care, she could go along with that. Evelyn saw her own legacy being eaten away but that was Evelyn's problem. She was not starving or even hard-up and quite ruthless in her conviction that she couldn't be expected to take on any of their mother's care. Even her patchy visiting had taxed her to the limit while Ginnie was away.

Fair enough. She didn't want to dim Evelyn's light as her own had been dimmed. The guttering candle of their mother's life had to be allowed to extinguish itself in its own time.

16

BERNARD HIGGISON gave his wife the same helpless, baffled look he always produced during one of their emotional crises. That of a man well out of his depth. One who could cope with war and politics in his morning paper but not the complexities of daily married life. His own father had gone out to run his minor silk mill at 6 a.m. and returned at 7 p.m. His mother had put the food on the table. Why had he thought life would always be so easy?

"I told you," said Mavis. "I said it all along. And now he's coming up with her to confront Arthur Blaney. To sort things out, he says. Couldn't they just have done it through lawyers, Bernie? He might have had some thought for me, his mother, just gone on HRT. I think I'm having another hot flush, Bernie — "

"Drink your tea." He found issuing small, dictatory phrases worked best with her in this state. He'd decided to take the day off, finding his mind kept bumbling off on the enigma of how two such conventional people as he and Mavis had produced this maverick son. Finding, too, that something hurt below the level of surface skin, a painful condition not unadjacent to parental love. Until recently he'd still cherished the hope that he could take Conrad to cricket matches. That they could find some common ground.

"They're here!" Mavis's sharp ear had picked up the sound of a car engine. She beat him in the rush to the window, in time to see Sylvia enter her own drive, then Conrad kiss her before he turned to come to his parents' house. With a rush of feeling for his wife, Bernard Higgison saw her mouth tighten and shoulders go back in the fight for composure. He was at the front door before Conrad had time to ring the bell.

Arthur Blaney let his wife through the front door of their residence at the same time. Like Bernard, he had arranged to have the day off. He was not prepared for Sylvia's new short haircut, a fluffed-out bob that gave her the look of a twenties flapper. She was thinner. The dark-green trouser suit was new, sharp as a tack. And she looked younger. The word *joyful* came into his mind and would not go away. He felt a grinding anger grow in tandem with a kind of weird guilt, that he had not been able to do this for her. At the same time, she seemed to recede in his experience, dwindle as though at the far end of a telescope till he could scarcely identify her as his wife. He made a massive effort to appear ordinary, normal. He did not kiss her, but took her coat and hung it up with a certain care. Then like a lawyer or a doctor showing her into a waiting-room, palm of his right hand extended, he indicated formally she should precede him into the sitting-room.

"Where's Tracy-Lee?"

"She's just Tracy nowadays. Working."

"What does she say about all this?" She shook a cushion before tucking it behind her as she sat down.

"Naturally, she's in my corner. What would you expect?"

She looked round the room a shade hungrily and he began to feel the first hint of a connection return, the tip of a distant reassurance. He hoped she would notice there were still flowers in the vases, as she had instituted and that he had polished the brass surround of the fireplace. Tracy had even added fragrant oil to the pot-pourri in the big crystal dish on the coffee-table. Nothing much had changed, he wanted to tell her. Your being away has not altered anything.

"Would it be in order for me to make us some coffee?" Sylvia asked. "I'm spitting feathers."

He had meant to say, 'You know where the kitchen is', but it came out, "I should go round there and smash him within an inch of his life. What have you done to us?" She had risen in alarm and started to make for the door but he put out an arm and barred her, inanely pleased to see the terror on her face. "You're no' going anywhere." The Scottish accent was in force. He felt his teeth bare like an animal's and she gave a little yelp, looking down to where he had grabbed her arm and keeping her gaze there till he released her.

"Arthur," she said softly, "for God's

sake don't let us let this thing get out of hand. Conrad wanted to come in here with me but I pleaded with him not to. He's got enough explaining to do next door." Their gaze locked, his raging, hers defiant. "But you and I have to talk calmly or not at all. Let me make the coffee. Please."

He wasn't going to let her go, that was all there was to it. The hardening of his resolution made him reasonable and he dropped his barring pose. "Make the coffee," he ordered. "One sugar for me. If you remember."

She brought the smaller of their cafetières in on a tray with cups and saucers, not beakers. "Is the new job working out?" she asked.

He laughed. "What would you care about the new job? Doubtless you thought I'd had it."

"No. I never thought that."

"You lying bitch."

"*You* left me, Arthur," she said evenly. "I hope you didn't think I wasn't hurt. Your going to Scotland like that hurt me like blazes."

"You've *betrayed* me. With that snot

next door. How do you think that feels?"

"I don't suppose it feels any better than having an illegitimate child brought into your life — "

There was a long silence. It had not been easy to arrange time off and perversely now trivial office matters obtruded on his mind and things like whether he had given Tracy a shopping list for the greengrocer's. He gave a shout of desperation and cried, "Things could have gone back to how they were. Tracy'll not be here for long — she's got boys after her already and she wants her independence." This was not strictly true. She was almost chokingly filial, wanting to be with him, wanting his approval.

"Tracy's not really the issue. I could get along with her, if I had to." Sylvia sighed, crossed her legs, looked almost reflectively down at her feet. "I have work now, Arthur." Her head came up with a deliberate actressy poise. "It's difficult to explain to you — maybe to any man — but I feel fulfilled doing it. It's really what I'm about and I want to go on doing it. I will go on doing it," she said mutinously. "No one is going to stop me. And in the circumstances I think it's better if you and I get a divorce." She gave him a look that plucked at something, some memory of truth between them. "Don't you?"

"Naw." Now everything came back, everything she was denying.

Raw pain suffused his chest, almost stopping him from breathing. He had wanted to talk everything through with her, to try somehow, he didn't know how, to rekindle what they had once known, to get her to deny that she loved Conrad Higgison, to admit that there had been misunderstanding on misunderstanding, to tell him the acting was just a passing whim. He couldn't seem to get through to her that he was back at work, that he was the provider again and that all she had to do was run his home on the same comfortable lines as before.

"Sylvia!" The plea came out as more of a groan. "For God's sake! Just tell me you regret all this, that you're sorry for what you've done."

"But I'm not."

"You don't regret tearing our lives apart?" His voice was dangerously low

171

and she saw that self-pity had brought him close to tears. "Did you ever want for anything? You only had to ask and you got it."

"I got what you wanted to give. But I never had the freedom to call my life my own." She was stunned into amazement at her own composure and certainty. "I'm not going back into captivity, Arthur. For that's what it was. We should never have married in the first place. The whole thing was a comfortable lie, but a lie it was."

He had never been good at sophistry, she beat him hands down at this kind of thing. He had tried his best. Now with a kind of weariness he let animal rage and the need for revenge sweep over him, pure and honest dancing sensation that fired his bones and blood. They said red mist, didn't they? Naw, he noted, the head got like a kind of compression chamber and there was a screaming somewhere, like that let off by one of the old-fashioned steam engines he used to go to see at Glasgow Central.

"I'll get him." Aye, he'd got through to her now. He saw it with a surge of triumph. "He needn't think he can take my wife and get away with it." She rose and ran alongside him as he swept through the hall and out of the front door, saying, "No, Arthur, no, don't let it come to this, please, please, stop, Arthur, stop." It seemed to take an eternity to reach the front gates, while her voice rose to the trees and was echoed, somewhere, by a school of rooks, and while his rolled-up shirt sleeves unravelled and flapped about in the breeze.

"Don't let him in," Sylvia begged Bernard Higgison when he answered the prolonged ring at the doorbell. But Bernard's detaining hands were shaken off like crumbs off a cloth and Arthur strode into the Higgison sitting-room where Mavis began a series of screams, knocking over the coffee she had been drinking, and Conrad got lumberingly and unpreparedly out of a deep armchair. Before he had time to remove the look of near-incomprehension from his face, Arthur had landed a right hook on Conrad's chin, followed by a series of blows that landed all over the place, shoulder, forehead, chest, stomach.

"Just a bloody minute!" Conrad at last

dodged away from the rain of blows, knocking over his mother who was behind him as he did so. From her position on the floor Mavis clawed at Arthur's trouser-legs. When Arthur responded by kicking out at her, Bernard picked up the nearest heavy object, a bronze art nouveau female figure and swung it wildly at Arthur's head.

"Father, no!" Conrad had just enough judgement left to see the terrible possible consequences of such a weapon and made to grab it from his father's hand. But Arthur was there first. As easily as taking a lollipop from a baby he wrested the bronze dancer away and swung it above his head like a knout. In the scuffling *danse macabre* that ensued it was Conrad's unfortunate temple that felt the impact. He stumbled and went down. Falling back on the settee, Mavis fought off waves of faintness. Arthur watched her face while Sylvia sobbed.

17

THE ambulance raced up Pinkmount Drive, the row it was making unnecessary from the point of view of traffic but allowed to go on because the driver felt a vague Trotskyist pleasure in desecrating the expensive quiet of those big complacent-looking stretches. In one residence, the gardener was already stringing some coloured lights through the tree branches in readiness for the coming Christmas. The two paramedics lifted Conrad gently on to the stretcher. He was still and pale, somehow innocent and almost childlike as he lay there. His parents insisted on getting into the ambulance with him. Mavis's hair hung in distraught little rat's-tails about her face. Bernard had had the nous to put on a jacket but it was from his business suit and the trousers underneath were his gardening flannels. He did not notice.

Sylvia helped to close the ambulance

doors, as though it were some kind of ritual and went back inside the Higgison house. She supposed it was all right. She could not go next door, where two policemen were in the process of interviewing Arthur. No doubt they would come and speak to her eventually. A woman constable was on the phone in the Higgison hall. He was swinging it wildly, she would say. The ornament. He didn't know what he was doing. Conrad sort of got in the way. It would sound as though she were supporting Arthur, which was in no way what she intended, but what was the penalty for murder, or even attempted murder? Arthur in jail was a terrible prospect. He never broke the law, not even as far as feeding a parking meter.

If anything — if anything, well, happened to Conrad, though, why shouldn't Arthur pay any penalty the law decided? She swung from an almost petty and mundane concern for Arthur's position to a dreadful, desperate and overwhelming anger over what he had done to Conrad and a wish to have it all undone. She realized she was crying again. "Oh, my poor baby, my poor lover, my darling." When she had wept like this in front of Conrad's mother, Mavis had screamed at her to be quiet, she had done enough. She acknowledged humbly that this was so. She had done a good deal more than enough.

She stood in the big encircling arc of the Higgison sitting-room windows and watched with a kind of life-saving detachment as the police led Arthur out to their car and drove him away. Would it be on the six o'clock local news, she wondered idly? It was always full of domestic tragedies, rape and snatched children and men driven to board themselves up with guns. Oh my God, what have I done? she wondered. The doctor had refused to be reassuring about Conrad. We don't know. At this stage we just don't know, he had said. The corners of his mouth had folded down. While she abandoned herself to weeping, noisily, out of control, Sylvia was aware of the woman constable entering the room and sitting on a chair by the door. She had her hair done up in some kind of bun and had a very pink, healthy kind of face. Eventually she came over and advised Sylvia that weeping did not do any good.

Across the wide road of Pinkmount Drive, behind the gates of the place where the gardener had been at work earlier on, the Christmas lights blinked on and off, red and yellow and pink and green, obscenely cheerful. A doggy young man who might have been a journalist rang the Higgison bell and was advised by the policewoman to take himself off, though neither harshly nor without some rough coquetry. Sylvia drank tea that appeared at her elbow and rang Wilhowbry General Hospital for news of Conrad. There was none. On the golf course, Bertie Macreevy hit his second last ball into a bunker. He was hooking again, his swing gone to pot because of the digressions from the norm in the Drive. Helen had forecast trouble. Women always could. Maybe those little random hairs they got after the menopause were like antennae, he thought. Women gobbled up trouble like profiteroles. One gulp, down it went. Sourly, because there was nothing he could do to help, he whacked at the damp sand.

Later, Tracy came home from work, where she had been contacted and scuttered through the front door. Sylvia saw her go and wondered whether she should join her. The Higgisons would not want to see her in their home when one or both returned. After consulting the policewoman, she decided her proper place was in the home she and Arthur had, after all, shared for so many years.

"What happened?" said Tracy. "Where's my dad? What are you back here for? Why couldn't you leave us alone?"

"This *is* my home."

"I don't want you here."

"Well, you'll just have to put up with me," said Sylvia, wearily. After that, they passed each other in the kitchen, in the hall, not speaking to each other, the anger between them palpable.

Sylvia sat in the far corner of the sitting-room, her wish to make herself as unobtrusive as possible. She wanted to shrink into herself, to gather the shreds of consciousness around her, maybe to drift off somewhere where the events of the morning had never happened. Reaction was setting in and she felt deathly tired. Perhaps she had actually slept for a short period for she roused herself with a start to see Tracy standing over her, a plate in hand.

"I've made a pasta salady sort of thing. Want some?"

She took the plate and proffered cutlery. "Thank you."

Tracy balanced a plate on her knee. "Can I talk to you?"

"You can."

"Will they let him out? He'll never get over it, you know. Going to the police station. Will they let him have bail?"

"Depends."

"On what?"

"How serious it is." Sylvia rose so precipitately she almost fell forward; leaving the untouched food on the arm of her chair. "I must phone the hospital again. There might be some news."

She came back from the telephone like an unsteady sleepwalker.

"There's no change."

"Will he die?"

"I don't know."

Tracy buried her head in her hands, making a strange screeching noise. "If he dies, what will happen to my dad?"

"I don't know."

"It'll be in the papers. My pals'll all know it was my dad."

"It was a terrible thing. And nobody meant it to happen. It just did. Conrad kind of got in the way — "

"They'll never believe that."

"I don't suppose so."

The police made it clear they could not as yet be very informative. Sylvia surrendered to the knowledge it was going to be a very long night. She and Tracy made interminable instant coffees and talked first in a desultory, defensive manner and then increasingly confidentially and compulsively. Gary came to the back door and was sent away.

"Should you contact your mother?"

Tracy looked anxious, then shook her head. "Not yet. Not till we know more. She's got nothing to do with him now, after all. Only me. I'm the only one who's got anything to do with him. I'll take care of him. If he needs bail, I've got my holiday money."

"If he gets bail, money won't be a problem."

"He might not take it from you." The comment was practical, not snide. Sylvia thought, as perhaps she had sensed from the beginning, that this was a genuine and straightforward girl, with good principles. She was like Arthur, the physical resemblance almost uncanny at times. She did not feel remote from this child, having known Arthur. If things had been different, she could have taught her a thing or two, about speech, posture, clothes; given her the right books to read, taken her to the odd gallery and concert . . .

From time to time, as much from frustration at the lack of news as from concern for Conrad's condition, they both wept, stemming tears as best they could with a supply of paper hankies, trying to hide their weakness from each other. Despite the central heating, the room seemed to become cold and Sylvia fetched two travel rugs from an oak chest in the hall and handed one to Tracy. They both appeared to doze and then woke to continue their disjointed compulsive attempt at getting to know each other.

Sylvia found herself saying, almost calmly, "I think all of it is my fault. I will tell the police that." Tracy looked at her intently, about to ask her what she meant and she went on, "But if your father had not been made redundant, gone off like that and left me . . . but he did and I was on my own and I didn't know what to do about it. I thought he was never coming back, you see."

"But you were his wife. Of course he was going to come back. He was worried about bringing me with him, that was all. So if anyone is to blame for what happened, then it's me. I should never have come here."

Sylvia looked compassionately at the girl. "Don't say that," she said quickly. "You're not responsible for the sticky mess we've got into. No way."

Tracy swallowed hard and then as though to discount the feelings of forgiveness that were threatening to overtake her said angrily, "Why don't folk stick to their marriage vows? Don't people mean what they say, when they say it? They say things in front of God, after all, solemn things like vows. And then have no intention of keeping them. I think that's rotten and contemptible, so I do. Better not to get married. Better just to say you'll try your best and if it doesn't work out, that's it."

"I think that too."

"Then why? Was it just sex?"

Sylvia almost smiled. "What do you know about sex?"

"I know about sex." Defiantly.

Sylvia sighed. "Well, I saw the sex go, I saw the love go, I saw even concern for me as another person. Arthur simply shut off. I couldn't seem to hear what he was trying to say and he certainly wouldn't listen to me. That becomes a kind of torment, you know. And in the end he just took off."

"And what about Conrad Higgison?"

"He was willing to listen."

Tracy shook her head, as though she had something in her ear she was trying to dislodge. "You should have given him another chance."

"I will be honest with you," said

Sylvia decisively. "I'm talking grown-up now. Once the bonds of faithfulness are broken, there is no other chance. Not in my book. I knew when I finally slept with Conrad my marriage was over. Sex to me is a kind of sacrament and what I have with Conrad is like a kind of marriage, in my mind. It's the final intimacy, the final commitment."

"You might have him taken away from you yet. Conrad, I mean," said Tracy in a low voice. Sylvia stared at her, realizing that the young, with their insistence on honesty, could be capable of great unconscious cruelty.

"He won't be," she said clearly. "I am going to pray for him and he is going to hang on."

"You don't know that," said Tracy. "But you pray. I am going to pray for my dad."

18

HELEN MACREEVY put her plump, soft hand on Bernard Higgison's shoulder and squeezed. "Now take up your soup," she wheedled, like a mother coaxing a reluctant child. "You've got to eat something. I wish Mavis had come back with you. She's going to wear herself out."

"She'll not leave the hospital."

"But the news is a little better."

"Only a little. Only in the sense that they've decided to do something. To remove the clot. To operate. But we still don't know — " Bernard ate his soup without knowing it went down, watched intently by both Macreevies.

"When did Sylvia Blaney turn up?" It was Bertie who put the question.

"This morning. Mavis decided to tolerate her presence in case our boy woke up and asked for her."

"And when will they operate?"

"Tomorrow maybe."

186

"You want to come round and do a hole or two with me this afternoon? Air'll do you good. Get the smell of hospital out of your nose."

"I should really get back. I just came back because Mavis wanted us to split duties and to pick up a few things. Mavis gets more out of the staff on her own."

"You come wi' me. Just for an hour." Bertie was imitating his wife's coaxing-a-child routine and Bernard looked at him gratefully, obediently, agreeing to be persuaded. "We'll take the portable phone," said Bertie reassuringly.

"I hate hospitals," said Bernard, standing at the first tee and inhaling with a desperate intensity. "I hate the smell, I hate the corridors, I hate the doctors."

"Thing about golf," said Bertie, "is you have to concentrate. You have to think about your feet, your shoulders, your whole stance." As his partner took a practice swipe he clicked his tongue. "See, you're never going to hit it any distance like that. All you'll do is twist your back. Head down and eye on the ball, lad." Bernard wiggled, swung, hit. The ball soared in a perfect parabola straight down the centre of the fairway. Bertie whistled generously. "That's more like it."

As the two men marched to the next hole, Bertie said, "Saved my bacon, did golf, when I first retired. Didn't know where to place myself. Wife got fed up wi' me organizing her life for her. I interfered in the kitchen, I took up this and that, but the golf wanted a bit of discipline and that were what I were missing, the discipline of daily work."

"Same when you get made redundant," said Bernard, with feeling. "Mavis said I drove her mad." Bertie noted approvingly he had lost the gaunt, exhausted expression he'd worn when they started the game and patted himself on the back for knowing how and when to distract. "I suppose that's why the golf courses of Britain are the one thing that's multiplying. Golf, the new religion."

"It's either that, or t'pub."

"Conrad would argue the arts should be more important, but he says we're a philistine nation."

"So-called arts don't cut mustard with the generality of folk, do they? Pile o' bricks don't amount to no more than a pile o' bricks. Not that I don't like t' *Messiah* at Christmas."

Moisture dripped from Bernard's sardonic beak of a nose. "Something in what he says, though," he persisted. The feeling that because Conrad was prone in a hospital bed he should be prepared to fight his corner for him would not go away.

"Something in poems wi' no rhymes and music that scrapes your insides? Give over."

"What about the likes of Shakespeare, then?"

"What about him?"

"There's insight in the likes of *Hamlet*, surely." Bernard's lack of sleep the previous night was beginning to tell and he felt irritable, unable to sustain this ridiculous argument. "Fact remains, we shouldn't need to get all our kicks from the likes of football. Get that?" he managed a smile. "Kicks from football?"

"Man United," said Bertie mischievously, "now there's poetry in motion for you."

"Fact remains, if we're going to get more enlayerment, more taking out of

189

whole sections of the hierarchy, more people doing less jobs — and it doesn't matter how the economic winds blow, that's the fact of the matter, more people doing less jobs, the rule of technology — if that's how it's going to be, should we not be devoting ourselves to some kind of enlightenment?"

Bertie stopped, took out his elderly pipe which these days was more of a museum piece, kept for rare moments of indulgence and taking his time about lighting it gazed with a querulous curiosity at his neighbour.

"Depends." Bertie did his best to hide his embarrassment, looking round to make sure no other club members were within earshot.

"Depends?" Bernard prodded him.

"On what you're on about. If it's politics, forget it. Politics is just another section of the bureaucracy. Folk don't identify themselves through politics any more. If you're on about the soul, the spirit, whatever. Enlightenment. When we used to have discussions about this, when I were a young man, one feller I knew, he died on the convoys, he did, young Ernest Brigman, clever young bugger he were, he called it the ghost in the machine. If it's the soul you're on about — and you don't get a lot about it on the television — I've got my own theory about that." Bertie drew on his pipe and waited for Bernard to prompt him further.

"When death comes near you and yours, you think about it, don't you?" Bernard's waiting, almost frightened face made him go on anyhow. "Whether there's anything — beyond." The arm with the pipe waved a semi-circle over the rest of the golf course and distant Wilhowbry. "And whether you've come up to scratch. Whether any of us has. And I'll tell you what I think: I think God died in Auschwitz, then got stamped on in Bosnia and Chechnya. I think we've put out the light. That's what we've done in this twentieth century, with its damned technology. Technology gave us the tank and the atom bomb. Now it's giving us permanent uselessness. It's taking away what little humanity we had left."

Bernard saw the old boy's face had

gone a dull red from the vehemence of his statement. He had not meant to start anything significant, he had merely been trying in some dim, half-understood way, to define what his son was about, to keep him close in his mind, to defend his image, even to himself, because most people in his sphere of life were about making money, about conspicuous consumption. He owned it was even what he and Mavis were about, up to a point. *Getting things*. And most thought Conrad soft because he wasn't about that, he was about things you couldn't touch and suddenly Bernard was glad this was so; loved his son utterly for what he was about and wished his own cast of mind had been otherwise. I'm deeply shallow, he thought, I like all the good, tangible things of life, fast cars, big houses, trips abroad, status, living in Pinkmount Drive, at least till the recession bit and the glossy life began to curl around the edges.

Bertie concentrated on a putt then gave a kind of shame-faced grimace. "These are the kind of thoughts you'll have yourself, come retirement," he offered, half-apologetically. "After you've checked your *Daily Telegraph* to see which of your contemporaries has entered in his final score. The joke is you check the obits to see if you're still around. I don't know myself about — after. About enlightenment. I've been as selfish as the rest, exempting Helen."

"Helen is kind," said Bernard. "This is what Mavis says. Mavis says Helen is the one person you can trust."

"Shall we have a quick half in the club-house?"

"Just a quick one, then."

Sitting drinking at the empty bar, Bertie thought he detected a welling of moisture in his neighbour's eyes.

"Right." He put down his half-empty glass. "We best be getting back."

★ ★ ★

Mavis was asleep with a dingy grey blanket pulled halfway up her body. Her usually immaculate hair looked as thought somebody had trawled it with a garden fork. A tiny mass of spittle had formed at one corner of her mouth.

Sylvia shook her gently. "The doctor wants to see us. Are you all right? We've to go to his office."

Mavis got to her feet. "What is it? What does he want to tell us?" Unthinkingly she grabbed Sylvia's arm, trailing half-bent after her, her limbs stiff and awkward, her mind only half-functioning. Outside the doctor's room Sylvia handed her a comb. "Want some lipstick?" Mavis shook her head.

"We're taking him down now, to surgery," said the young doctor. "I'm afraid we can't delay."

"Is he worse?" demanded Mavis fearfully.

"Put it like this," said Dr Anderson, "there's been a development we're not one hundred per cent happy about. But he's in good hands with Mr Black-West. The best." He tried to beam at them reassuringly but it came out as a wry and tired grin in his white, overwrought face. His dark hair looked as though it had been combed by the same garden fork that had raked through Mavis's. He couldn't quite remember how many hours he had been on duty, but it was

too long, to the point where he envied
his patients their beds.

Mavis began to weep. A nurse led her
out of the room and offered to bring
her the inevitable cup of tea. Sylvia
sat beside her, her own feelings numb.
She had wanted to ask if she could see
Conrad before he went down, just to
touch his hand, his hair, perhaps to kiss
his cheek, but she did not feel she could
do so when Mavis did not. And in an
emergency you did not make demands.
It was singular, this sharing of terror
and grief with Conrad's mother who
had once been quite a close friend but
enough for the moment that Mavis did
not take exception to her presence. She
tried not to think of London, pink silk
nightgowns and Conrad's blissful grin.
After a time Bernard came in and sat
holding hands with Mavis in a kind of
exclusive trance.

There was the sound of footsteps in
the corridor and she looked up dully to
see Tracy standing there.

"Why have you come?" she demanded.

"To see if you were all right," replied
the girl and it was only then that Sylvia

gave way to her anxiety and wept. Tracy put a tentative arm around her. "Wheesht," she said. "He'll be all right, you'll see." Carefully she avoided Mavis's red-eyed glare.

19

THE streets they drove through were revving up for the final Christmas onslaught. Plastic Father Christmases rolled and tee-hee-heed in shop window displays, hastily erected trees above the smaller retailers leaned at precarious angles over the shoppers, turkeys that hadn't been frozen displayed their naked carcasses, babes in pushchairs pointed at the myriad pinpoint lights twinkling among the greenery, at Disney Mickeys and sickly Snow Whites. But there wasn't a lot of Christmas spirit about. People looked dull-eyed as they wandered aimlessly in and out of one price-slashed emporium after another. They had money, enough to raise the flag of celebration, but they were being cautious, mindful that mortgages might rise, that the recession would deepen again, suspicious of so-called bargains that were merely the crap remainder of lost sales, knowing their precocious young wanted the ever-more expensive technology in the toy department.

It wasn't all like that. Tracy, sharp-eyed in the passenger seat, saw young lovers looking in jewellers' windows, seeing some reflection of the Christmas dream in each other's faces and wished fleetingly for the time when such true romance would be hers. But for the moment, no. Gary had wanted to be privy to all her worries, but she had shut him out, not wanting gossip carried back to the set in which they both moved and to which she might never return. He was kind, Gary, and his big hands sought to pat and reassure her, his puppy eyes pleaded. But as for the love scene he craved, she was not ready, she had too much to fret over. But she tended the hank of hair, grown to fall precipitately over one eye, that was so essential to his image. She was brilliant with that. She had other, more pressing ambitions, to do with courts and pleas and police cells and her father. What she wanted more than anything was to get him out of there, into a bath with a very great deal of Dettol and then fresh clothes from the skin out.

"I can't get my head round Christmas," Sylvia said.

Tracy thought she had begun to look dowdy, a faded flower with all the delicate colour drained out of her to be replaced by greyness, limpness. That was what the daily attrition of going to hospital had done, the not knowing what you were going to hear when you got there. The news had been good, then not so good, then better once more. At least Conrad was conscious, asking for things. But they'd been warned a long road lay ahead, with pitfalls, nasty possibilities. The reassurance that everybody had wanted, that Conrad would get back to his former state of health, would be none the worse, was patently not forthcoming. The doctors merely wheeled out a daily bulletin of wait and see.

"Will they let Dad out?" Tracy knew she had asked the question before but now they were on their way to court she had to ask it again, as it was increasingly the only thing she could think of; that and how it would be if Sylvia stayed on in the house.

"Kellerman, the lawyer, thinks the

charge will be reduced to grievous bodily harm, that because of your dad's previous good character and the fact the prisons are full to bursting anyhow he might be remanded on bail. I've sold things — I've told you that — shares and things and I've got the money, unless it's prohibitive and even then I'll get it somehow."

"OK." Tracy composed herself, conscious she was living through one of those police things on the telly. *The Bill. Taggart.* Her role was to be the daughter who never gave up. If she thought of how she felt, really, of her towering fear he would go again, of being totally on her own, she would just run away at the edges. Melt. Dissolve. Be a nothing. So better to be the daughter who never gave up. She breathed deeply and Sylvia gave her a quick, encouraging half-smile.

In the court Tracy saw that her father had dwindled. Not only was he thinner, to the point of gauntness, but he was less of a presence; he made hardly any impression on the air around him; his eyes were blank and expressionless. She turned with a little moue of frightened protest to Sylvia and saw that she, too, had registered how remand in prison had brought Arthur down, degraded him. Pale-faced both, they sat while the court procedure took its formal course. To the officials, there was nothing about this morning different from any other. Fright and dislocation were their daily fare. The lawyers and barristers had grown set and cynical in their ways from it, the police puffed up with their own immunity. But at least at the end bail was granted. Arthur's eyes went from his daughter to his lawyer and his stiff pose eased into jerky movement, his head going up and down, his tongue wetting his lips. Tracy smiled and waved at him and he almost smiled in return. Sylvia's heels clattered as she walked forward to discuss the settlement of bail with Kellerman. And then eventually they took Arthur home.

Tracy sat in the back of the car, talking incessantly so that Sylvia should concentrate on the driving. A sudden burst of hail hit the windscreen and then harsh, driving rain. "Conrad's getting better," Tracy assured her father. "Honest, he really is. I know he's still in the hospital, but — "

"I didn't realize it was nearly Christmas," said Arthur. "You don't think about these things in jail."

"Don't talk about jail. You'll soon forget about it. I've got bacon and egg for you, you can even have fried bread and you don't need to have tomato for the vitamin C if you don't want it. Just this once, you don't need to have it."

He walked through his own front door and into his own sitting-room with the air of a man who doesn't quite believe what is happening to him. Old Sinbad came forward to greet him, wagging his tail so hard he all but unbalanced and making wheezy, growling sounds of joy and welcome.

He had not spoken to Sylvia. Now he said, "You sorted the bail. Thanks for that. You're not staying here, are you?"

"I thought one more night."

"She's had to stay, Dad," said Tracy apologetically. "I didn't like being on my own."

"Fair enough. But you can go now."

"Is that what you want? I thought we could talk — "

"I have nothing to say to you. I

don't want you here, that's all there is to it."

"Dad — " Tracy protested.

"I don't want to be here," Sylvia's voice was cold as ice. "I should be in London, rehearsing. We'll have to sort things out, some time. Practical things." She waved her hands. "I'll get my clothes together." She looked at Tracy. "I'll be in touch."

"Make her a cup of tea before she goes," Arthur instructed his daughter. "Maybe she'd like a sandwich."

On being referred to as though she were not there, Sylvia's colour heightened. Quickly she ran from the room and upstairs, where they could hear her moving about. She took the smaller of the two cars from the garage and Arthur and Tracy watched as she drove away through the rain.

★ ★ ★

In the week before Christmas, Tracy was busy at the salon. Every matron in Wilhowbry, it seemed, wanted a new style, a perm or a special colouring. The girls had less time to dance about to Radio Two; their backs and shoulders ached and they grew jaded from hearing about Christmas dances, new frocks and office do's. But the tips were good and Tracy hoarded hers jealously, counting the money in her purse every night. She loved Christmas, the warm knit of conviviality, the bustle, the mince pies with morning coffee, the carols, the lighted trees in windows; above all, the pure storybook quality of it here, in the well-doing and comfortable heart of England as opposed to the harsh and hard-up and Scottish milieu where she had been brought up. Even the nightmare of what had happened to her father could not spoil things for her. She was going to buy him all manner of things — a shirt, a wallet, aftershave, a book on cacti, which he grew, fondant mints, red braces with golfers on them. She'd bought stuffed turkey breast from Marks and Sparks, with a small Luxury Pudding that would just do the two of them, and a miniature bottle of malt whisky so that he could finish the meal in style. At her insistence he'd lugged an artificial tree from the lumber room and she had spent hours improvising ways of decorating it without spending too much — tying red ribbon into tiny bows, painting fir cones with old white paint, making a cardboard fairy with a handkerchief skirt. The effect pleased even her unrelenting eye.

Gary was good: she had to admit it. By dint of persistence he had managed to worm his way into the house for the odd cup of coffee. He was always deferential to her father. She could sit and listen with half an ear while he fantasized about taking Kick The Moon to Wembley. He had a lot of day-dreams, Gary, and not many listening ears at home where his mother and father argued endlessly, his big brother slept late — he was jobless — and his little brother had a lot of earache. He said he would love her till he died but she did not pay much attention. She would never let him go too far, either. Just a kiss and she didn't like the open-mouthed variety.

It all helped to take her mind off the hunched and uncommunicative figure she left at home each day. After Sylvia had gone, she'd only once brought up her name and he'd refused to take the conversation any further, simply closed his eyes and turned away.

One or two of the neighbours had brought Christmas cards, their noses sharpening inquisitively when she'd answered the door to their knocks and dealt with their enquiries as to how Arthur was and their assurances that they'd be pleased to see him for a noggin, though they'd not specified days or times. At least it was something and helped to lighten his mood. Dougie Walker came round for a long chat and Ginnie Carter brought a pot plant with the Sainsbury label still on it. He made much of these visits, telling Tracy they were proof that some folk did not condemn him without a trial. It was important for him to know this because Steve Grant and Gordon Pershor were shilly-shallying about whether he could come back to work for them. Maybe, they suggested, he should stay away till the trial took place. He pointed out that could take months and asked what happened to his mortgage payments in the meantime? It wasn't that they didn't know he could cut the mustard. It was just that things got round, they couldn't allow anything to endanger the small amount of growth they were beginning to nurture, he knew how hard things were and how old-fashioned some firms could be when you got down to it. He settled for half-pay on a consultancy basis and did a little from home. Gordon Pershor called a couple of times and was breezily polite to Tracy. She was intrigued and a little frightened by the emanation of male energy that seemed to surge from him. As Arthur's body seemed to contract more and more into itself Tracy assured him he could have nearly all her pay, she could buy tights and things from her tips. Then Sylvia got her solicitor to write and inform Arthur that as she was in work she wished to pay half of the mortgage, the house being after all in both their names.

He had no option but to accept: he could not manage otherwise. He told Tracy that eventually the house would probably have to be sold unless the trial went his way and things improved greatly after that unquantifiable time.

She had loved the house from the

minute she entered it but they could, of course, live in a much smaller place. All the more reason, with all this uncertainty, to have a proper Christmas, their first as father and daughter. Womanfully, Tracy tidied and sponged down kitchen surfaces she had neglected; scrubbed out all those unidentifiable marks on the carpets. It wasn't a chore, it was a kind of propitiation.

Sylvia sent her a silk teddy. It was nearly as good as she had hoped on Christmas morning when her father opened all the presents she had so carefully wrapped, each one of them individually. He kept shaking his head, saying she shouldn't have done it. Then he gave her an envelope with money in it, saying she could buy what she wanted, clothes, the clumpy boots that, it seemed, were high fashion. She would have regarded this as a bit of a let-down had she not known he had sold a good watch and bought a cheaper one, so that the sum in the envelope would not be risible.

For Tracy it was a good Christmas, despite everything. Gary brought her a box of chocolates in the shape of a red satin heart. If she ever took up with him seriously, if they ever went Far Enough, she would have to teach him a thing or two about taste.

20

IT was Jane Banks, the director, who suggested Clapham. Sylvia did not find its curious *fin-de-siècle* seediness to her taste, but at least there was the Common. She could walk briskly there, stopping to watch model powerboats overturn on the lake and be fished precariously back by embarrassed owners, or to see the ducks that reminded her of the mere back home and the day Conrad had quoted Keats. There were youngsters playing football and plump, dark-jowled men jogging, children being recalcitrant about getting in and out of prams, ginger dogs skittering after sticks or burst rubber balls. (Sometimes she missed old Sinbad, his devoted doggy face and the ruff of thick hair just under his collar. Did he wonder sometimes where she had gone?)

Her bed-sit was at the top of a tall, thin Edwardian house of yellow brick owned by a small, old man with an unpleasant, leering expression, who over the years had made no concessions of modernity to suit his lodgers. The loo on the landing was a dark hole under a stained wooden seat. The cooker was prehistoric and the gas fire plopped and hissed like a prop in a thirties movie. She felt better when she had taken every item off the bed and had it washed and dried in the nearby launderette. But in the main she was scarcely aware of her shabby surroundings. It was just a place to lay her head and keep her tea, her sliced brown bread, and her reservations about what she had done. Her life, her new life, her resurrection if you like, was in the television studios, where she was practising her craft, where she lived easily in her skin and did the things she had wanted to do for such a long time, without ever acknowledging it was so.

She was at home with these articulate, nervy, touchy, insecure, funny people and she liked being Louise Albury, the mother of two daughters, in the well-written soap. She liked wearing Louise Albury's flashy clothes, the too-tight jeans and low-cut blouses, the skirts above the knee and high-heeled boots, the kind of clothes she would never wear in normal life. Louise Albury was assertive, scrapping, ingenious, adaptable and held her household together by will-power and elastic bands. She could be touching, silly, devious, pathetic and emotional and practical disasters accrued about her defenceless shoulders, but it was Sylvia's pride to keep her just this side of parody, to give her a kind of integrity that meant she couldn't be dismissed as just another cheap and easy piece of characterization. The *Mail* critic had spotted her in the pilot show and given her a kind word. (Critics had no idea how powerful they were or how one took out these few words of praise and polished them when things went badly.)

At weekends she shed the motley and drove or took the train north so that she could visit Conrad. She could not have gone to Pinkmount Drive, but when he was well enough Conrad had turned down his parents' pleas to stay with them and rented a room near the hospital, where he had to attend for physiotherapy. Once he began to mend he did so quickly, almost as though will-power did the job for him. With an overdraft, he wanted to get back to work. They began to talk of finding a place they could share together, Clapham, Camberwell, anywhere would do.

They were glued, bonded to one another now, seeing nothing that could keep them apart. He argued against her helping to pay the mortgage of the house in Pinkmount Drive that was no longer home to her, but she explained that she was looking ahead to the dissolution of the marriage, to the splitting up of assets and she did not want any arguments about her half-share. Once she had that they could afford something decent, even at London prices. She put the divorce in hand, pleading unreasonable behaviour. She did not admit to Conrad that there was a remnant of loyalty towards her old relationship, that she did not want to see Arthur ground in the dust. Of the two men, she did not know who had suffered more. Of course, Conrad had been through a testing and frightening time. But the image of the crumpled man she had seen in court, had driven home through rain-sodden streets, would not fade from her mind. She wanted Arthur rehabilitated, but all she could think about was the blueness of his fair skin underneath the prison pallor and the way flesh had fallen from his bony arms. When she spoke to Tracy, occasionally, on the phone, she listened deep inside herself for any hint, any glimmer that he was climbing out of shock and despair. But even while Tracy said defiantly that they were fine, they were managing, she also indicated that the waiting to come to trial was something Arthur battled with from day to day. He didn't go out much. He read a good deal. She got him books from the library.

Jane Banks took her in hand when she got down in the mouth. The director had a haphazard, book-stuffed flat in Islington where she entertained friends and colleagues to impromptu suppers, spag bol or other pasta with red wine, and where her declared relaxation was sorting out the tangled emotional lives of others, her own being placed on hold after a spectacular break-up from a man she had loved and wanted for years.

214

He had not been able to cope, others said, with her massive competence, her incisiveness, her sheer cleverness that had laid bare his silly infidelities and posturings. Yet, when he had finally gone, he had left her as crushed as any sixteen year old and Sylvia sometimes glimpsed behind all the bravado a vulnerable, lonely girl who needed loyal friendships badly at this stage in her life. She was willing to offer her own and in exchange Jane stiffened her backbone about people taking responsibility for their own lives, about not taking old, ingrained attitudes on board, about remaining positive, ditching the guilt trip, not being a victim. It was how women comforted themselves these days when a new template was being fashioned for them, when cold winds blew down the corridors of freedom. And to think she had once been a wife who practically only had to wish for something to have it granted: a wife who sat on a cushion and sewed a fine seam. It had not been insufferable at the time. Now she looked back and saw her existence as a kind of limbo and with her present deep sense of who she was, what she wanted to do, a painful limbo at that.

Once Conrad's convalescence was complete, they found a temporary place just south of the river, dusty, charmless but convenient. He began filming his commissioned series, intensely preoccupied and happy; she opened her eyes each morning, seeking the patch of sky outside their small bedroom window and hummed a greeting to the coming day, a day when by being somebody else she would be most deeply and fulfillingly herself. Patchily she would remember Arthur, think of the strange situation he was in with a daughter he hadn't known for the first seventeen years of her life; of how he would hate the present lowering of his status in the Pinkmount Drive community, the status bought with this and that club membership, the years of dinners and dances and other functions and the big house with emerald lawns.

Then she would remember also the times he had been harsh and cruel, not just in leaving her, like the time he took off for Scotland, but in turning his back on her commiseration before that. And she would remember his intransigence when she wanted to talk over how she felt with him. Demonstrable show had become everything with him: feelings increasingly beyond the pale. She shook now, sometimes, with the fine rage she must have felt for a long time. The difference now was that Conrad was there for her, ready to listen and comfort and talk. They took long walks along the river or through Battersea Park, arms about each other's waists, stopping to kiss and marvel at the bonds of loving that bound them ever closer yet did not seem to constrict or cut.

She was happy, no doubt about that. Fervently happy. Yet every so often, like a stone into a clear, tranquil pool, there fell the dire question of what would happen to Arthur, and how far she was guilty of provoking his behaviour and whether duty and honour still existed and selfishness could turn itself inside out into abiding love. She often thought of Tracy then and her sturdy loyal qualities. She did not quite know why remembering the girl's fresh, pink-skinned face with its ingenuous honesty of expression should tear at her like a wound, except that there was so much of Arthur in her and except that — except that she had always felt this cherishing in her, towards the girl, towards Arthur's girl, who might after all have been theirs, their joint child, had things been only a little different.

★ ★ ★

"You can't go on spending money like this." Bernard repeated the words like a mantra. The credit-card statement had come in and Mavis had gone over the top again. This time it had been for new garden furniture, the latest rustic wood replacing the now out-of-favour wrought iron, and for a series of expensive light fittings throughout the ground floor.

"I thought the business was establishing itself." Mavis's face was like a small, scrunched, beige sock, the dark eyes like holes. "I can't run a decent home without some refurbishment."

"We're into a new era," said Bernard patiently. "We can't go out and spend any more like there is no tomorrow."

"Back to make do and mend?" Mavis

demanded. "I didn't marry you to make do and mend. I used to be the style-setter in Wilhowbry. Now you expect me to have old-fashioned light fittings and blistered garden furniture. God knows, what with our Conrad and the bitch next door, my standing has sunk low enough." She turned her zealous, burning gaze on her husband. "You won't get business if we are seen to be hard-up — "

"We're not hard-up." He did not meet her eyes. "We have to wait to get this Europe business settled, till the market stops going up and down and the economy is really on the upturn. It'll come." The reassurance was more of a plea than a certainty.

"I hate having to count every penny," said Mavis. "This suite needs recovering and as for the curtains — "

"Hold your horses," said Bernard, in the same patient tones he had used earlier. "That's all I'm asking."

"When did our Conrad last ring us?" Mavis demanded.

"Not so long since."

"Ages since. After all we did."

"Well, *c'est la vie*."

21

WHEN houses have not been occupied for some time, it shows. Small things, unexceptionable in themselves, begin to add up and pronounce a state of mild dereliction — windows unwashed, doorways not swept of decaying leaves, weeds poking up through pathways, neighbourhood cats padding through without stopping. Rooms that have not been lived in should not be able to communicate this fact to the outside world, but somehow do. Faces are not seen, curtains not drawn, life is somehow suspended. Plants neither wither nor flourish on sills. And there is a faint hint of reproach hanging over all, that sometimes catches the passerby unaware.

Ginnie Walker was going round to visit Dougie and saw the two big men in dark suits walk up the drive of Judy and Frank Radcot's unattended mansion. They have been away quite a long time, she thought absently. There had been one postcard from the Florida Keys and then nothing. Only the other day Helen Macreevy had spoken of her mild concern: no more than that, for Judy and Frank were always on the move. Ginnie stopped, a flutter of purposeless anxiety in her chest. One of the men rang the doorbell, then knocked, while the other, careful of the rosebeds, peered through the front windows. One of the men saw her hesitation and ran down the drive to address her. "Are your neighbours at home?"

"Doesn't look like it." She wasn't going to say any more: you didn't give information to strangers. They might be coppers, she thought, then became convinced of it. Plain-clothes men. They had that look of heavy complacency.

"Seen them recently — ?" the man began, but Ginnie began to move off, murmuring an apology, saying she was in a hurry and the man let her go.

The house was making its own statement, after all, for anyone who cared to note: no living soul had cared for it, no breathing creature had run up its stairs, opened its windows, played its radios. The men nodded briefly at each other and exchanging some kind of pleasantries, plodded down the drive and drove away.

When Ginnie told Dougie he said, "I hope Frank's not been sailing close to the wind again."

"I've never known exactly what Frank does," said Ginnie.

"Put it like this: he looks after other people's money." Dougie shook his head. "I'm sure he's a shrewd enough cookie, but if I had something to invest I'd make sure he never got his mitts on it."

"They did look like coppers," Ginnie reiterated. "But I wouldn't say so to anyone but you."

They put the incident to one side. They had other things to think about. Since their return from Croatia one consideration after another had demanded their attention. Dougie had to decide when, if ever, he was going back to teaching. They could not keep the post vacant indefinitely at the High. But Bosnia was haunting him. He felt that perhaps he should become a full-time aid worker. Yet that was an enormous commitment. He wasn't sure either his physical or nervous strength was up to it.

As for Ginnie, her mother had been at the forefront of most of her waking hours. The old lady had caught some virus that was going round the home and ended up with pneumonia. She had been very ill indeed, yet such was her constitution she had fought back and made a good recovery. There was no doubt the home was an efficient one and looked after its elderly patrons with skill and dedication. Yet if her mother was to remain there, Ginnie agreed the house would have to be sold. Daddy's house. There were simply no funds to go on paying the considerable fees and Social Security would not subsidize property owners.

Ginnie was out on a limb. She had to face up to the fact that she would never reopen her own business. Even if she could raise a loan she did not think she could take the uncertainties of her trade. It had been different when her father had been alive and able to subsidize her. Now she supposed she should get a job, but it would have to be part-time so she could continue her daily visits to her mother. She would have to find a furnished room somewhere, use the last of her savings, sell the last of her jewellery. It was a daunting prospect, but Bosnia had changed her perspective on things and she knew you did not need *that* much to survive.

After the intimacy of the Croatia trip, Dougie and Ginnie had been curiously inept with each other. Recently, some kind of almost angry tension had been building up between them. Of course they had meals together, went out together, saw each other most days, but even over Christmas there had been this reserve, almost fear, between them. Of course they had been caring of each other, attentively listening to each other's worries. Really good mates, as Ginnie told her sister. She began to wonder if after all the sexual energy she had felt released in her during the Croatia trip was some kind of aberration, that she was, as she had thought before going away, intended to spend the rest of her life celibate. Every reproach Sydney had hurled at her about her inadequacy as a wife came back to haunt her. She couldn't be sexually attractive, she was too plain and ordinary and mother-orientated. Then she remembered holding the Aids babies in Croatia, the warmth of substitute maternity and she knew she wasn't dried up, she was like everybody else, with love to give. And she had not forgotten holding Dougie, liking his body, wanting his endearments, his kisses. But somehow, back in normal surroundings, it had seemed a little ridiculous.

They sat down today, finishing a hearty soup Dougie had made from leeks and lentils and he gave her a long, quizzical look. Outside, there was a lightening in the air, a freshness that spoke of spring coming. Some way off, perhaps, held back by the cold, but coming nevertheless.

"Virginia." Sometimes he liked to use her full name, as though he were the schoolmaster calling her to attention, she thought. "Virginia, I have been coming to some decisions. And conclusions. Would you like to hear about them?"

"Uh-huh." She mopped the last of

her soup with the bread. Dougie often started conversations off with a kind of preamble. You never knew where you were going afterwards. But she liked meandering talk. Being a listening ear. Maybe it was one thing she had always been good at.

"I think I'm finally over Connie's death. Properly over it, I mean."

"That's good, Dougie. Not that you want to forget Connie — "

"No, no, no. You know that. I'll always have my memories of her. They'll never leave me. But seeing people die, out there, like we did, even little children, even babies, made me realize life, when you possess it, is for living."

She gave a sigh of agreement.

"Back in the house, I've been testing myself. I don't get wound up the way I did before; I don't go over what Connie suffered. It's over. Part of me, but behind me. And the other thing I've decided is that I'm going back to the school."

"Really?" This took her by surprise. He had hedged away from the subject whenever it came up recently, but now she judged it must have been because he was fighting some kind of private battle. She gave him an anxious look.

"Are you sure you're ready for it?"

"M'mmm. As ready as ever I'll be. I'm conceited enough to think I'm quite a good teacher. And that teaching matters. Not so much as parents, perhaps, but there are values to pass on."

"These stroppy kids! I've seen them. They don't give a tinker's cuss for authority. They smoke; they go into the supermarket at lunchtime to buy cans of lager; they have sex before they're ready for it — "

"All of that." He laughed a little at her vehemence. "But they're also good kids in some ways. Ready to help. Quite a lot won't eat meat any more. They're not beyond the pale and we should not give up on them. I used to like the challenge, you know. And just recently I've felt the bite again. Do you think I should try, Ginnie? Will you support me?"

"You've talked of doing more aid for Croatia," she reminded him.

"I won't give up on that. I want to take supplies out during the holidays and meantime I mean to work on this town and get people to give more. I think I can do as much here as in full-time aid work. And I am a teacher. I shouldn't, I feel, give up years of useful experience. I want to be able to look back and say yes, I did it, I fulfilled my potential, I did what I set out to do."

He stopped, seeing she was having trouble taking it all in, that she had probably decided he would never go back and he said with a fresh diffidence, "There's another reason I want to earn a proper salary."

"What is that?"

"I want you to think about marrying me. I want you to come and live in this house and bring your femaleness with you — it needs it. It needs a woman."

She looked at him, almost totally aghast.

He put up his hands, a comical expression on his face. "What have I said?" It was meant to be teasing, but it came out rougher than that, a lot more uncertain. As she still said nothing, he went on, "You're such an independent soul, I can't always read you. But it was a wonderful experience, *for me*, being with you on the Bosnia trip and finding out how tough and resilient you are, underneath all that fragility. I got to care about you a very great deal. You can't be all that shocked. Are you?"

"I don't know about marriage, Dougie," she said slowly. "I'm really not all that good at it."

"At this one, you might be," he said encouragingly.

"We haven't — " She couldn't say it, couldn't talk about intimacy, about feeling she could die sometimes for want of the physical expression of feeling.

"No," he admitted. "But you don't find me totally repellant, do you?"

She began to laugh. "Not repellant!" she repeated. There was chagrin and a wild relief. She thought irrelevantly that she liked being in this ramshackle conservatory at the back of Dougie's house, with its view of bare apple trees and borders with the spears of daffodils coming up. She felt at home.

"Well?"

"Of course I don't think you are repellant! What a thing to say!"

"Come over here then." It seemed a

long way to go, like walking in sand dunes or marshland, but it was only a few feet, and she went.

He pulled her down on to his knee, looking up at her. "I feel like a bloody awkward sixteen year old. But I do want to kiss you." She put her mouth slowly down on his and it was tentative and unpractised but it was also good enough for neither to wish to end it, it got better all the time. When they broke away he apologized. "Sorry. I've been wanting to do that for ages."

She turned his head back towards her gaze. "Me, too. I love you, Dougie." There, it was said. It was comparatively easy.

"You want — us?"

She rubbed her hands up and down his back, loving his solidness, meeting the challenges and demands in his eyes with wild and happy promises in her own.

"Yes, Dougie. I do."

"And you think we should get married?"

She jumped up and moved away.

"That I'm not sure about. Let's wait. Let's see."

She could see he had been thinking

hard about the whole proposition. And that he was disappointed she was not more enthusiastic. But he managed a smile and he held out a hand to draw her to him again. They put their arms around each other and held each other so tightly it hurt.

22

LINDA EVERET never came into the hairdressing salon she ran without a little thrill of pride. Tricked out in eau-de-nil and palest peach, with just a touch of gilt here and there, it was elegant and yet business-like. She liked the thrum of gossip, the easy camaraderie between her girls and herself and the background trickle of radio. But this particular morning she had an unpleasant task to perform. The lease had gone up, since Christmas business had fallen away drastically. So, last come, first go. She called Tracy Blaney into the back room where they kept the towel supplies and kettle. There was no doubt in her mind that Tracy was the right choice. Linda did not like any whiff of scandal affecting the salon and everyone knew Tracy's father was on remand for thumping a neighbour — in Pinkmount Drive, of all places. It was one thing rolling the latest piece of juicy gossip round your tongue, another if it involved your personnel. For this reason Linda could be deeply judgemental. Although she liked Tracy, she was cool. "Just work the week out, Tracy. I'll get your cards ready. I'm sure you'll find something else."

Tracy walked out there and then. She walked home, crying carefully. It was because she was Scottish. It was because she had fatter knees. It was because she'd left the tannin marks in the mugs when she washed them. It was because of the scum on that one wash-basin. It was because she said Wheesht and didn't smoke. By the time she reached home she was in a fine old state, the skin under her eyes bobbled and the rims all red.

Arthur was in the room he called the study, sleeves of a clean shirt carefully rolled up, face close-shaven, so that he was ready if Mr Anybody called. That was their little joke. Mr Anybody. Nobody did, except couples bearing religious magazines or crouch-backed men with pamphlets for double-glazing or ironing services.

"What's up?" He heard her come in

and followed her to the kitchen, where she was dashing cold water on her face.

"Sacked."

"What for?"

"For nothing, that's what for. She says it's the recession. Places are closing, even. What are we going to do? We need the money."

"We'll manage. You'll get dole money."

"I'm not going there. Living in this big house — and going there."

"Come on now, ease up. You'll get something else. A smart girl like you."

He had noticed it before, how prickly she was, how little able to take suggestions or offers of comfort. He understood how it came from a low estimation of herself and knew guiltily how difficult it must have been, growing up without a father to praise when you succeeded or urge you on when you failed.

He gave a rueful laugh. "We're a fine pair, aren't we?"

"Is it because I talk different?" she demanded.

"Differently," he corrected her. "Talk differently. Don't be silly. It's what she says. I've tried to explain to you how the world is changing, Tracy. How there are going to be fewer jobs to go round. Unemployment is going to be built into the system. Some kids will never work. It's why I wanted you to go to college, take some extra qualifications."

"Gary's got certificates. He can't get a job."

"He should try cutting that hair. In the technology revolution, everybody can suffer. Till we work out new ways of organizing things."

"You would think people would always need their hair done."

In the days to come, they went over the same old ground. Tracy conned the local paper, put cards in the post office offering baby-sitting or cleaning services, but nothing came up. In desperation, she went for shop jobs which were snapped up so quickly she suspected applicants of inside knowledge. It seemed, at the moment, within a five-mile radius of Pinkmount Drive, the labour market had all the workers it needed and a ready army of job seekers waiting to fill any post the moment it became available. In the end Tracy took dole because there was no help for it, but she hated the whole process, the dichotomy between the seedy poverty of the place where she 'signed on' and the splashy comfort of the house on Pinkmount Drive.

"Maybe I should phone your mother in Miami, ask if she can raise the wind to get you out there." After a particularly black day, when she had been turned down for two jobs she had fancied, he brought up the whole business of having her with him.

"Don't you want me here?"

"You know I do. But what is there to offer you?"

"I don't need offering anything," she said truculently. "Being here is enough. He doesn't want me around. Out there. They just want to be together. I got fed up playing gooseberry."

"Your mother's your mother. She loves you."

"I know that. I'll go out and see her. When I'm ready for a holiday. When I'm a success."

He gave up badgering her. At the moment, with his court date coming up, with the divorce papers arrived from Sylvia, she was the only light in his existence. He liked seeing the resemblances to members of his own family in her, the way her fair hair peaked on her forehead like his mother's, the well-developed Cupid's bow of her upper lip that all the women Blaneys had.

She was his. His kin. Because he had never shared her with Ida, she really did seem to be his, solely. She laughed in a Blaney way, she ran in a Blaney way, she got het up in arguments in the very same way he had done, as a young man, before a kind of veneer of rationality had been laid on him.

While they did their careful shopping and ate their careful meals, they shared confidences with each other. To his anger, though he never disclosed it to her, she revealed how Ida's mother, the righteous female who had separated the two young lovers in the first place, had insisted on strictures on her upbringing that would not have occurred to Ida. She had not been allowed to play with local children. She had on occasion been hit with the tawse which the old martinet had kept hung up on the kitchen door after her own brood had flown and habitually hit about the head for 'cheek'. She had been made to wear hand-me-down, old-fashioned clothes from the house where the grandmother had gone cleaning, something she had desperately hated. "I felt I was never myself in these clothes," she said now. "They were supposed to be good but they were thick and heavy. And I had to wear a liberty bodice and flannel with wintergreen on my chest in the wintertime."

"She wouldn't have done it if I had been there," he said uselessly. Or perhaps it wasn't useless. The look of a kind of wonderment, a vulnerable surprised pleasure at this late, verbal cherishing, made him turn away with something suspiciously like a lump in his throat. Somehow he had to look after her now. She was the little girl who had grown up through all these harsh years as well as the dreamy, sensitive, unaccommodating girl she was now. God, they were alike. Day by day he looked at her and saw his own Scottish bap face, a face with no guile in it, no cupidity, with those honest blue eyes that, his grandmother had once said, would earn you a ringside seat on the Day of Judgement itself.

In the end it was Gordon Pershor who offered her a job. He came to see Arthur and viewed his daughter with unconcealed curiosity.

"She'll not get a lot," he told them. "But we'll train her up. Janet'll teach her filing and introduce her to the word processor. Are you quick?" he asked Tracy.

Her father answered for her. "She picks things up easily."

"Then as long as you're willing," said Gordon Pershor, "I'm sure you'll earn your corn."

She was a little in awe of him, but it slipped out almost unthinkingly: the way words did with her, all the time, "You make me sound like a chicken."

He gave her a kind of half-amused, half-warning look, then broke into laughter. Even Arthur smiled strainedly. With her coif of golden, streaked hair she could look, on occasion, as if she'd just pecked her way out of the shell. There was this innocence about her. An old aunt of his had had a mawkish saying which she used when she thought someone in need of protection: '*Who could hurt her?*' It came up quite often in his reflections on his daughter. *Who indeed?*

★ ★ ★

"You getting along OK?" Gordon Pershor stopped by the cheap, utilitarian desk where Tracy was learning the ropes. Janet, a stringy matron with grown-up children of her own, was quite pleased with her. She had, she reported, a natural aptitude for typing and her spelling was better than most.

"Fine," said Gordon Pershor. He leaned over Tracy and she could smell his aftershave like spicy carnations. His dark, jowly face had a day's heavy growth and his hair was cut almost brutally short. She could feel a physical response as though someone was rattling a wooden spoon up and down her ribs, making it hard for her to breathe. His brown eyes smiled into hers. "Keep it up, chicken." She blushed and hoped nobody had heard.

From her father, from Janet and from the two other girls in the office she gleaned what details she could of Gordon Pershor's life. She wasn't very interested in Harry Grant, the other partner, a tall, thin individual she thought of as a slidey kind of man — he slid in and out of half-closed doors, into his office chair, even into conversations. Pershor had caught her imagination, with his square, thickset body that he moved with an athlete's grace, his gravy-browning voice and his deep-set eyes that seemed to sparkle and warm when he looked at you. He wore polished loafers, fine wool slacks, bomber jackets, interesting ties. Occasionally an Italian suit.

"Well," said Janet, one day when they were having their afternoon coffee, "the boss lives the other side of Wilhowbry, on that stretch of country road on the way to the airport. It's a white farmhouse, old Cheshire, beams and all. He took a degree in business studies at Manchester University, then went to America for a few years. He likes classical music and motor-bikes."

"What kind of classical music?" demanded Tracy. Her voice had a hopeless kind of fall. She knew nothing about classical music, scarcely the definition of what it was and she didn't know anybody who had been to university. As for old farmhouses, with black beams . . .

"He's married, of course," Janet went on.

"Uh-huh?" Tracy willed it to be nonchalant, while part of her lay as doggo as a collie outside the sheep-pen. This was the important part. "I don't know if they hit it off all that well. She goes away on a lot of language courses. They have a son at boarding-school."

"What does she look like?"

"Tall. Thin. Good dresser."

Tracy rubbed her palms over her chubby knees.

23

SYLVIA turned up one afternoon out of the blue. She had decided to do this so that Arthur would have no time to build on either anger or sarcasm. Now that the divorce was going through, she did not want them to part in bitterness. If there was anything she could do to help during his court case, she would do it. She also wanted to discuss with him the selling of the house. So her face was arranged in planes of propitiation as he opened the door.

"It's you!"

She agreed. "Yeh, me. Can I come in?"

"I thought you were busy."

"Break in production. So I thought I'd come and pick up a few things. Dresses for the summer. My navy jacket. Is it OK?"

"I suppose so." He couldn't help but be grudging. He had been having a cup of tea and offered her one off-handedly, but she accepted gratefully.

Mentally they were circling each other, like wary dogs with the hair on their backs refusing to lie down. He thought with a mean satisfaction that she was looking a little strained, older, her fingers working nervously in her lap. But unshakeable too. More defined and sure of herself. She thought detachedly that he was a good-looking man but like a book with a seductive cover in whose contents she no longer had any interest.

"How's everyone?" She gestured to the neighbourhood at large then narrowed it down. "Tracy?"

"Tracy's fine. She likes her work."

"Still seeing Gary?"

"I've told her there's no future for her there. He's left college, but he can't get a job. They go out a bit. He's a dozy oik. He seems keen."

"And the neighbours?"

"Dougie Walker and Ginnie Carter are an item."

"Never!"

"Go about hand in hand, can you believe?" He gave in, sat down and began to look more relaxed. "I think the law have been round, looking for

Frankie Radcot. Ginnie saw 'em and said they had Fraud Squad written all over them. Pinkmount Drive is not what it was. Maybe this *is* the time to get out, though prices are sticking. I dare say you want to discuss selling the house?"

"It will have to come to that." Her hands clasped resolutely in her lap. "And the court case? How do you think it will go?"

There was a pause, while he decided against losing his composure. Instead he said in a steady voice, "I'll go down."

"Are you sure?"

"Pretty sure. Probably I deserve to. It's Tracy I'm worried about."

"I can see you might be. But she's pretty sensible. She'll be OK."

"It's not for you to judge."

"No. Tell her I would like to keep in touch."

He did not answer this but said instead in what he intended to be a business-like manner but came out hectoring and rough, "So you'll marry lover boy?"

"Probably not."

It caught him off-balance. "Oh?"

"Don't think so. Failed the test first

time. Best to leave things as they are."

He could feel something akin to warmth move at last in a slow tide through him: something that reassured him his marriage had not been worthless nor thrown away at no cost. For the first time he felt a grudging respect for the slender woman sitting opposite him, a relinquishing of a mindless sense of ownership. He knew then that he had loved her, but in the wrong way. It hit him like a brick. He caught her eye and wondered how many of his thoughts she might divine and saw her colour rise.

"You know the Higgisons are away on holiday, in Barbados? So Ginnie tells me."

"One of the reasons I came up now."

He wanted to ask 'And how is he?' Even in his own mind he could scarcely name the Higgisons' son, think the name *Conrad*, with all its connotations of hatred and suffering.

Sylvia said, almost as though in a hasty aside, "He's all right, you know. Made a good recovery. That should work in your favour. In court, I mean."

They were awkward with each other

now, knowing that all kinds of things could be said which should not. She rose and said nervously, "Can I get my things?"

"Of course."

He heard her opening drawers and wardrobe doors in the room that had been her bedroom. She came down with jackets over her arm and smaller things crammed into two plastic shopping bags. In the hall they had an embarrassed conversation about how much the house might fetch, whether some decoration should be done before putting it up for sale. It was in their joint names and there was no quarrel about splitting the proceeds down the middle.

"Get Tracy to put some flowers about the place, when anyone views," she offered tentatively. "And they say the smell of brewing coffee works wonders."

In the end they were still awkward. She thought about kissing his cheek but settled for touching his arm. "Good luck," she said. He closed the door abruptly and did not watch her walk towards her car. He poured himself a large whisky. The bottle was nearly empty.

★ ★ ★

The court appearance was a day away.

"C'mon," said Bertie Macreevy. In his golfing plus twos and tartan cap he looked like an elderly version of Bertie Wooster. "You're not sticking in t'house all day, are you? Get your clubs out of t'mothballs."

Helen had talked him into it. Arthur Blaney had been in her mind all week, the thought of his imminent trial tormenting her almost as though it were happening to one of her own children. When Bertie's regular partner had gone down with the virulent bug attacking larynxes and bronchi that spring, she had seen it as the perfect opportunity for a quiet gesture of support for their beleaguered neighbour.

Arthur had taken some persuading, but eventually dragged out his golf bag and the two set off on a fresh Cheshire morning to attack the recently rain-soaked greens. Bertie's trolley, a power one, stopped and started erratically, misbehaving.

"Don't know where it's at," said Bertie,

248

kicking it lightly. "Like government on Europe."

"Like the rest of us," said Arthur.

"If worst comes to worst," said Bertie, "what'll happen about t'little lass?"

"She'll go to stay with Janet Macintosh, Gordon Pershor's secretary. They get on. Janet's Scottish on her father's side. House is going up for sale."

"All change, eh?" said Bertie regretfully. "Thousand pities it ever came to this."

"You think I don't know it." Arthur tee'd off. It wasn't much of a shot. His arms fell uselessly to his sides. "Don't know if I'm up to this."

"Aye, y'are," Bertie insisted. "Keep your eye on t'ball, is all." They played through green on muddy green, the very condition of the course demanding their denunciatory irritable attention. "I could be in sunny Portugal," Bertie grumbled, "or a decent course in Spain. What keeps me here in this Goddamn-forsaken country?"

"You tell me."

"'Cos I want to die here." Bertie coughed his customary wheezy cough. "I don't want some foreigner sticking a tube

249

in me bladder, some old foreign nun-girl crossing me arms on me chest."

"You might get some foreign doctor doing the necessary in this country," Arthur pointed out.

"True." Bertie's blue eyes gleamed behind his silver-rimmed specs. "But I'll die in a British bed, thank you very much. Coughing up British phlegm." He punched his chest dramatically.

"Why are we talking funerals?"

"I'm trying to cheer you up. Like I cheer up t'wife. When she gets one of her downs, when t'family have forgotten to phone or she's burnt t'dinner watching telly, I cheer her up talking about the hymns we'll have, when we die, like. She wants 'Old Rugged Cross', I'm for 'We Shall Gather at t'River'. 'Mazing the cheering effect it has, concentrating on your own mortality. Last great taboo of modern man." His sardonic but compassionate gaze swept over the younger man. "Just you remember, lad. We're all like the chimney-sweeper. Come to dust in th' end."

"All the same a hundred years from now, you mean?" suggested Arthur.

"Aye. That's really cheered me up, Bertie. Thanks no end."

They were chortling as they walked towards the lake where wild ducks were engaged in disgraceful rowdy quarrellings. Slightly ahead, Arthur heard a noise and turned to see Bertie's power-trolley give a convulsive leap in the air, a bit like a mechanical kangaroo. The old man let go and the machine, going round in circles, twisted and turned towards the edge of the lake and then threw itself dementedly in, contents and all.

Cursing heavily, Bertie ran after it, with Arthur behind, robbed of movement by paroxysms of uncontrollable laughter. He helped Bertie retrieve the trolley in the end, even its contents, lying deep in the duck-muddied water.

"Bloody machine," swore Bertie. "Never been right since our Helen had it out. Death to machines, that woman is."

"Crrrmmmmm," said Arthur, bent over an aching stomach.

"Bloody cheered you up though, hasn't it?"

24

THE magistrates' court did not feel able to pass sentence on what was seen, after all, as a grave assault. Conrad could have died and although it was acknowledged he might have been hit accidentally in what had been a confused tussle for the *art nouveau* ornament, he had been attacked, punched, battered and caught off-balance before that. Arthur had clearly gone round to the Higgison house with the intention of causing grievous bodily harm. The Crown Court took on the onus of sentencing and Arthur 'went down' for six months. He had been hoping against hope for a suspended sentence.

The tabloids ran the story. Sylvia did not escape their lurid attention. '*Soap star in marital punch-up.*' So she was a star now, was she? The publicity did not hurt the ratings of *Barrington Place*, but the company wanted to convey a more up-market 'feel' and Sylvia was warned:

no bedroom confidences, no 'My new life with young lover' journals, even if the inducements were high. She had no intention of making any disclosures, anyhow. She was too appalled by the way your life could be twisted out of all recognition and the people you cared about paraded like cardboard cutouts. Most of all she hated the cheapening of what she and Conrad had between them and shed bitter tears when he was not there, tears of rage and terror that their life together could be ruined. His stoic attitude was that it would soon blow over: that next week, somebody else's life crisis would hit the pages, somebody else's suffering laid bare to sweeten the readership's morning coffee.

Because of his previous blameless record, Arthur was sent to an open prison. In a strange way he was not quite so wretched as he had envisaged. There was relief of a sort in coping with a real situation instead of fighting off the demons of conjecture. But for a man brought up in a tight-lipped little community, where John Knox was never very far away and national hubris cultivated as a way of overcoming poverty of every sort, the shame was like a creature eating into his very soul. He could not bear it when Tracy came to visit and begged her to stay away, assuring her that he would soon be home. After a little, seeing that his fellow prisoners were, in fact, mostly abject but normal human beings like himself, he became less prone to self-condemnation. He remembered Burns' lines about gently scanning your fellow-man and about 'stepping aside' being what humanity, by and large, was about and began to breathe, eat, sleep, exercise without the tensing of muscles and endless mental chastisement.

What he reproached himself about most of all, as time went on, was the fact that he had brought Tracy down from Scotland to start a new life with him (and he had hoped, Sylvia) and then had let her down so calamitously. His daughter's calibre became clear to him in her frequent letters. There was no mention of how hard it must have been for her, first the court appearances then the publicity, but it was clear that everyone in the office, from Gordon Pershor downwards, had bent over backwards to be kind and supportive and Gary had told a nosy local reporter to clear off or he'd bust his nose for him. Although he had told her he regretted butting in to her life, she assured him he was the best dad ever and he must never think she did not want him. All during her childhood she had dreamed of finding him and nothing could change how good she felt about having him now.

He realized that what was giving him strength was the thought that he could still make it up to her, keep his nose clean while incarcerated, get some kind of job when he got out (he was pretty sure Grant and Pershor would be lukewarm about him and not certain he wanted to keep up the connection anyhow). They'd get a new place, he'd buy her a little car and teach her to drive; with luck her cooking would improve. He would give her stability, be there for her, keep an eye on young Gary and maybe one day, in the fullness of time, he would take her down the aisle on his arm and she would make him a grandfather. That was the scenario.

Sylvia did not come into it. Even if sometimes in his cramped, if only faintly malodorous room, he remembered the twining of their languorous young limbs in the early days of their marriage, heard, like an echo somewhere, that unaffected, riff-like laugh; saw how much she had given to him in terms of sensibility, awareness; even then he did not allow himself to think anything could happen, between the nisi and absolute of their divorce, to allow any rapprochement. Could it? He could not quite close the door. It caused him anguish, but he could not. But he wrote no scenarios. He remembered how she had looked at Conrad Higgison and acknowledged that no matter what his own feelings might be, she had taken her love elsewhere. It was largely his own doing and if he ever did have her back, he did not know how he could change. He was run-of-the-mill, ordinary, a man's man. It was strange how he now saw himself: much as he had been when he first came south, raw, unsophisticated, ignorant, out on a limb.

Almost as though Sylvia had never been. He would have to start all over again.

When Tracy had gone back to work after Arthur's last court appearance, Gordon Pershor had come up, touched her arm and knitted his brows at her in commiserating fashion. "Any worries, just come direct to me. I'm there for you. You'll be fine." She had felt her miseries shrink and dwindle to manageable proportions. She was determined, in any case, to work as hard as she could, so that no one could have any criticism of her. It was more vital than ever that she kept her job.

Janet Macintosh had a little terraced house where she had brought up her two daughters after her husband died. The girls had married young and lived locally, dropping in on their mother several times a week. The house reeked of cleaning fluids, polish and steam-iron. The nets at the windows were washed every few weeks, the cushion covers changed, flowers carefully arranged at the window in a cut-glass vase. Tracy recognized the old working-class ethos of never being caught out. You had your standards. But Janet had holidayed abroad, liked serious documentaries on the telly and worried intelligently where the politicians were taking the country and how she should vote. She was not, Tracy noted with relief, the narrow-minded sort and did not condemn 'the youth' out of hand for wearing big boots or funny locks. In her little back bedroom decked with crinoline ladies and country ducklings in plaster and print, Tracy felt like a squirrel in a nest. She tried very hard not to chip or break anything in the kitchen and she made the evening cocoa so that Janet could put her feet up on the pouffe and rest her varicose veins. She was very glad of this undemanding haven where she could mark time till Arthur was freed.

Into the second week of the new order, she stayed late one evening to practise getting up speed on the word processor and had told Janet she would probably then go to see the John Travolta at the Three-in-One cinema complex. She knew both bosses were working late. She saw Harry Grant slide into his camelhair coat first and heard him call a brief goodnight to his colleague. She was walking from the building when Gordon Pershor caught up with her. "Late bird, aren't you?" he queried. She blushed. "I was trying to get up my typing speed." "Good. That's good."

They walked along in silence till he asked, "What do youngsters like you do of an evening?"

"I'm going to see *Pulp Fiction*. I missed it first time round."

"It's a bit — a bit — " he protested.

She laughed. "I like to see everything and make my own judgements."

"Well, that's as it should be."

"Have you seen the film?"

"No," he admitted. "Maybe I should. Look, would you mind if I come with you? Can we go somewhere for a burger or something first? I'm starving. I'll pick the car up later."

It was a bit like being bumped rudely from first gear into third. Everything in her seemed to be operating on a different level. She was noting the outlines of trees, hearing birdsong as though someone had just turned up the radio. She was crashingly, blunderingly, almost blindly happy. She was remembering the sensation of wooden spoons rattling her ribs the first time he had stood near her in the office, the smell of spicy carnations. After a little, these heightened sensations quietened, leaving her on the point of trembling.

"Won't your wife be expecting you for dinner?"

"She's away at present. No, I'm footloose and fancy-free," he said jocularly. For the first time their eyes met and he was the first to look away. She thought she saw something bruised there and something in her immediately denied it. *Oh, no, no, no,* she thought, I shouldn't be doing this. What would they say in the office? What would Janet say? But she knew also she would never tell Janet and that nothing would stop her going to the movies with her companion. In the empty burger bar they tucked into chips and burger. "Better than going home and opening a tin," he vouchsafed. "Haven't you heard of the microwave?" "Whatever," he said. "This is still better. Better company."

As they walked towards the cinema,

she felt it was like a kind of procession, something important. She was very aware of the brown suede of his jacket sleeve occasionally rubbing against hers and of his profile, alight with animation as they discussed films, how they had changed, how the shock barriers had been pushed further and further out.

Before they reached the complex he stopped suddenly and said, "I shouldn't be doing this. It isn't fair."

Again their eyes met and this time no one looked away. Yes, hurt. Yes, bruising. Both there, she thought. She had no idea what had caused them but she wanted to offer him the remedy of her understanding. She could do this. She could understand. A voice at the back of her mind restated that he was married but a much stronger voice (at least at the moment) was saying that it didn't matter, it didn't matter in the least, it was irrelevant. She was getting so deeply into something, some nexus of feeling, it was like being lost in mist and at the same time going down into a springy bog and the helplessness was overwhelming and at the same time the best sensation she had ever had.

"It's only going to see a film. For goodness' sake."

"Well, look, maybe I should push off home." He was looking down at his shoes now but his head was jerked up as though on a string and their gaze was locked again. "We know this is innocent enough but somebody might see us and think differently. Do you mind very much?"

She said miserably, "Yes, I do." She could feel tears come up in her eyes and she seldom if ever cried. Not her.

"What would your father think?"

"My father's not here. It's us. To do with us."

He tossed his head in sudden resignation and led the way into the cinema, buying both tickets despite her protests. It was not a busy night and they had the back row to themselves. Neither of them took in much of the crudely violent film. She waited impatiently and eventually he held her hand. After a while he put his arm round her shoulder and she leaned momentarily against him. She turned her head and he kissed her. "This has not to go on. This has not to happen again," he said into her hair. "But it is happening," she responded. "Did you know? Right at the beginning?" "The minute I came to your house." "In what way?" "The way you were put together. You looked that milky white, with your hair so fair and your apple-blossom skin. And so kind of honest. You would never do the dirty on anyone, would you, Tracy? It bounces straight off you, you know, whatever it is. And I want it. But this is madness, pure madness. Where is everybody going? Is it the end of the film?"

She got up, laughing, leaning over him so that her hurrying, panting, terrified breath mingled with his. "Yes. The end."

He grasped her and she fell into his open jacket, his shirt-front. Smelling carnations. As, struggling to his feet, he caught a clean, soft odour from her hair and the smell of Comfort from her recently washed lacy jumper.

25

AFTER their night at the movies, Tracy did not know how Gordon Pershor would react to her in the office. She need not have worried. Apart from the customary formal good-mornings, he ignored her. She thought he was waiting for an opportunity to say something when they were alone, but it never happened. He did not call her into his sanctum and although she waited late a couple of evenings, on the pretence of practising her typing, he left with the others. She was upset and bewildered. What kind of a mixed-up person was he? Had the other evening been some kind of sophisticated leg-pull? Had she done something to annoy him? In bed at night she wept tears of utter frustration and despair, hating herself for having fallen into some kind of man-trap yet also longing to feel Gordon Pershor's arm around her again and the touch of his lips on her cheek. More than that, she longed to talk to him, because it seemed to her they were on the same mental wavelength, that they could talk freely together in a way she had never known with anyone else. In her more sobering moments, she remembered how he had tried to renege on his first impulse to go to the cinema with her and how, when they had been sitting close, he had called it madness. Pure madness. With a lurch of despair, she realized that these reservations must have taken hold of him. He was older, he was supposed to be sensible and, of course, above all, he was married. It wasn't on. She had this glimmering, this understanding, of the true situation. Yet what was true? What about the immensity of her need to see him, be with him? What about this wailing that seemed to go on endlessly at the back of her mind, destructively pulling her apart?

"Had a row with the boy-friend?" they asked her in the office, meaning Gary, but she wouldn't see Gary, wouldn't go to the disco with him, would only permit the briefest of telephone calls. Janet Macintosh diagnosed some kind of reaction to her father's predicament. She let her go to her room with a book. She was no stranger to teenage moodiness. She made her light meals and milky coffee.

Into the second week, he fell into step beside her one evening as she was walking home. It was all she needed to be instantly restored. She could feel the blood begin to course round her veins again, the world swing back on to its axis, her whole being pulse with a proper life. He was smiling at her, his eyes pleading. "Hi, hon," he said. "I've missed you."

"Me you."

"Of course we shouldn't. We really shouldn't see each other. I've been trying not to. Honestly. I feel the world's worst shit."

"But here you are. And people might see us."

"They've all gone home." The back of his hand rubbed against hers and sent electrical currents through her. "And just once, I don't care. Have you missed me a bit?"

"Yes." She could not dissimulate. "I've been in the pits of miserableness. What are we going to do, Gordon?"

"I don't know. I guess I've been in a kind of low state for a long time. Mel — my wife — and I don't seem to register with each other. I don't know what's wrong, but something is. I would put it right if I could."

"That's honest." It hurt to hear him mention his wife. Tracy did not like to think of her, but if she was the trouble, then they had to.

He gave her a tormented look. "You have to believe me, Tracy. I'm not the kind of guy to go off the rails. But I'm in love with you. I've never felt like this before. Just bear with me, darling. Let me talk about it." She could see his brown eyes were brimming and her own began to fill with tears. She grabbed his hand, then remembering they might be seen, immediately let go. "Let's go somewhere," he pleaded, "somewhere we can talk. Wait here. I'll go back for the car."

The car was a glossy, dark-coloured Jaguar. She stretched her legs in guilty appreciation. He drove, expertly and easily, away from the confines of

Wilhowbry and out into the Cheshire countryside, the farmlands douce in their evening reverie. They found a small deserted pub that did not do meals. He ordered her a small sherry with ice in it. His drink was a single malt with water. Across a well-scratched table they were able to hold hands. His were cold. He had neat nails. Not like Gary's, which were bitten. She felt a pang for Gary that was genuine but fleeting. He might as well not exist and that was a hard thing to feel and he did not deserve it.

"If you'd said to me," said Gordon Pershor in a low voice, "that I could sit in an out-the-way pub and feel like I'd won the National Lottery — "

"I thought you were never going to talk to me again. It was awful. I didn't know what to do."

"I couldn't trust myself, see?" His working-class, Bolton accent was coming out a little more clearly. "I've been someone who's worked his hide off, Tracy. Mel says it's part of the trouble. But I find my work exciting, a challenge. Every day I get up and I want to get in there. Harry and I have been mates since school and he's sharp, the sharpest brain this side of the Pennines, though you might not think so. We've ridden this recession and beaten it and that's taken some doing."

"You helped my dad," she said emotionally. "When nobody else would."

"Your dad could sell moccasins to Red Indians. What I'm saying, Tracy, is I never expected this. I didn't know I had all this feeling in me. I want to buy you things, darling. Tell me something you would like. Let me buy you it. A necklace, a locket? You say."

She smiled. "Don't be silly. This isn't about you buying me things."

He looked chastened. "No. I agree. It's just me. Loud and flash. But I'll get you something. I want to."

She looked around. "I should be home by now. I'd better phone Janet, case she's worried." She found the pay-phone in the pub's foyer and told Janet she'd met a neighbour from Pinkmount Drive and was going to have a meal with her. Her face pink from lying, she returned to the pub interior. It was cold and getting dark. The landlord came in and switched on some miserable mock candle lighting and threw a couple of logs on the fire.

"Can you do us a sandwich?" Gordon pleaded. The man brought some unexpectedly good bread with cheese and butter and his wife brought coffee in big, clumsy cups. The fire continued to improve matters by blazing up and casting its warmth towards their legs. Perhaps the owners thought they were in need of cheering. They turned on the muzak, but low, and Tammy Wynette assured the world she would stand by her man.

The settle to the left of the fire had been inviting them to sit together and they did. He held her, lifting the little strands of her yellow hair and delicately touching her cheek and shyly she kissed his cheek and then his mouth. The kiss lingered, asking and answering questions, and insisting, when they broke apart for breath, that there had to be another, and another.

Afterwards, when the dark was lighting up with a pale theatrical moon, he drove the car on to a patch of grass near a farm gate and they sat and talked. He'd had a tough upbringing, he told her, short on both love and material things. You did as you were told, or else. His father had been a roisterer and his mother, though not without spirit, held down by ill-health and lack of means. Out of four brothers, he was the only one who had gone on to higher education and it had set him apart from the others. He'd met Mel at university and she had come from the same sort of background so it had seemed natural they should stick together.

"Do you love Mel?" she asked in a subdued voice, cutting across his monologue.

"There's something there. Whether it's habit, loyalty. And there's the boy — there's Jonathan. But she's got sort of cut off from softer attitudes, has Mel. She's got very ambitious. Into politics and perpetual studying. I mean, we sort of put up with each other because we don't see all that much of one another. But I don't want to talk about Mel. I want to talk about you." He took her hand and held it to his mouth, kissing each finger in turn. "How am I going to be with you? How am I going to see something of you? Truth to tell" — his voice began to break down — "I should be saying the opposite — that I don't mean to have anything to do with you. But I can't say it. Maybe you should say it for me. Maybe you should send me away."

She was silent, going over the moral arguments in her mind and finding herself unable to acknowledge them. Every time what happened was this rush of tenderness and feeling, this ocean of love flowing in an inexorable tide towards the man next to her. She didn't know how it had happened. That was the crux of the matter. He had simply come and stood next to her in the office that day and some alchemy had turned her bones to water. Resistance didn't work. Resistance only made the tide press harder.

"You're not saying anything," he reproached her.

"I don't know what to say. What do people like us do?"

"I could leave Mel."

"No!" It broke away from her before she had time to think. "I don't want you to do that. What's Mel done to deserve it? And there's your son and your home and your job." She was crying, in a helpless, unresisting way. "There's my dad, too. I don't want him to hear about it — "

"Right. Right. Spot on." He put his arms around her and dried her tears with a large handkerchief. "We got into this, we can get out of it." He kissed under each eye. "Come on, hon. No damage done. I've stepped out of line, but I no more want to hurt people than you do."

"Should I leave the office? Find some excuse — "

"You need the job, don't you? No. I'll be away a lot anyhow. We'll not see all that much of each other. It should get easier."

"You mean," she said sadly, "you will forget all about me."

"Never that. But I have to do right by you, don't I? I'm older and supposed to be wiser. Not that age seems to come into it. To me, we seem the same. You make me feel young and I've put an old head on your young shoulders. Haven't I?" he asked regretfully.

She managed a smile. "We are the same," she acquiesced. She put up a finger and touched the corner of his mouth. "I like everything about you. That little curve there." She laid the palm of her hand on his cheek. "My skin on your skin."

"Come on," he said, letting in the clutch. "Let me get you home. Before."

"Before what?"

"You know what before."

The road snaked ahead of them in the moonlight and the cat's eyes winked through a blur of light evening rain.

26

HELEN MACREEVY liked to walk the length of Pinkmount Drive at a certain time in the evening, before television sets were switched on for the 7.30 soaps and curtains were drawn in upstairs windows as younger children were settled to sleep. It seemed to belong to her then more than at any other time. In the daytime it was often featureless as people were out at work and their offspring at school, with maybe only the occasional odd-job man or part-time gardener to be seen in desultory occupation. She liked to think of belonging. Middle England. Middle class. People moderate in thought and behaviour. Dependable. She was even fond of the milkman, because he was dependable, never getting an order wrong or leaving a pint too little, and of the postman, because he shut the gate behind him and rang if an envelope was too big for the letterbox, rather than mangling it by shoving it through.

She and Bertie had the meal they called tea — Bertie's mother had called it 'us tea' — at 5.30 and nothing after that except a hot drink before bedtime. It was working class, of course, and the family ragged them about it when they came home — in their trendy southern habitats they were known to have dinner as late as ten — but Bertie was adamant it was better for his digestion. It was a proper meal, of course, fish or chicken more often than red meat nowadays, and a pudding and afterwards, guiltily, Helen could nibble something chocolatey during the evening, while Bertie had his malt.

She took old Sinbad for his walk. She and Dougie Walker had been horrified when Arthur Blaney had talked about having the old chap put down and agreed to share looking after him. Dougie (or Ginnie) had him most of the day and she took him for his evening stroll. His rolling, slightly overfed gait suited her very well and they had interesting conversations. "I see the Grayshotts are away to Tenerife again," she would say, or "Mabel's got her new curtains up" and Sinbad would signify by a flourish of his long tail or a contented snuffle that he was taking in every word. If he started and put his ears up at the sight of the occasional grey squirrel or territory-marking cat, he had no intentions now of chasing them. He was a good old boy, with eyes as dark as the Bournville Plain Helen was so fond of and Helen had become convinced that, from the intensity of the expression in those eyes, the way he could supplicate, laugh, even apologize with them, that animals must have souls and be candidates for Heaven. These kinds of useless but absorbing ruminations were a strong feature of Helen's walks. Nightly she also thought, collectively and separately, of her sons and daughters, her grandsons and granddaughters, recollecting them from infancy to the present time and sorting out when to phone whom, whose birthday was imminent, who might be coming up soon on a visit. When she began to long for a sight of the latest baby, or the feeling of those distant small arms around her neck, or for one of her girls to say "Sit down, Mother, I'll get it", it was time to go in. Bertie would have finished reading the *Telegraph* leader and be ready with his comments on the state of the country. Not good, as a rule. But Helen would know the hedgerows smelt the same, and the gardens of Pinkmount after rain. Even with those permanent-seeming *For Sale* notices up at the far end and the two empty new houses that had 'in-filled' a once desirable site, she had had her fix of reassurance.

On this particular evening she had noticed the low-slung car stationary under some willows near the new houses. Nothing unusual about that for people were always coming to look them over, putting in low offers that they were hopeful of being accepted. But there were no lights on in the houses, so if there were prospective buyers, where had they gone? Sinbad was turning for home now. He knew the parameters of his evening walk better than she did and wanted back to his bone. Helen felt, she didn't quite know what, but it was an irritation, a sense that something wasn't falling into place. When she got to Candelbarra, which was the Radcots' deserted residence, she was convinced she saw two dark-clad figures whisk out of sight behind the elaborate conservatory. She *had* seen them, hadn't she? She wasn't the sort to imagine things? With her heart thumping in uncomfortable fashion, she walked quickly up her own drive, or as quickly as the arthritic old dog would allow. When she got in she called loudly to her husband, "Bertie, get on the phone to the police. I think there are burglars at Candelbarra."

The police knew Pinkmount Drive quite well. Thieves regularly dipped their hands into jewellery boxes, neatly abstracted expensive videos, helped themselves to the occasional smart car left in a drive for a so-called joy-ride and made quick getaways to Manchester or Liverpool. The Force were on the scene with commendable alacrity, two young coppers with tender pink skin rubbed sore by their helmet straps. They soon came down the drive with two figures between them, a man and a woman. Bertie had gone to his gate to see what was happening and was greeted loudly by one of the figures.

"Tell them," begged the figure, "that I'm who I say I am, Bertie, for God's sake. That I've been in my own house — "

"Frankie Radcot!" Bertie found it difficult to believe his eyes. But Frankie and Judy Radcot it was. But why had they been sneaking into their own home by the back, like two thieves in the night? Why was Judy crying, her mascara all over the place, and wobbling about as though her legs had given up on her?

"Constable," he addressed the senior of the two policemen, "this man is my neighbour, Mr Francis Radcot. This lady is his wife Judith and behind you is their home. May I ask where you think you are taking them?"

"No sweat," said the officer. "This gent is helping us with enquiries, is all."

"What enquiries? What bloody enquiries am I supposed to be helping with?" Judy screeched hysterically.

"It was yourself who insisted on coming with us to the station, madam," said the policeman coldly.

"Yes, so that I can bloody make sure

you let my man go." Judy was out of control, but she turned to Bertie in her frenzy. "Tell them! Tell them, Bertie! We're law-abiding citizens, I am chair of the Three Charities Annual Ball, I am — "

"Why didn't you tell us you were back?" demanded Bertie.

"Why don't people mind their own bloody business?" Frankie suddenly thrust his face forwards towards his neighbour, a face as pale as daybreak. He, too, had reached some breaking-point. "Sod off, you interfering old bastard."

Helen, who had put Sinbad indoors, appeared belligerently supportive at her husband's side, but seeing Judy's distraught appearance immediately put her arms around her and supported her.

"Can't you see she's on the point of collapse?" she appealed. Judy leaned heavily against her, eyes shut.

"Can I take her into the house?" Helen asked the policemen. "Make her a cup of tea?"

"Jude!" There was desperation in Frankie's cry but the policemen urged him inexorably towards their car. One of them turned and nodded hastily in Judy's direction. "See to her," he ordered Helen. "We'll send down a woman PC." Both young officers were behaving like pups with a hunting trophy. Frankie's bloated, chagrined face glared through the steaming glass of the police vehicle. The engine jolted into life.

Bertie helped Helen take Judy into the house. Her feet in their expensive strapped shoes dragged like a reluctant child's and her eyes fluttered open then shut. She was making little guttural noises of infinite distress.

Bertie made the tea while Helen sat on the pouffe by the big chair they had poured their visitor into and chafed Judy's unresisting hands. The tea was sweet and hot with a smidgeon of Bertie's Glenmorangie in it and after a little a hint of colour came into Judy's cheeks. She sat up, straightening her shoulders, running her fingers nervously through her expensively coiffed long hair.

"Better?" Helen smiled her ready, non-judgemental smile. "You don't need to say anything if you don't want to, dear. What I mean is — "

"We're not snoopers. You know that," said Bertie angrily. He was still smarting at being called an interfering old bastard. On all counts. *Old*? (Not inside he wasn't.) *Interfering*? (He prided himself on keeping out of others' private affairs. He'd have thought he was known for it.) And bastard he most certainly was not. He should shake that ignorant, disrespectful son-of-a-bitch till his teeth rattled. Good job the coppers had taken him out of his sight. Towards Judy he felt no animus. He'd always liked her blatant sexy cheerfulness. It was the kind men responded to because they knew it was safe, beamed at the world at large.

Not that she was cheerful now. She was sobbing with pitiful little hiccuping sounds and Helen said concernedly, "Would you like me to get a doctor, lovie? You're doing yourself no good. Try and breathe evenly. Relax your shoulders. You're all right here, you know." After a few minutes, it seemed as though her advice was having some effect. Judy became calmer. She lay back in the easy chair and said with her eyes closed, "I don't know where we're going.

He keeps saying we'll be all right, but it isn't all right, what he's done. It can't be, can it?"

"Get him a good lawyer," said Bertie.

"We've had lawyers." Judy's eyes were open now. She made the statement sound as though you had lawyers like you had measles. "We've been back in the country for some time, you know. Trying to sort things out without — without it getting to this stage. We couldn't come straight home because we knew the Fraud Squad had a bead on the house."

"Fraud?" said Bertie, testing the word.

"Fraudulent conversion or something," said Judy tonelessly. "I've never understood the world of finance," she appealed to Helen. "I'm just a dumb-cluck who thinks figures are what you keep if you want to keep your man." She sat up, suddenly sharper, angrier. "He's got one of those clever, niggly little minds that can spot a loophole in something a mile off. Frank, I mean. Only sometimes it's not there. The loophole. We were supposed to be having a holiday in the sun and it was pure torment. He knew he'd screwed up and he couldn't rest. Then he got

284

sunstroke and lay and shivered for three days, like he'd had a real burn, which I suppose it was."

Helen clucked sympathetically. "It happened to Bertie once. In Bognor Regis, of all places."

Judy smiled automatically at the banality of a holiday in England.

"He wanted some books and letters, to help him get sorted. That's why we snuck in tonight. I was sure nobody had seen us. I was sure everybody would be having their evening meal or watching telly."

"We eat early," said Helen, "and I'm not into soaps. Apart from the Archers on radio."

"I'd forgotten that," said Judy. "Was that Arthur Blaney's old dog you had? It looks as though my poor Frankie will be joining him. In the clink. Arthur, I mean. Not the dog."

"Now, don't." Helen pulled her up short. "The police are only making enquiries. It's a long way from that to a court appearance."

"Get a good lawyer," Bertie reiterated.

Judy hung her head. "You don't

understand, Bertie, Helen," she said quietly, formally. "It'll all go. The house. My little gym in the second garage. The swimming pool."

"You don't know that," Helen offered helplessly.

Sadly Judy shook her head. She was almost back to her old self-possession. "Oh," she said softly, "but I do."

27

TRACY finished writing the letter to her father, wondered whether she should start one to her mother in America and found herself instead beginning what she thought of as one of her 'Dear Gordons' — letters which were written though never posted, ending up instead in many careful shreds in her wastepaper basket.

She could never send them. They were just a way of bringing him closer to her, reactivating the meagre store of memories of being together. He had stuck to the letter of their decision on the night of the country pub, that what they were doing was out of line and should not be pursued any further. He had been away a lot on business, anyhow, as he had told her he would be — was away in Brussels at the moment — and she had tried to keep her side of the bargain by seeing Gary again, by trying very hard to revert to the person she had been before

287

Gordon's overtures.

But it was hard. There was something so fatalistic about her feelings, so impermeable were they by regret, anger, determination, diversion. 'Darling, darling, darling,' she wrote now, 'I think of you first thing when I wake in the morning and you're in my mind last thing before I fall asleep. Life only makes sense if I'm with you. I remember your kisses, your voice, your breath and I want it all again, the time of being together. Precious, precious, precious time.'

Her writing hand moved swiftly over the page, her breathing coming in short little gasps, almost as though he were making love to her and tears rushing up through their conduits towards some kind of easing, some kind of exorcism of her pain. The front doorbell went and as Janet Macintosh was out doing the Saturday shopping she went down. It was the postman with a package that would not go through the letterbox. It was addressed to her and there was a foreign postmark. As she carried it back up to her room she saw the stamp said 'Brussels' and her heart began a mad tattoo. She made sure her door was well shut and tore at the paper. It came away to reveal a book. *An Anthology of Love Poetry*. She turned it over and over in her hands. Inside the front cover there was a small, flat package, something wrapped in tissue paper. A fine gold chain. She shook the book out for signs of a note, scanned its front pages for an inscription. Shook out the wrappings. Nothing. "I want to buy you something," he'd said. It had to be from him. The postmark said it all. She was to make her own deduction. It was the same for him as for her. She was there for him, first thing in the morning, last thing at night, in his thoughts and in his dreams. *Darling, darling, darling.* She put the chain round her neck, held the book to her bosom. Was invaded by a warmth that could only be happiness, a reassurance that what mattered most was still there. The worries would come later. Would he look her way when he got back to the office? Would there be any more furtive assignations? They had said no to those. But it wasn't over. Whatever it was wasn't over.

She worried about the implications if

Janet had been at home and had taken in the small parcel. Like everyone else she knew where Gordon was. Could Janet have put two and two together and made four? But then Tracy was sure no one in the office had the remotest idea of what there was between herself and Gordon. He must have wanted to send her something very much, just the same, to take the risk.

She went dancing and for the odd burger with Gary just to keep up appearances. Sometimes they slumped in front of the telly at his house (his parents were seldom in evidence) or he would moodily strum his guitar. He had a terrible chip on his shoulder about others his age who were in jobs, calling them wallies, conformists, slaves to money, but he hated his own impecunious state. She knew the days when he had visited the job centre: he was even spikier than usual, rubbishing everything he was offered. Other days he was full of brave talk of setting up his own band, doing a demo, writing his own songs. But she saw him change from a larky, amusing young man into someone moody and irascible. They fell out increasingly about the love-making she would not permit and when he started seeing another girl, called Sammy, Tracy knew the friendship would probably peter out. They still enjoyed talking to each other, teasing each other, even the odd disco date, but she knew very well that Gordon stood between them and she found Gary's black moods increasingly hard to take.

* * *

"The boss wants to see you," said Janet. "You know he's off to Malaysia at the end of the week?"

"What does he want to see me for?" Tracy kept her voice monotonous though she knew the colour was draining from her face. The boss meant Gordon, of course. Although Harry Grant was the equal partner, it was Gordon's presence that dominated.

Janet smiled reassuringly. "Maybe he wants you to run the show while he's away," she joked. "Go on. Don't keep him waiting. I expect he wants to check on your progress."

She hadn't been face to face with him for so long. As she closed the office door behind her she wondered how much longer her trembling legs would support her. Gordon rose immediately and stood with his back to the door, holding the door handle as if to prevent anyone coming in. "Hi," he said. "I want to ask, quickly, before anyone interrupts: can you come out tonight? I'll pick you up at six outside Germaine the florist." As she made a demurring sound he added, "Please. We can go to the same pub."

"All right." At her agreement they both suddenly relaxed and laughed. He touched her arm quickly as he walked back to his desk. Once there he toyed with a pen, hardly daring to look at her. "You look lovely. It's been so long. And I'm going away."

The Jag crawled along the pavement edge like a great, crouching beast, the door opened and she was swallowed up as he drove swiftly away.

"Thank you," she said, "for the book and the chain. It was you, wasn't it?"

He smiled. "You're wearing it. The chain. That's nice. And the book? Did you like the book?"

"I read it all the time."

"What's your favourite?"

"The Elizabeth Barrett Browning one: 'How do I love thee, Let me count the ways'. And the 'O my America' one. And oh! loads of them; all of them."

"Doesn't go away," he said, hopelessly, "does it, the feeling? I couldn't get on that bloody plane without talking to you. So much for all my good resolutions."

She touched his arm, a little shyly. "It's all right," she said. "I wanted to come."

He drove with a fast, dizzying skill through the outskirts of Wilhowbry and into the countryside, playing a Wagner tape at full volume. Now trees were sporting a gauzy green and in woods there was the seductive spread of bluebells. He moved up a road that was little more than a track and turned into a little curve of unofficial lay-by, protected by hawthorn. There he turned off the engine and the tape and took her into his arms. She wound hers around his neck and responded without thought or reservation. It was as though they had to touch wherever they could, for comfort, for reassurance, for the signal to go on living. They were breathing like runners, murmuring, calling out, kissing. The Wagner music ran on in her mind. He kissed under her chin and the inside of her wrist. When they came up for breath, he said, "I won't hurt you. Just let me, I need to — " and he was touching her breasts, unfastening her brief skirt, pushing his hand down between skin and her tights and panties, lifting her bodily to him, groaning with need and then wrestling her round so that he was on top, so that for the first time she was taken, scarcely knowing what was happening to her except that the sky suddenly fell in and he was in the wreckage with her, scrabbling to reassert order out of disorder, calm out of chaos.

He buried his head in her shoulder, his remorse painful to her. "Oh Christ, I shouldn't . . . oh God in Heaven . . . oh, I've wanted . . . how I've wanted." He took her face between his hands and kissed her eyes and then her mouth. Seeing her expression, the delicious look of entrapment, tenderness, relinquishment, he became emboldened, touching and kissing her once more, gathering her up the way she had once gathered and held wild flowers herself, or puppies, or babies, anything precious or treasured. At last with much reluctance he allowed her once again her own containment, smoothing down his own clothing while she tended hers.

In the pub it was almost a straight repetition of last time, down to the empty room, the broody logs, even the reluctantly served bread and cheese, but all they wanted anyhow was the privacy.

"Malaysia is such a long way away," she said. "I won't be able to picture you there."

"Oh, I'd like to take you out there some time," he promised. "You'd love it. I'm very fond of the people."

"But you'll be careful," she pleaded.

"How do you mean?"

"All that travel. You'll get tired." She really wanted to say: you'll be unhappy, as I will be, because we won't be together.

But she didn't need to say it. He knew what she meant.

He drank his one glass of whisky reflectively. "When I get back, we have some sorting out to do." He blew out his breath through puffed cheeks.

"Do you really mean that?"

"I do really mean it. If you knew me, you'd know I don't resolve to do something and then forget it."

"But I *don't* know you! Is that what you're saying?" She was a little peevish from the thought of him going away and it made him laugh and reach out to grasp her hand. "After what happened? After what just happened, you know me better than anyone ever has in my whole life. You had all of me back there. I would trust you with my soul, girl, and I hope you would put the same trust in me."

"I'll wait, then," she said, with a very serious face. "I'll wait till you get back and we'll talk about things."

"I won't stop loving you in the meantime."

"Nor I you." The same serious face.

28

CANDELBARRA was up for sale. "Even if he walks free," said Bertie Macreevy to his wife Helen over the toast and cherry jam, "he's not going to want to come back here. They'll fetch up somewhere in Spain, is my guess. Somewhere on the Costa del Crime."

"Poor Judy!"

"Well, she went along with it. She knew he sailed close to the wind. She as much as said it to me once, at one of their poolside parties. When she'd had a skinful."

Helen looked at her husband consideringly. "You know, men *are* less charitable than women. I'm sure a lot of so-called business men blur the edges a bit. Do dodgy deals. Hope for the best. You ask Bernard Higgison. He knows all about the high-flyers who have come to rest in some of the country properties around here, the taxes they've avoided, all the rest. 'All you need is a good accountant', he says. 'Or a crooked one'. Bernard will tell you."

"Bernard's judgement is tainted with the sin of envy, fuelled by that airhead wife of his."

"Mavis isn't so bad since they got recession-hit like everybody else. Nor since Conrad's little bit of bother."

"Mavis hasn't learned a thing. She'll be the same conspicuous consumer till the day she drops!"

"What's one of those when she's at home?" demanded Helen mischievously.

"Greedy cow," said her husband. "Not to put too fine a point on it."

"Pass the jam," said Helen. "I might as well finish this toast."

Helen retired to the kitchen, thinking without rancour that age was making her husband more explosive. She wondered when she should tell him about the Asians. She had seen the flash of bright blue sari and the bob of dark heads getting out of a smart Espace and going in with the estate agent to Candelbarra. She wouldn't allow that her husband was racist. It was more that he was dyed-in-the-wool English, in the way that Scots and Welsh were passionate about their countries, but the English by and large regarded as uncool . . . She thought the war had done it. He had had a hard war, losing two brothers, many friends, and then there was this strain of romanticism in him, that few saw but his wife knew was there. It was old-fashioned to be a patriot but that was really what he was, she decided. He saw an England where people kept their word, hung on to standards, did good by stealth; an England that was bathed in a kind of prewar sunset glow that encompassed cricket matches on village greens, children in pinafores, wives with big laps and which maybe had never existed *then*, never mind *now*. But it was in his head and that was what counted.

But racist? Maybe a little behind the times. She had done battle with the idea of a multi-cultural society herself, but it had been put paid to the night she saw a small West Indian boy on television, crying in a heart-broken fashion because his father could not find a way of making him white. He had thought that one day he would wake up and be the same colour as his school-fellows. That night

299

Helen had acknowledged what the Bible said about a broken and a contrite heart and had wanted to make amends for all the reservations in her own nature in the past.

In more practical terms, she thought that some people were a bit less adaptable than others and took time to assimilate new notions of what country and community meant. Her husband moved among the comfortably-off where racism was more casual and unthinking than cruel and deep-dyed. If an Indian doctor came to one of the golf-club dinners, for example, he would be treated with total courtesy and respect. If an African footballer covered a Northern club in glory in the Cup Final, he would be praised this side of idolatry. But casual asides like 'our coloured brethren' in arch-sarcastic tones revealed harder attitudes.

She decided not to put Bertie to the test. The Asians might only be looking. But it was Bertie himself, coming in from golf a few days later, who confirmed that a non-white family would be moving into Candelbarra and Pinkmount Drive.

Bernard Higgison was worried about the effect on house prices. Dougie Walker had had an argument with somebody at the bar over a remark that had included the expression nig-nogs. Bertie's own face was flustered.

"What difference will it make to us, who moves in?" Helen challenged him.

"We've never had non-whites in the Drive before."

"So?"

"It'll affect house prices."

"But we're not selling," she pointed out sweetly.

The changes at Candelbarra were not the only ones. Ginnie Carter got tongues wagging again by deciding the family home had to go to pay her mother's nursing-home fees. She had moved everything that was hers into Dougie's bungalow. People were in two minds about Ginnie.

There were those who affected to be puzzled by what they regarded as lowering of her standards. She was plainly living (and very happily by what everyone could gather) with Dougie Walker, but what would her late father the alderman have said and if her mother were not so frail, would she not also take exception in no uncertain terms? There were others who quietly said hurrah for good old Ginnie. It was time she thought of herself and why shouldn't she have some fun out of life?

Ginnie herself would not be rushed. Slowly but surely she was bringing changes to bear on the bungalow. For one thing, Dougie had to get rid of the piles of ancient periodicals and newspapers he had 'filed' to help him with the occasional articles he wrote about education — he could take cuttings, she suggested, which would take up far less room. He in fact liked squirrelling information away and liked the cosy, nest-like feel of old print piled around him, but after Ginnie found a mouse nesting in one pile, admitted it was no contest. He was prepared to do more than this to please her. The bungalow lounge was transformed by a new set of curtains and fresh cushions and in the kitchen Ginnie threw out old equipment and brought in her own. Sometimes Dougie looked pained at these procedures and Ginnie back-pedalled. It wasn't that she wanted to change Dougie himself in any way: it was just that clutter had always offended her aesthetic sense and that she liked to keep reasonably up-to-date and in fashion.

Even with her clothes she was finding a sense of renewal, discovering younger styles like leggings and tunics that suited her and a shorter hairstyle that took years off her face. Dougie was transfixed by these transformations, both to his home and the woman he loved. Connie had been someone who hated change and defied fashion. But after a while he began to go along with Ginnie, even allowing himself to be smartened up with a new casual jacket and trousers. He looked younger, but it sat a little oddly on him, for middle age had always suited him well.

"You won't change old Dougie too much, will you?" Helen Macreevy pleaded.

"I won't," Ginnie promised. But she washed and pressed his beloved pullovers more frequently and made him go to a decent barber to have his hair cut. After such renovating tactics Dougie retired to the garden to dig, to plant and prune and sow without the gardening gloves Ginnie suggested. "The whole point is you get your hands dirty," he pointed out. He wouldn't allow any tidying up whatsoever in the garden. Ginnie could feel a strong tide of reproach and argument rising up in her but saw clearly that the cluttered hut and untidy piles of logs could prove her Waterloo. These adjustments, these periods of intransigence on both sides, were what made Ginnie wait before entering into definitive talks about marriage.

Her mother's house sold with surprising speed, bought by a nursing-home chain who had been looking for a suitable place to convert to their needs in this affluent area. The grumbles grew about the changing face of Pinkmount Drive. How commerce itself was intruding, because commerce was certainly what the home was about, with its disgracefully high fees and trade in the frail and vulnerable elderly. Mavis watched the ambulances and minibuses blunder up the drive of what had once been the flashiest residence in the neighbourhood and sighed that it should come to this.

The only consolation she could find lay in the thick cypresses and rhododendrons which partially screened the sight from the road.

* * *

Helen, who was sneaking an afternoon cup with a bun after the rigours of a dieting lunch, opened the door to a peremptory ring and found the blue sari on her mat. Edged in gold and swelling over a rather splendid bosom, it was topped by some gleaming white teeth stretched in a smile and a pair of sparkling brown eyes.

A graceful brown arm was extended, a little imperiously.

"Meera Singh. Doctor. We're going to be moving in next door. Thought I'd say hello."

Helen carefully wiped the butter from the corner of her mouth with her hankie, extending her own arm. "Helen Macreevy. Housewife," she said. "Won't you come in?" She supposed she should really have taken her guest into the sitting-room but the tea was in the kitchen. "Will you join me?" she asked.

"No. No, no, no. I have to watch my figure." Meera Singh's eyes lingered fractionally longer than necessary on Helen's generous proportions. "As we all do."

"It's a lovely house," Helen volunteered. "I hope you'll be happy there. Do you have a large family?"

"Six. Three boys. Three girls."

"And your husband?"

"My husband is a businessman. His mother lives with us, of course. It is useful. I can work. I specialize in paediatrics."

"Well, anything you want to know. About the neighbourhood shops. Who delivers." Helen was suddenly floundering, not knowing what to say. She was often like this with people she felt were self-important. She saw the other woman's eyes dart around her kitchen, taking in everything, the tiles that were due a freshen, the hand-towel that needed changing. Even the bun. She felt a curious defensive anger.

"You're too kind." Meera Singh looked — what? — a little deflated. "Just wanted to say hello, you know. Now I must go. Lots to do." Her thonged sandals flapped hastily up the hall.

"I couldn't think what to say to her," Helen told Bertie later. "I don't know whether I like her or not."

"Let 'em get on with it," he growled.

29

BERNARD HIGGISON went into his office in Wilhowbry, the new office that was going to make his name as one of the county's premier financial advisers, admiring as he always did the techno chic of the layout, the slender gilt lettering on the door and the nameplate. At first, it had lifted him, made him think anything was possible. Now it was different. Mavis was getting to him, going on about the lack of results, the restrictions he still had put on her spending, wanting to know what had happened to his flair. Well, failing banks were what had happened. An uneasy Europe was what had happened. Public unwillingness to put savings at risk, to opt instead for boring bonds, certificates and even the proverbial under-the-mattress. How could you advise a public with no imagination, no courage? The bounce had gone out of things. It brought on that fluid feeling below the belt and the constriction above, so that he was continually trying to take deep breaths, to come up for air.

Mavis shouldn't do it. Twit him. Nag him. She would only stay on in Pinkmount Drive, she assured him, if she could have the exterior of the house done up and grey and cream cobble tiles laid on the drive instead of the common tarmac she had come to find insupportable. She was suffering again from acute indigestion, from headaches and a nervous inability to attend large gatherings unless, for example, she had an aisle seat at a concert or was near the door in a restaurant. She had hot flushes and palpitations and seemed able to cry at will (though she could also stop, it seemed to him, as soon as she had won her point, such as the expensive course of yoga and relaxation for which she had just signed on).

In his impatience Bernard knew he was open to the charge of not loving his wife, but the truth was otherwise. He did. He always had. Her haggard, anxious face and tortuous thought processes were dear to him, her physical presence could still excite him. He had not been at all certain of his own power to attract when he was younger and a woman who was too healthily assertive, free of neurosis, not needing him so much, might not have brought out the man in him the way Mavis had. He would protect her to the last hour, humour her, consider her. They were looped together in their interdependence like the chains of DNA. But she should not nag and denigrate to the extent she had been doing recently. The affluence of the Singh family had been a spur to her further ambitions. Meera Singh had her own magnificent Porsche; the eldest boy had his own natty sports. Their Conrad had never had that when he was at university said Mavis, but Conrad hadn't deserved it, in retrospect. Mavis did not hide the emotional bruises still there after her son's defection.

Bernard drank his morning coffee brought by Ella, his secretary, noticing abstractedly the bounce of her middle-age spread. He took out an indigestion tablet and sucked it after his drink. Mavis had been down to the car showrooms and spotted a new BMW. They hadn't changed their main car for four years: *ergo*, they should be thinking seriously of the new model. Bernard had been telling her recently that things were picking up, the economic recovery was under way, so why did he have to sit on their savings like some frowsty old squirrel on its nest? They weren't going to leave their money to Conrad and his inamorata, were they? Mavis should be able to keep up with the neighbours. Did Bernard know how shaming it could be, the suggestion that her financial wizard of a husband made her cut corners?

He sifted through the portfolios of elderly clients: so many thousand in gilts, so much in unit trusts and then the fail-safe stuff, tucked away in bonds and annuities. Most of it would lie there till they died. Money was inert stuff to spend your life looking after. He wished he had been blessed with Conrad's imagination. Before the slump, he had at least been allowed to use his intuitive flair. Now folk wanted certainty, even for smaller returns.

He had lied to Mavis anyway when he assured her things were getting better.

The government insisted they were, but markets were still jittery, people who had thought themselves entrenched for life in comfortable careers were still finding themselves jobless in middle age, ruthlessly excised by the new technology they had often been involved in setting up. Maybe God was trying to tell the world something, that it should be less materialistic, that it should scale down its demands, but try telling Mavis that. He had a sudden vivid picture of her, back in the early eighties, when they had really been riding high and she'd had *carte blanche* to spend what she liked. The house in Pinkmount Drive done out in soft, expensive pastels; the kitchen humming with every new gadget; the wardrobes stuffed with designer clothes, designer shoes. Bernard sighed, thinking with a fierce nostalgic ache that took him by surprise that his wife had possibly been really happy then, her every wish satisfied. If he could only do it again! But he was more cautious now. Caution came with thicker socks, and thinning hair; with knowing you could not lift lawn-mowers bodily or drive sleepless across the Continent any more. But it had been good to remember her smiling, dancing, spending, that anxious, grievanced face when it had been vivacious and pretty.

He turned at last to the morning mail which Ella with her love of formal order had placed four-square on the corner of his desk. It was like regurgitating yesterday's dinner; same old pap. No wonder the sourness spread from his middle to his chest and arms, filling him with a chronic apathetic disgust. The last letter was on thick, crackly paper. From his landlord. He couldn't at first believe what was set before him. At the back of his mind for weeks had been the thought that the lease on his office was due for renewal, but Herbie Benson was a friend of his, he had never thought the terms would be anything other than reasonable. Not so. Herbie was sorry, but in view of his own galloping overheads, he was obliged to quadruple his terms. Bernard would know that his locus was now a fairly sought-after situation and Herbie felt in view of this . . . The rest became a blur. Ella, Tim Scott and Vic Hudson, who occupied the other desks, were aware of a sudden upsurge of movement in the boss's corner, as Bernard's chair crashed into the radiator behind him.

"That's it! You can start working your notices now!"

Three appalled faces stared at him. Sometimes Ella read the mail; this morning, in a hurry, she had not. She was no more aware of what had happened than the other two. Tim Scott, the senior, moved forward. "What's up?"

"The lease! Unless I can negotiate some sense into this bloody man." Bernard waved the letter in front of him. "He's quadrupling the rent. Benson. Herbie Benson. How can we be expected to take that on board?"

Tim shook his head. He was a thin, pleasant, shabby man, whose jackets were always at odds with his trousers, but who picked up useful information as a jammy piece might pick up fluff. "I heard he'd sold the yacht," he volunteered. "And the shops in Manchester."

"The domino effect," said Vic Hudson. They crowded round Bernard, seeking the confirmation of print. "The shops

314

have gone because of the new out-of-town trading estates. I dare says the man is in *stück*."

Ella had begun to cry and Bernard waved a desisting hand in her direction. "No use getting upset. Come on, Ella."

A wailing cry issued from Ella's crumpled face.

"We've been there! My Jack was made redundant a year ago. He sits about like a zombie. We only cope because I work."

"We're all in the same boat." Tim patted her back, his voice sepulchral. "But the boss will do his best for us, eh, boss?" He looked directly at Bernard, who responded with a nod. "Goes without saying," said Bernard, shamefacedly. "Shall we get on? I've got some calls to make."

He did not eat at lunch-time. Instead, moved by some imp of perversity, he walked to the car showroom and looked at the car which Mavis wanted him to buy. A lovely machine. In a perfect world, everyone should have one. He looked at the Mercs, the Rollers and the Jags. Flash cars were his Achilles heel. But obviously, in view of this morning's bombshell, he was going to have to deny Mavis her wish. If the business were to survive, he was going to have to execute much tougher economies than that. Vic would have to go; he couldn't do without Tim's nippy intelligence. If only he could persuade Mavis to come back and do a stint in the office, as she had done once, he could dispense with Ella's services. But you're on a losing wicket, old man, a deep, disengaged voice echoed in some subconscious chamber. Wouldn't it really be better to cut and run? But what would Mavis say then? Eh, eh? The office and the gilt lettering had at least impressed her bridge-playing chums, the rich widows and pampered wives with whom she ate cake.

He wandered idly through the graveyard of the old twelfth-century parish church, indulging his sense of having failed — he was no stranger to it, after all. The urgent spring day plucked at his consciousness, as if to say look, here be flowers, here be fluttering new leaves, see how green they are, feel that tender, warming breeze. Someone had opened windows in the rector's house and music came forth, something by Bruch — the violin concerto? — that somehow heightened his growing feeling of apprehension, the same feeling that had stopped him eating, that had warned him it would be irrelevant. He bathed momentarily in the soft, sad tide of music, thinking it would be good to listen to it more — people, Conrad maintained, were at their human best listening to great music, nicer than they knew. He felt an affinity for his son that brought tears to his eyes and a sad ache of longing for something, he did not know what. He knew he would have to sit down. No matter how it might look, if someone he knew came by. Old Bernard sitting in the churchyard. The great pain came then and smote him, almost cleaving him. Someone in the rectory turned the music off and closed the window.

★ ★ ★

Mavis crept into the hospital room where her husband looked like some half-inanimate object with wires and tubes coming out of him. She made no sound — the sounds were all inside, screaming around in her mind — but somehow found his hand and held it. She had been scraping potatoes when the phone went and there was a minute blob of clay under one thumbnail. And a mark on her skirt, which she'd not had time to change.

They wouldn't tell her what might happen. They didn't think the indications were very good, the heart attack massive. She sussed that much. She was wearing her gardening coat. She was in a great, white, disinfected wilderness, with no sign-posts. Somebody came and shoved a carton of tea into her hands.

At some point Bernard opened his eyes and gave her an earnest, searching look, followed by the ghost of a smile. She knew he was comforted because she was there. And then he was gone.

Eventually there came Conrad and she in her turn was comforted. Because a son was a son.

30

THE death of Bernard Higgison affected the rest of Pinkmount Drive in various ways. Bertie Macreevy thought even more frequently about his own mortality; Helen remembered the small acts of neighbourly kindness Bernard had shown her, the cuttings for the garden, the saucers of raspberries or strawberries. Dougie Walker and Ginnie guiltily felt that in their own new-found contentment they had bothered less than they should with all of their neighbours, and Bernard and Mavis in particular. Judy Radcot wrote a tear-stained letter from goodness knew where, mentioning the heavy Hand of Fate.

Mavis was coping. She was going to be very comfortably off in her widowhood, Bernard had seen to that. Her women friends clustered around her, bearing pot plants, tonic wine, titbits specially made or bought in the more expensive delis. Some, widowed themselves, knew the well-ordered paths where comfort lay, the phrase that would linger, the gesture that would count. One or two in their temerity suggested Mavis might move to a flat, somewhere smaller, at any rate, but she rounded fiercely on those, saying Bernard was everywhere in their home, she could never leave it. While everyone marvelled at her stoicism, Helen did not. Mavis had always been able to cope with the practicalities. It was the shadowy, the imagined, she was not very good at.

Coming out of prison, back to Pinkmount Drive, Arthur Blaney felt a searing regret over Bernard's demise. Despite everything, including a permanent and instinctive dislike of Mavis, he had never regarded Bernard as any kind of enemy. Soft, petticoat-ridden, perhaps, but basically a fair-minded and reasonable kind of bloke. He wished he could express his sorrow, his genuine feeling of a space left in the neighbourhood, and emptiness, but of course there was nothing he could do or say. Soon, anyhow, as soon as the house sold, he would be moving away. The Pinkmount Drive years were over, the years when it seemed the sun had always been on his back. He brought Tracy and her suitcases home from Janet's. Tracy put flowers at the window and on the tables. She was glad to be home.

"Don't," she said, the first day. "Don't say you'll make it up to me. I don't want you to say that. It's just enough that you're home. We've got to make the most of it."

He walked through the rooms, out into the garden, touching things here and there as if to make sure of substance, reality. Once in the West Highlands an old woman had told him there was a day when the trees dressed to the nines for summer, a special time, and it seemed to be happening now, everything was freshly shaken out, scents were keen, birdsong sharp, melodious. When Tracy wasn't around, he wept or drank.

She saw he had picked up a habit in prison of sitting, sleeves rolled up, chin on hands, as though attentively waiting for thought, for revelation, or inspiration, to come to him. Sometimes he would shake his head, as though to reassemble one of those cheap puzzles you had as a child. He would hug himself as though cold. "Dad," she demanded, "are you listening?" "Yes, I am listening." But she was far from sure that he heard.

She was waiting to tell him about Gordon.

Once, visiting him while he was still incarcerated, she had thought he suspected something. He had looked at her and said, "There's a kind of bloom on you. Are you in love?" She had denied it, blushing and laughing. "Whatever it is, it suits you," he had said. "You are one bonnie bird." Now he was going to have to know. Everybody would know. Gordon was not yet back from Malaysia, where contracts had dragged on interminably, but she knew from the memory of his face that when he did get back it would be crunch time. Decision time. And she wanted him. Whatever. Mel might exist and the boy Jonathan, but she wanted him. There was no alternative to this. They had to be together. The ruthless nature of her need for Gordon assailed her daily, fretting at the straightforward moral code of her upbringing. She did not feel as though there was a bloom on her now. She felt embattled, frail, whiny as an ailing child inside.

It was Gary who in the end precipitated matters.

With Tracy's return to Pinkmount Drive, he had reinstated the practice of the casual call. The brief fling with Sammy had come to nothing and he wanted to know from Tracy why they couldn't see more of each other. It wasn't that she didn't like him, even that she didn't find him quite attractive, it was just that with Gordon uppermost in her thoughts Gary didn't quite register any more. She felt sorry about this and tried to be nice to him and that was maybe a mistake because he became moodily questioning, even suspicious. In the end, when he was trying to kiss her, she told him there was somebody else. His stunned look prompted a stream of apologies and then she made the decision to try and explain properly. About finding this new person who touched her in a way no one ever had before, about her certainty that this was for life, about her own bewilderment that made it easier for her to understand how Gary must be feeling now. "Please," she begged, "try to understand. Maybe one day this will happen to you too."

"Who?" he demanded. "Who?"

She shook her head. She wasn't going to give him any kind of hint. To placate him, she merely said, "He's older" as though that explained everything and he asked, "How old?" She said she was not sure. (She was. Gordon was thirty-two. They had discussed the age difference and agreed it did not matter.)

"He's got money," Gary said jealously. "That's what it is. He spends on you. It's because I haven't got a job."

She felt his misery. "Let's still be friends," she said disingenuously.

He got up. He had grown tall and stringy during his disillusioned search for work, his face pimply from too many cans of soft drinks, too many hours indoors. "No," he said, "I don't think so."

She went with him to the door. "See you around?" she suggested.

He went, his face bleak, his eyes unforgiving.

Her father came out from the study

where he had been filling in late tax forms.

"What was that all about? I saw your Lothario go. You upset him or something?"

"I told him I was seeing somebody else."

His head went up. "Oh? Who would that be?"

"Dad, it's Gordon Pershor."

* * *

"I've met Melanie Pershor. She's a nice-looking, pleasant woman. What has she ever done to you?"

They were going over it. Over and over it. He couldn't understand and he didn't want to understand. They were both distraught, their voices pitched high.

"I'm not saying she isn't pleasant. I'm not saying she isn't nice. I think Gordon feels she leads her own life. Maybe she's had to, while he's been busy. She does aerobics, self-improvement classes. Looks after Mel. He says there's been no emotional input and he's a man who craves affection."

"Let him go elsewhere, then. What's he doing with a young girl — "

"Daddy," she protested angrily, "I'm all of eighteen. My mother had me when she was my age. I've just grown up, that's all. What I feel for Gordon makes me a fully paid-up member of the human race."

His exasperation made him speechless, but not for long.

"What about us?" he demanded. "We've hardly any time to get to know each other, as a father and daughter should. It was what kept me going, while I was in there — "

Eyes large with pity and contrition, she protested, "What difference will it make to us? I'll still love you, be here for you. It wasn't my fault, Dad, that you weren't there while I grew up, was it?"

His blue eyes flashed, a nerve touched. His hand flew towards the telephone.

"What are you doing?"

"I'm going to ring your mother in Miami. She should be here. She'll sort you out — "

She tussled with him and succeeded

in drawing away the book of telephone numbers, the big, hot tears flying like her protests. "No, no! Daddy, please don't!"

"Will you stop seeing him, then?"

She stood, mutinous and rigid. "How can I? I love him."

And they were off again. How could she love him? How dared she love him?

The long night drew towards bedtime and still nothing was resolved. Sweatily and gradually he calmed down, reproached by her pallor and her dignity and in the manner of fathers immemorial saw he could play for time.

"You have to promise me you'll not rush into anything," he pleaded.

"How could I? Gordon is still married."

"He has to explain to *me*. What he's done behind my back. I find that hard to forgive. He was a man I trusted. I'll never work for him again, that's one thing for sure."

"He hopes you will. You know what he thinks of you. Dad, he didn't let you down. He employed you when you were made redundant — "

"I'll find my own job. Anything.

Anything. I'll dig roads first — "

"Well, that's your choice."

"You see what he's done to us? You and I never fell out over anything, did we? I know you'll want to go off some day, I've faced up to that, I want grandchildren and all that, but not yet, I don't want to see you settled yet, you've too much to learn, to see. What about work? Some kind of career?"

She said helplessly, "How does knowing Gordon knock all that on the head? Dad, I feel as though my life is just beginning. Everything is possible, through knowing him."

"It's not how you were brought up."

"How can you say that? Look at you and Mum."

"We were young and we wrecked things. You'll do the same."

"I don't see that." She was stubborn. Unmoved now. Unmoveable.

"You're breaking up somebody's marriage. You're taking a father away from his son."

"The marriage doesn't exist. He'll see Jonathan just as much."

He shook his head. They were both hoarse, exhausted. "Away to your bed," he ordered, using the Scottish idiom. "I can see I'll get no sense out of you this night."

31

THE lines of the transatlantic telephone whined like the wind then Ida's voice answered, clear as if she was in the room next door.

"Is my bairn all right?" she demanded immediately.

He said, "She's OK. But she's got herself in a tangle with a married man. I want you to come home and talk some sense into her."

There was a long silence at the other end then Ida's voice, altered by shock and outrage, demanded, "I thought you promised me you would take care of her. How did she get herself entangled? Where is she? She's not pregnant, is she?"

"No, she's not pregnant. More by luck than good guidance, though. She's at her work. I don't want her to know I've phoned you. Just come."

Another silence. "It's not as simple as that."

"Why not? She's your daughter."

"And you're supposed to be taking care of her. I've got my own problems out here, Arthur — "

"Such as?"

"Such as things not being quite as we expected them to be. Financially I mean."

"But you're still with him. What's he called again?"

"Norman." Her voice changed again. The inflexion told him much more than she realized, hopes dashed, options closed, then her voice rose, flyting and scolding in the old working-class way they'd both grown up with. "You canna expect me to take the first plane out of Miami. Get Tracy to ring me."

"She won't."

"I'll ring her."

"She'll not speak to you. Ach, I'm sorry I rang. Go back to your Norman and the best of British to both of you." He hung up the phone. His hands, his body, were trembling. He was even shedding tears. Appalled, he wiped them away with the back of his hand and reached for the whisky bottle. He should

331

not be drinking in the morning but he had to get a grip somehow. He was hopeless at anything to do with the emotions. Sylvia had always said that. If only he could convey to Tracy how much it had meant to him in prison, knowing that they would have a life together when he got out. In a sense, the betrayal he felt over this was worse than the concern he had over his daughter's involvement with a married man, but that too, rankled deep. He had wanted nothing but the best for her. No messy affairs.

He had always liked Gordon Pershor. That was the salt in the wound. He had thought him a man you could trust with your life. Showed you how wrong you could be. You couldn't even trust him with your teenage daughter. After the incident with Conrad Higgison he had examined his character as searchingly as he could for the explanation of the violence that had erupted and had vowed that never again would he allow anger to get out of hand. Yet rage threatened his autonomy now. He wanted to attack Gordon Pershor physically, to 'take him on', to beat him into the ground, annihilate him. That's what the shaking was about. Suppressing all that anger. He was sorry now he had brought Ida into it. He had broken his part of the agreement, that he would take care of Tracy. There had to be some other approach. He had to be a bit statesman-like. But prison, if not breaking him entirely, had somehow taken him apart. He needed mending. And so far the whisky bottle had been his only ally. After a time it conferred a haze, a blurring, so that raw edges no longer met to impose intolerable hurt. Stopped rational thought, too, though. That was the trouble. Should he have one more drink? Probably not. But then, maybe yes.

Tracy's feet were not touching the ground. That was how it felt. That was how forms of speech began. Somebody realizing something. Neither did she appear to be touching anything around her. Floating. The strangest feeling. A kind of bliss. It lifted the corners of old women's mouths with smiling magic; it made babies' faces look like the cherubs on the record sleeve for Handel's 'Water Music'. It made her look at skies. The bus seat held her in a kind of embrace and the big rain-soaked Labrador sitting with a blind man made her think of caves, forests, older animals and the damp primeval mist that married land to sea. It was like a madness, a good madness that made her see the faces of the children they would have, a dark boy and a fair girl, and the houses they would live in, the holidays they would take. How they would grow old.

He was coming home. There had been a phone call to the office, asking her to meet him at Manchester airport. There had been funny looks. It did not matter. Soon they would all know. Everything. The tide of her happiness would knock them all down. It would carry her to the airport as he had requested and they would meet, never to let go of each other again.

He came bearing gifts, perfume, a hip-hop tape (now he knew her taste), a gold bracelet and a length of yellow silk, his face bemused by travel. Their mouths collided painfully in the first eager kiss. "I missed you," they both said and their faces became realigned, losing the strain.

They went to a hotel near the airport, to talk, to hold hands, to plan.

"I'll talk to your dad," he promised.

"I don't know if it's a good idea," she temporized fearfully.

"I'll not have him making you miserable."

"He doesn't mean to," she said loyally.

"I want him to know I'm serious about you. I've never been more serious about anything in my life."

"He sides with your wife. He says she is a decent woman. He makes me feel bad about her."

He sighed, taking a sip of the tonic water with lemon he had ordered.

"Trace, I don't know why Mel and I got married in the first place. I liked the way she looked, we did a lot of the same things but we should have waited. We were too young. There's very little animosity between us. We've just grown apart in an inexorable way I can't do anything about. Nor can she. Believe me, we've tried. I think she's ready to let me go. I'm certainly going to ask her."

"What if *I'm* too young?"

"Do you feel that?"

"Not at all. I feel as though everything is cut and dried between us."

"Don't frighten me. I don't see you in terms of age, of experience, of anything. I just see you as inevitable. That's the difference."

"Don't be scared." She could have been talking to a co-conspirator in some childish game and her hand came out to touch his. "We'll have to be careful with Dad, is all. He thought I was going to be there for him, you see, and I've tried to tell him I will be, in a way. But not the way he thinks."

"You'll be there for me."

"I'll be there for you."

They could not part till he had driven to a secluded spot on the edge of some nearby woods where he made love to her. They were in danger of being seen, for there were dog walkers not far off, plus the occasional jogger, but they could not be kept apart. Her gold-speckled hair, growing longer, fell across his face, tickled his nostrils; her gentle soft-palmed hands pulled him insistently closer.

The essence of her seemed in danger

of getting away from him in his terror of not having her, possessing her. He could feel himself gasp at tender skin and peachy breath and strained for ever greater containment of her. All the while in Malaysia he had thought of her; not, of course, when he was working, not over the planning dinners and the plotting receptions, but when he was on his own in his hotel room or swimming the length of the long blue pool. Then he had known she had danced through his pores and under his skin, she had fastened her shy elusive smile into every page of his mental album. When he had known regret — and he had — it had been washed away by a certainty that was stronger than upbringing or convention. Love had shown him her face and he could only be grateful the experience had not passed him by. He was sure that what he felt was rare, maybe only granted to a few. He threw himself away from her now, leaning back on his seat, almost languid from the power of his longing and she crept over him, bestriding him, crushing him, so that libido crashed effortlessly through him again and he held her roughly; he took her, there was no way he could not, and then before they left they consummated their feelings once more, when he was gentle, confident, brilliant, there was nothing but affirmation, nothing but joy.

* * *

"Tracy, come in here."

"I'll be late for work."

"Never mind work. We have things to settle."

Arthur Blaney was wearing the blue and white striped shirt with a white collar and the grey suit which had been his business armour in the days when he had a job. He was well shaved and his hair brushed down with a slick of gel. He held open the sitting-room door with an almost theatrical flourish.

"I know where you were last night."

She was pale-faced, not so happy now about facing questions and gossip at the office, though Gordon had told her to explain nothing. A wave of sickly fear attacked her at her father's harsh expression. She went obediently into the pretty room and sat down on the smaller settee.

"I phoned him last night. After you came in. Janet put me on the alert. Said you'd gone to meet him and they were all wondering at the office what you were up to. You've certainly filled their mouths, haven't you?"

"Daddy — "

"I'll do the talking. You're my responsibility. I don't think he'll want to see you today, anyhow. It was Melanie I spoke to first last night. Yes, Melanie. She had no idea. She was expecting her husband back from the Far East in the normal way. Do you see what you are doing, girl?"

"You had no right." The violent protestations of her mind came out in a wavery voice that dismayed her, but she ploughed on, "Gordon was going to tell Melanie. Why did you interfere? Daddy, I'm not going to stay here unless you are going to be reasonable." She insisted to herself she would not cry, but she could feel herself go puffy and red with the effort. "I'm not a minor, you know. I can choose my own life."

"Well, we'll see what your mother has to say about it."

"Mum? You haven't been on the phone to her? Tell me you haven't."

"But I have. And she rang me back. She'll be here this afternoon."

32

HELEN MACREEVY walked up the drive to have coffee with Mavis Higgison, her face heavy with reflection. She had just had a letter from her middle daughter Elizabeth saying she had left her husband and wanted a divorce. Elizabeth lived in Maine, in America. How many thousands of miles away was that? Even if she could go and see her, Elizabeth would not take her advice, which would be to fight for her marriage. Elizabeth had never in her life listened to her mother about anything. She had been a small, sickly girl who had never eaten anything she didn't fancy, done anything she didn't want to do. She would not be any different now.

She would not mention the matter, she decided, to Mavis, in case it started her off again about Conrad and Sylvia. Better if she talked about Bernard. She said Helen was the only one of her friends who really understood that she *wanted* to talk about Bernard. She did not want him marginalized. He was still very much *there* for her, she wanted people to realize. She wanted to remember his wisdom, his jokes, his funny little ways. Helen felt terribly sorry for Mavis in her grief. Sometimes she could not bring herself to look her neighbour in the face, for fear of seeing there what would happen to her herself if she were widowed. They were in muddy waters during her little visits, with Mavis as likely to be laughing immoderately at some remembered incident involving Bernard as crying soundlessly into an endless succession of paper hankies. And sometimes, hardest of all, Mavis railed, against every remembered slight, real or imagined, and against Fate and its hardest of hard faces, that could not be softened by tears or chipped away by reproaches.

Helen opted for diversionary gossip. The little nugget she had was that she had seen a woman go up the drive towards the Blaney house, a kind of cheap-smart, youngish woman carrying an airline bag and sporting white shoes and a very short haircut. There had been something faintly familiar about her and then Helen had had it — she was like Tracy, that's who she was like. This would surely have Mavis's attention. Mavis was very good at putting two and two together. Maybe she'd even put out the biscuits.

In the Blaney household, Ida and Tracy were both crying tears of rage and it was Arthur who had to bring in the tea and biscuits; summarily, in mugs with the spoons in and the biscuits left in the packet.

"I've warned you," Ida said to her daughter. "You saw what happened to me, left high and dry. You had no business getting in with a married man — "

"He shouldn't have rung you." Tracy could not forgive her father's betrayal, as she saw it. "Gordon could have got the divorce and then it would all have been different, wouldn't it? Well, I don't see what the difference is. What Gordon and me feel for each other wouldn't change. I can't explain it, Mum."

"Aye, it's bigger than both of you," said her father, with heavy irony.

Ida identified it. "It's infatuation. The first time you've ever been smitten. And as for him — I haven't met him, but I can see what he was after. A young, unprotected lassie, that he can throw over when he's had his fling."

"It wouldn't be like that."

"Wouldn't it? Wouldn't it just! You're coming back to the States with me, girl. Is your passport in order? If not — "

Tracy was about to run out of the room in tears when the front door-bell went. She could see the form of the visitor through the glass and knew that it was Gordon. She flung the door open and propelled herself into his arms.

"Steady," he said into her ear. Then, in a voice heavy with angry intent, "I've come to speak to your father."

"What do *you* want here?" Arthur demanded from the hallway.

"I've come to talk. Can I come in?" Brooking no refusal he stepped over the threshold. Ida came slowly from the sitting-room into his line of vision. "I'm Tracy's mum," said Ida. "I take it you're the Gordon in the case?" She gave him a look filled with contempt. "I hope you're proud of yourself."

Refusing to be deflected by any of this, Gordon strode into the large room beyond, drawing Tracy with him by the hand. As always, his expensive loafers were polished, his shirt and tie immaculate under the leather bomber jacket. He looked from Arthur to Ida and then to Tracy's tear-stained face and drew in a protesting breath. "What have you been doing to this poor girl? What has she done except love somebody?" As Tracy sobbed, he said harshly, "Come on, love. I'll take you away from here. You don't have to take this kind of thing from anyone, even your parents." He looked at Arthur. "You've done such a great job looking after her, haven't you?"

It was Ida who was galvanized into response. "Leave him out of it. I brought her up and it's me you've got to answer to." Her escalating tones held a note of hysteria and he gripped Tracy's hand harder as he sought to take control of the situation.

"Look, can we sit down?" As though energy had suddenly flowed out of his body, he was the first to follow his own injunction, but the others followed suit.

"Arthur," he appealed, "I've come here this morning to clear up any misapprehensions. I have spoken to Mel and told her I want a divorce — "

"But what about her?" Arthur seemed to have lost the power of speech and it was Ida who put the question, her face a mask of tiredness and scorn.

He kept his voice low and conciliatory as he answered. "I know I've hurt her. But we've been two people leading two pretty separate lives for a long time. She has her own job, her own money, her own friends. I wouldn't be leaving a helpless little woman, you know. Not Mel."

"And what about my daughter?" Arthur spoke up at last. "Did you think of the plans her mother and I had for her? She's too young to settle; she needs to get herself a career or some qualifications at the very least?"

"You've got a funny notion of modern liaisons," said Gordon. "I wouldn't stop her studying. I wouldn't stop her working."

"But it's the very thing that's come

between you and Melanie. All this independence. Tracy needs time to think about what she wants."

Tracy pulled her hand away from Gordon's grasp. "I'm here, you know. Tracy is here. Don't kick my name about between you like — like a football. I can speak for myself. I love Gordon." She gazed passionately at her mother. "I do, Mum. I love him more than I've ever loved anybody. And I'm going to be with him. Whatever anybody says."

"I feel the same." Gordon affirmed it. "I didn't ask for it to happen. It just did. I'd lay down my life for this girl. I am going to marry her. Mel will come round, given a day or two to think things over. She'll see our marriage for the farce it was."

"Have you thought where that leaves me?" Arthur's voice was flat, toneless. "I've got no job, my home is for sale, my wife has left me. Correction, my wife is now my ex-wife. The divorce is through." He looked at his daughter. "I was going to teach you to drive, wasn't I? When the house was sold we were going to have a holiday together. What happens to all that?"

"You can still teach me to drive!"

"No! If you persist in seeing him, that's it. You can clear out. Why should I care about teaching you anything. You've shown your mother and me, both of us, what you think of us."

"Don't," Tracy pleaded. "Don't be like that, Daddy. I want us to have a good relationship, for you to be friends with Gordon — "

"In the old days, he would have been horse-whipped," Ida intervened.

"I never thought, when I brought you down here to live with me, that you'd be off at the first whistle." Arthur scarcely heard what Ida said: he was focusing only on Tracy. "You were what kept me going through all my trouble — "

"But you didn't think I was going to stay with you always, did you? Daughters go out into the world and do their thing. It doesn't mean I don't care about you. You know I do."

Ida had had enough. She rose, scattering the contents of her handbag as she did so, but leaving them where they lay as she stood in front of Gordon and Tracy.

"You," she said directly to Gordon, "can get out of here. You can get your divorce and sort yourself out and come back in a year if you still have the stomach for it. If you think I'll let my daughter see you in the meantime, you have another think coming."

Ignoring her, Gordon said to Tracy, "Do you want to go back and stay with Janet? I can arrange it. Or we'll find you some other digs." He then addressed himself to Arthur. "Look, there's work for you at Grant and Pershor. We can sort everything out, with a bit of goodwill on all sides."

Arthur made a lunge at him and both women screamed. Gordon dodged and hunched up his shoulders defensively, but began to make for the door.

"Are you coming, Tracy? Just get your coat and come."

Ida put her arms around her daughter, imprisoning her. "You're not having her. I haven't come home here at great expense to myself, expense I could ill afford, for you to take her away out of my sight." More sensibly she said to Tracy, "At least wait and talk to me."

Gordon's arms fell to his sides. "No coercion," he agreed. He put out his hand to touch Tracy's hair. "I'll be in the office all day. Ring me when you can." She nodded, her lips trembling. She could afford to wait till later. She knew when she left she would not be back.

Helen Macreevy was going home after her visit to Mavis Higgison. She saw the man in the leather bomber jacket get into his flash car. Something had discommoded him. She bet it was something to do with Tracy. Some girls had that kind of aura about them. They called it sexy nowadays. In Helen's day it had been oomph. She sighed. She had not exactly had a large measure of either.

33

THE old lady, Mrs Grace Carter, Ginnie's mother, had grown quite fond of the pink candlewick bedspread. It was worn and soft to the touch and she bunched it up under her fists and squeezed it. They put trays on top of it, the kind with legs, and fed her toast, soup and milk pudding. Sunlight and shadow passed across her face, she slept, and sometimes a figure sat beside the bed, and smiled and smiled then sailed away into the far corner of Mrs Grace Carter's consciousness.

One day she felt for the bedspread and it didn't appear to be there. Nothing was there. Mrs Grace Carter felt and felt and found nothing. Her breath leaving her was like no more than the fall of a rose petal from the flowers arranged on the window-sill, no greater volume of air disturbed by her going. First there, then not there. The ward maid coming in to dust her room had seen it happen before, gave a little sigh and went in search of matron.

For Ginnie, the relief was great. 'For the best', everyone said and up to a point it was true. But her mother restored to her, in full possession of her faculties, would have been better still. That was why she cried in Dougie's comforting arms, remembering her mother's strong hand pulling her up hills, adjusting the hems of dresses she had made for her, pouring her tea when she got home from school (her other hand always on the lid, in case). She'd been a mother's girl. And now there was relief almost outweighing the sorrow and guilt sitting imp-like on her shoulder. Could she have done more?

Dougie assured her she could not and that the feeling would pass. He had been down that road after Connie's death. Once the formalities were over he took Ginnie away for a short break in the Welsh hills, where in ever-renewing closeness he hoped to get her used to the idea of marrying him.

"They'll say I was just waiting for mother to go," she demurred.

"Who are *they*? What people say matters sometimes, but not in this case. We can do it as quietly as you like."

She did not know what was holding her back. Maybe the fact that they were happy as they were. People did live together now, 'over the brush' as her mother had called it, 'living in sin' as her grandmother would have described it. Maybe it was the naughty edge of irresponsibility that she liked, the flouting, after so much attention to respectability. The feeling that she could get up and go. Dougie managed to put on a grey mask of hurt when she said this, to age ten years before her very eyes, so she stopped saying it, knowing she was being cruel. But she could not give up thinking it. Not after Sydney.

Just before the summer holidays, the headmaster sent for Dougie. The head's name was Chris and he had an easy, commanding way with the boys. He and Dougie were on Christian-name terms though Chris was barely forty and Dougie could not resist the notion that the younger man should be calling *him* 'sir', which was patently absurd. Nonetheless, it masked a deeper conviction, that Chris was more front than erudition and it hid a kind of fond contempt for the trendy products of training colleges these days.

Dougie took up a seat in the head's study and twiddled his thumbs forward, then backwards, wondering which piece of forward thinking was about to get an airing.

"Do you think we should point a moral path?" Chris brushed his carefully cut fringe forward and adjusted his metal-rimmed specs, giving Dougie a sideways look.

"In what way, Headmaster?"

"D'you think the bandwagon has rolled on far enough? That there's been enough erosion of family values? I mean, Dougie, we see it here, don't we, the kids we have to refer for counselling, marriages breaking up? I think the moral backlash has reached Wilhowbry High and I have to take a stand. I have to reassert family values. I think it behoves those who teach moral values to be in stable relationships themselves. What I'm saying, Dougie, is I've heard the boys are referring to your — your private situation since Mrs

Walker died in less than respectful terms and this seems to me bad, Dougie, less than desirable, wouldn't you think?"

"What about your hot affair with Angela, the gym teacher, two years ago?" Unworthy of me, Dougie acknowledged it, but it had just come out.

"We were discreet." Chris was embarrassed, but not too much so. "I'm saying: the moral majority would not have approved and I acknowledged the fact. I am asking you to do the same, Dougie. Can't you regularize your illicit union?"

"It's not illicit! We're two free agents. But I take your meaning. You want us to get married. No big deal, Chris; I'm working on it."

"A certain amount of girding of loins, I think," said Chris. "The trend is back to the text, eh, Dougie? Good old-fashioned, copper-bottomed family values. This is Middle England after all. Janice and I are expecting our fourth, by the way."

"Congratulations. Hope all goes well."

"You won't regret toeing the line. Not when it comes to staff cuts, if you know what I'm saying. The governors will like it."

"I know, I do know. I know moral blackmail, too, when I hear it." But he smiled to show he couldn't possibly mean it.

★ ★ ★

"So you see, Ginnie. I'm in a hard position."

They were eating what she called his bachelor soup, made with a round-up of softening vegetables and a lot of lentils and she was thinking how much she liked the extempore mode of much of their living, the sharing of chores which he took for granted, the postponement of things like ironing if they felt like listening to his latest classical CD. And the love-making. Ah, yes, that.

Sydney swooped into her mind and out again, like a bat. She said with a sense of strain, "I don't see why we should get married just to please the headmaster."

He was silent, his mouth in a thin, straight line almost disappearing into his face. At last he said, carefully choosing his words, "You know it isn't really about that. Not when you come down to it. It's that I'm a conventional kind of bloke, with a sense of responsibility. Not a flouter."

"Well, maybe I am, a bit. I don't think I want to be tied."

"You know that isn't so," he argued. "You know you're as conventional as I am."

"Not now my mother's gone. She was the conventional one, who always worried what other people thought. Maybe I want time now to work out my own ideas."

"We are for each other, yes?"

"Of course."

"We're committed. Don't tell me you haven't been happy, because I know you have. I know you like being with me — "

"Why are you doing this to me, Doug? I don't want to leave you, ever. But I've been through one divorce and I never want to go through another. Why can't we just say to each other: yes, we *are* committed, we *do* love each other and that's that?"

"Is it because you think I have my

sights on the money from your mother's estate? You can't think that, can you?" He caught a glimmer of something in her look that made him burst out in fury, "Ginnie, what would I want your money for? I have enough of my own. I want nothing to do with your money."

"Well, he would. Sydney would. He would have taken me for every penny." She glared at Dougie as though holding him responsible.

He shook his head in despair.

"You can't shake him off, can you?" He was too angry to take the conversation further. He threw down his soup-spoon, gathered up the bowls and took them into the kitchen. He stood looking down the garden, feeling he was looking down time's avenue and seeing in his mind's eye the patient figure of his late wife, bending over the border flowers to behead them. Serve him right for forgetting Connie. He should never have thought he could cope with another one.

Ginnie stood at his shoulder.

"I might as well tell you. I'm going to start another business. Another gown shop. With the money."

Without turning to face her, he said stonily, "I thought all that was behind you."

"It's my insurance. So that if ever anything went wrong again, it would be me. I'd have something behind me. I like clothes. I like fashion. The rag trade's in my bones."

"Funny you didn't discuss it with me."

"This is what I mean." Her face could not have been straighter. "Some decisions I'll always want to make on my own. In marriage you give all that away."

"Not with me." He turned away so that she should not see the extent of his hurt. "But go ahead. Do what you like. This whole thing is becoming impossible." He opened the kitchen door and walked blindly down the garden.

"Dougie," she appealed. She washed the soup bowls, her tears falling into the sink.

34

"WHAT do you think I should do?"

Helen Macreevy looked down at the small, huddled figure of Ginnie Carter and felt an uncharacteristic surge of impatience.

"About opening another shop? Oh, I'd think hard and long about that, Ginnie." She sought for a way of putting it delicately, found none and took the plunge. "After all, the last one went down the pan. Is there the money about for the expensive stuff you used to sell?"

"Oh, I'd go for middle range this time. Classic country stuff. There's always a market for that. I'd do just a few ball gowns for the fun of it — "

"And what does Dougie think?"

Without thinking, Ginnie stretched for one of Helen's ginger biscuits and bit into it, sharply. Helen realized they were coming to the nub of the conversation, the reason Ginnie had appeared on her doorstep at an unconventionally early hour, eyebrows arced in a plea for company, time.

"He's anti. He doesn't say so, but he thinks it's frivolous. I'd still do my work for Croatia. I'd do the buying but I'd have a manageress for the shop."

Helen looked at her perplexedly. "Pardon me for asking, but are you two thinking of marriage? I was sure it was on the cards."

"He wants it."

"But you don't?"

"It's not what you think. I do love him. It's just — " She paused.

Something bitter and wintry took over Helen's expression.

"You younger ones, you don't commit any more, do you? I've just heard from our Elizabeth. Her marriage has gone for a Burton. In my day, commitment was what it was all about. Loyalty." As Ginnie looked at her in concern, the older woman began to cry, plying her eyes with a hankie. "Why must you make your lives so complicated? Elizabeth wanted it all and now she has nothing. Her husband is going to fight for custody of the children. She'll lose her lovely home — "

"I didn't mean to start you off." Ginnie went round the table and put her hands on Helen's shoulders. "Sorry, Helen. I'm afraid I regard you as a rock. I shouldn't. It's not fair."

"No, perhaps you shouldn't." Helen looked at her with a pink, accusatory face. "But then everybody does. I don't really mind, except when you get taken so much for granted."

Ginnie managed a rueful half-smile. "And even you must feel like breaking out sometimes. Throwing your dutiful pinny out the window. Come on, don't cry. Elizabeth will sort things out."

"She's so far away. And I do worry so."

"Then don't. Loosen up. I'm sorry I brought my grotty little grumblings round to you. You're so good at listening, you see."

"Marry him, Ginnie."

"And what should I do about the shop?"

"Don't know." Helen wiped her eyes, then said, "Maybe you should go for it.

Maybe it's best not to put all your eggs in the domestic basket. I don't know any more."

"But you do think I should marry Doug?"

"I think you should make him happy, then you'll be happy."

"Sounds simple."

"Does, doesn't it?"

"If only it were."

★ ★ ★

Going home from his morning on the golf course to have lunch with his wife, Bertie Macreevy saw the tall youth come out of the Blaney's drive. He had time to notice Gary's dejected air before their paths almost collided.

"Sorry," said the boy. He took his hands from his pockets. It was this small gesture of unconscious respect that touched Bertie.

"Miles away, were you?" he said jocularly. "Thinking of your girl-friend?" He and Helen were not sure of the state of play in the Blaney household. He hadn't spoken to Arthur in weeks. There was a strange woman in residence but Helen had commented that she had not seen Tracy or the man they presumed was a new suitor for some days. Maybe his reference to girl-friend had been injudicious. Certainly from the boy's miserable face it seemed to be.

"No bike?" He tried again.

Gary shuffled his feet in their elderly trainers, hands back in pockets. "Had to sell it." Head down. The hair was cut pudding-basin fashion. They called the style curtains, Bertie believed. Didn't do a lot for them, that was for sure.

"Times hard, then?"

"Unbelievable, man."

"Can't you get a job?"

"Nope." Now the level, blue, not-unintelligent gaze met his and did not look away. "Just been up there" — Gary jerked his head towards the Blaney residence — "to get back a list of college courses I lent — I lent to, you know, Tracy. Thought I might do another."

"What course have you done?"

"Computers. Too many of us, though."

"You tried anything else?"

"Course. I just want a job. I'll try anything."

Bertie felt some chord of memory vibrate, so that he was suddenly in touch with his younger self. A lot had hurt in those days. Hard bosses, unfeeling females. Until he'd met Helen. The boy had drawn the short straw with the girl Tracy, too. Daft haircuts and strange allegiances or not, maybe the young today had their pangs and sufferings.

"Look, you heard of the cash-and-carry warehouse on the Mondle Road?"

"Yeh. I know it."

"Go there, ask to see Mr Perce Attershaw, tell him I sent you. Tell him you're ready to start at t'bottom and train up. Y'are, aren't you? You just said so."

"Did I?"

"Said you'd try anything."

The boy seemed to sink into a trough of intransigence. Bertie said nothing. Merely gazed at him good-naturedly till he was forced to answer.

"Who will I say sent me?"

"Tell him Bert Macreevy. He'll see you. It were me gave him his chance.

Now he's boss, like I was."

"Not much point."

Bertie grabbed the young man by the arm. "Give it your best shot," he said vehemently. "What's your name, lad? I'll phone Mr Attershaw when I get in. Put in a word."

"Gary Barker." The face, animated at last by something, some response, was quite a pleasant face, not sullen really. "D'you think I'm in with a chance?"

"Aye, I do. You'll be able to buy a new bike. Good luck, Gary." Formally, the two shook hands.

Just before they parted, Bertie pulled the boy's sleeve again. "Something to remember about women, Gary." He looked significantly up the Blaney drive. "They're like buses used to be. Another one along in a minute. Take it from one who knows. I can guarantee it."

When he repeated the last part of this conversation to Helen, she smiled at him and said, "What would you know about women?"

"You forget I were once the Adonis of the dance-hall, co-respondent shoes, fag-case and all."

"But could you do the dip and the scissors?"

"That and all."

★ ★ ★

Mavis Higgison had been having a good day.

She had been shopping and bought two new dresses, a swimsuit and some shoes. She had booked a cruise to the Greek Islands with her friend, Helga, who was also a widow. Although unfortunately Helga's fair skin showed more wrinkles than her own, they were quite a personable pair.

What am I thinking, thought Mavis sadly. We are not men-bait. Yet there might be some older available men on board, who would be ready to fetch a scarf or a newspaper or join a hand at bridge. Would she remember how to flirt or, for that matter, discourage, after so many years? Did she want to? She was not averse to male charm.

It was as though Bernard were still at her side and she needed to keep giving him reassuring pats. Letting him know he was still *numero uno*. Would always be. It was strange how the many annoying traits he had had while alive had melted away into thin air. The Bernard she remembered was the one who never really lost his temper with her, who brought her cocoa in bed, shared the paper, took care of the bills, laughed her out of her silly little animosities. The realization had come to Mavis that Bernard had really loved her. And, face it, that was an accomplishment in itself, for sometimes, she knew, she could be a trial. Tiresome, vain, spendthrift, dog-in-the-manger. But could she be all that bad, given Bernard had thought her worth staying with all these years? Had he known how she felt about him? That worried her a little now. Exasperated, niggled, infuriated a lot of the time by his calm passivity while alive, she now looked back and saw him as a kind of saint, good and selfless beyond the call of duty. She had noticed she was not alone in this: her widowed friends all tended to raise their husbands' memories to a level of sanctification. Was that good or bad? She only knew that there was a large corner of her heart that was

Bernard's garden and which she guarded tigerishly. Always would.

So if on the cruise she wore her new dresses and laughed at some elderly colonel's feeble sallies, it would only be out of loneliness. Today had been a good day. Mavis patted Bernard's ghostly knee. He'd never minded the buzz she got from buying something new.

35

THE phone rang and for a moment, Ida thought she was back in Miami and it was Norman ringing to say when he would be home. Sleepily she picked up the guest-room extension and it was Tracy's voice on the other end. Sleep quickly deserted Ida as she sat bolt upright.

"Tracy! At last! I've been out of my mind. Where in heaven's name are you?"

"I'll tell you later. Mum, can you meet me? Don't bring Dad. He just won't listen. Meet me outside the Midland Bank in Wilhowbry, eleven o'clock. We'll have a coffee."

"Are you all right? What's been happening?"

"Eleven, Mum. Got to go. See you then."

She needn't have worried that the phone had woken Arthur. He had not closed his bedroom door and she could see he was still sound asleep, his head buried beneath the clothes. He had probably been sitting up drinking again. She had heard the muffled buzz of the television downstairs into the wee small hours. She did not feel she should be responsible for him. They had had a brief teenage affair and she had been left to bring up their baby on her own. End of story. When they had met up again she had remembered what it had been like to feel attracted to him, but the later Arthur had seemed to her terribly conventional and stick-in-the-mud for his age. Though with something about him that made you want to mother him. She wasn't about to do that now, though. She'd had enough of Arthur and his mid-life crises. She wanted back to Norman, who was garrulous and amusing and diverting. And young. Ida felt she had missed what being young was about and yearned to roll back the years again and find out.

Meeting Tracy, it was brought home to her how the move south had changed her daughter, given her a kind of poise and even elegance. She'd always been a quick learner. Now her once-chubby offspring

371

had long elegant legs, long, glossy hair. Maybe only someone as young as Tracy should wear black. It set off the petal softness of her skin, the poreless-seeming, immaculate purity of it challenging the dark shade. *I made her*, thought Ida, with a quick spurt of maternal pride. They can't take that away from me. I worked in those dreary places, I rose to comfort her in those dismal hours, I did without those clothes, those meals, those opportunities. She marvelled that she did not feel envy, but she did not. A sense of owning, though. That she did feel. And anger that she had not been made privy to Tracy's movements over the past two days, since she had sneaked out after the row.

She could barely wait to stir her coffee. Around them the affluent wives of Wilhowbry had parked their second cars to meet for gossip. "What's been happening?" she demanded. "Where have you been?"

"Gordon found me a B and B. It's OK. It's fine."

"What's wrong with home? I came here, Tracy, at a cost I can ill afford, to be with you and you just ran out on me the other night."

"I can't take Dad at the moment. I can't handle him. He wants to tell me what to do. Look, Mum, he thinks I'm going to stay with him, shop for him, cook for him. Well, it's not on. What do I owe him, after all? If I owe anyone, it's you. You brought me up. You and Gran."

"It's not what it's about." Ida looked severe, almost ferocious. "It's about you and Gordon Pershor. The man is married, Tracy — "

"Not for much longer."

Ida gave her daughter a long, searching, reproachful look.

"Has it ever occurred to you you're exchanging one father-figure for another? He's far too old for you, too experienced. And he's got a son. Kids should have their parents around and don't cast up my one mistake; I still know right from wrong, good from bad."

More humbly, Tracy said after a pause, "He didn't need to bring you back all this way, you know. I want to sort out my own life. And that means Gordon."

She raised her clear, youthful eyes and gazed at her mother with utter candour. "Gordon first, last and foremost."

Ida made an elaborate play of cutting up her toasted tea-cake. She licked buttery fingers. "When you first met *him* — your father, I mean, I'm talking Arthur now, not Gordon, you were swept up by him much the way you're swept up by Gordon Pershor now. You thought he was a great dad, the cat's thingy, the whole cheese."

"I still do!" It was Tracy's turn to look reproachful. "Ma, I still think it was the best thing ever, getting a dad after all these years. I don't want to stop seeing him, being a daughter. I do love him. I feel . . . I feel more solid, because I can look at him and see the genes that are in me. I mean, when Sylvia left him and he got into that dreadful bother — " She looked carefully round the tea-room, terrified anyone should by chance telepathy pick up the word prison. "I stuck by him, didn't I? It's not been easy since he came home — from *there*. He's been spaced out, Mum. Drinking far too much. What am I supposed to do?" Tracy put a hand up to her cheek in case any tears might have slipped their mooring.

"I can't stay indefinitely," said Ida, more briskly than she felt. "Arthur isn't my responsibility, any more than I was his."

"But could you try?" pleaded Tracy. "Could you try to explain to him, Mum, what the position is? Gordon has seen Melanie, his wife." She did not quite meet her mother's vigilant eye. "I think she's going to institute proceedings."

"You only think? Will she name you?"

"What does it matter? It's only a name on a piece of paper. Nobody much knows me down here, anyhow."

"He might have spared you that."

"But a divorce by mutual consent would take two years."

"I can't believe it. You talking like this."

"Divorce is commonplace. Gordon says."

"Just you remember his words, when he divorces *you* in ten years time."

"No. That won't happen."

"Why not? If it's commonplace."

"Because we're different."

"Oh God!" Ida appealed to her Maker, somewhere up there in the tea-room's high and well-lit ceiling. But all that came back to her was the pitch of chatter from a hundred mouths and the shrieking laughter of matrons busy denigrating the husbands who paid for their meringues and the second cars in the busy car-park.

"Come home!" she pleaded. "I can't stay in the UK much longer and your dad needs you. Please, Tracy. Do it for me. Learn to wait."

Tracy bit on a trembling lower lip. "Can't," she said. "And if you loved me, Mum, you wouldn't ask me."

★ ★ ★

Ida was not in the least looking forward to her return to the house. If only she had been there on a straightforward visit, she could have got a lot out of her attractive surroundings, the rooms furnished and embellished with such care by the shadowy Sylvia and the garden with its pretty lawns, bowers and garden sofas swinging under fringed canopies. Like living inside *Homes and Gardens*. A long way from the cheerless estate back home and she didn't blame Arthur for his despairing plaint about the prospect of losing it all. She knew very well how hard he must have worked to attain all this — and how lucky he must have been to find the job that best suited what talents he did have. But she didn't know how much longer she could take his moods and diatribes. How should she know what he ought to do next? She had come over because Tracy was her concern, not Arthur. If she could have afforded it, she would have moved out, like Tracy, into some bed and breakfast and left Arthur to his whisky and self-pity. But as it was, she had to watch what she spent.

As she got off the yellow neighbourhood bus and began to climb the gradient of Pinkmount Drive, Ida saw a somewhat haughty-looking Asian woman drive past in a gleaming car. That would be the Dr Singh whom Arthur had mentioned: the one nobody had spoken to as yet. Back home, the Asian kids would have been out playing in the street with the Scottish kids. Money insulated, Ida thought. But then, she thought, feeling an uneven paving slab cut through the thinning soles of her trainers — Tracy had looked a bit askance at them — what would I know? I've never had any. It hardened her resolve to be tougher with Arthur, to point out to him he had had years of gracious, easy, money-cushioned living and shouldn't whine because now he had to suffer the restraints — face it — that most folk knew. She wasn't being vengeful, was she? She hoped not. She had enough failings of her own not to be too harsh a judge. Just the same, Arthur tried her patience.

And her loyalty. There was that, too. In a lifetime of erratic but voracious reading (in search of wisdom, mainly, and some kind of insight) she remembered something she had noted with particular care: some character or other saying the man who took your virginity always remained special. Important. In her mind, she had added the coda that you felt a kind of almost loyalty towards that person. As though you owed them something. No. It wasn't love, thought

Ida, reaching the gates thankfully. It was some kind of exchange of self, though. The sexual act was charged with more significance than most people nowadays acknowledged. At least the first time was. And having reached this conclusion Ida charged in the back door calling out her one-time wooer's name, even as she wished she could be instantly transported back to Miami with tiny waves at her toes and Norman putting sun bloc on her shoulders. For there was loyalty there too.

"So is she coming back?"

He had been waiting for her. Drinking, too, by the look of it, for the blue eyes were puffy and his skin colour heightened.

She put down the few bits of shopping she had picked up and laid her two-toned shell jacket over the back of one of the fatly upholstered chairs.

"She's OK. She's in a bed and breakfast. He's spoken to his wife, apparently, and the divorce is going ahead."

He lowered his head like someone going into the teeth of a storm.

"Right," he said. "I'm going to see him and I'm going to have it out with him."

She felt her stomach heave in apprehension.

"At least wait till you're sober," she said, and thought she sounded like the wife she had never been.

36

THE voice on the office phone had asked for Tracy Blaney and now it said in clear and unambiguous tones, "You know what you are, don't you? Not to put too fine a point on it, you're a slag, a slut, a whore and an adulterer."

"It's Melanie, isn't it?" Tracy could scarcely get the words out for the shock that had her trembling from top to toe. She had just enough presence of mind to cup her hand closely round the receiver and to turn her chair away from the rest of the office. "Look — look, can we meet so that I can try and explain? I'm very — "

"Sorry, are you?" The voice maintained the same disdainful tenor throughout. "I wouldn't meet you if my child's life depended on it. I wouldn't be in the same room as you. You would taint the air I breathed. Just wanted you to know what I think of you, Miss Blaney. Before

I let you have him and welcome to him. I hope you'll both be very unhappy."

The line went dead. She got up on tottering legs and walked across the office concourse to Gordon's room. When she did that nowadays every eye was upon her, but this morning all she was concerned about was getting there before she broke down. Once she had closed the door she gave a low gasping cry and he rose and led her to the chair across from his own.

"It was Melanie. I spoke to Melanie." Close to, she saw a sallowness under his eyes and a tiny tuft of hair under one nostril that his razor had missed. His shirt collar looked crumpled.

"What did she say? No, don't tell me. She had a go at you. She's upset because we met Jonathan yesterday and naturally, he's not for the divorce, he'd rather we stayed together."

"I'm not those things she said I was. I wanted to explain to her the way it happened — "

"Of course you're not," he said grimly. "But I'm what she told me I was yesterday."

"And what's that?"

"The lowest form of animal life. Dirt and worse." He touched her hand across the desk. "Maybe I am. For getting you into this. For making Jonathan happy. He can't see his mother as anything but perfect."

"Oh Gordon," she said, "I feel I know her now. She wouldn't have said these things if she hadn't wanted to hang on to you."

He took his hand away from hers. "She wants to hang on, but for the wrong reason. Only for Jonathan's sake. What I need or want doesn't come in to the equation." He picked up and then threw down his pen, saying with a heated rush of impatience, "Oh, some day I'll tell you a little bit about her manipulative little games. As for my son, well, I trust he knows I love him and will provide for him. I'm not deserting him. He'll come round. He has friends with divorced parents, he knows where it's at."

She looked up at him, her face a mixture of trust and dismay. "Why does she call me these names?"

"To hurt. To turn over the playing field."

"She wouldn't. If you meant nothing to her. If she wasn't hurting like hell."

He said nothing for what seemed to her like an eternity. He walked to the window and flicked the blind. She looked at his silhouette and noticed he had the merest beginning of a protruding stomach. For some reason this saddened her but did not make her love him less. Perhaps more. Because she could do nothing about him growing older; growing, perhaps, sadder.

"Marriages don't end without casualties," he said at last. "Of course there are emotions all over the place. But the main element between Melanie and me for the past few years has been boredom. Whatever she may feel now, the marriage has been a dead parrot. So," he went on, with a conscious lifting of his chin, "we go on. I'm asking you to be brave and not let anybody put you down. Dry your tears and let's get back to the drawing-board."

She shook out her hair, fighting for composure.

"I'm meeting your dad, at lunch-time," he said. "Just before you came in he was on the phone." He looked down at her, not quite smiling. "You can't say I don't meet trouble head on."

★ ★ ★

They had agreed to meet at the Pinkmount Golf and Country Club, in the smaller restaurant and bar. It being mid-week, it would be relatively quiet. And both men had seen the need to impose a background that would demand circum-spection. Gordon's stipulation was the talk should be restrained and civilized. He thought Arthur had come down from the high of anger of their last meeting.

From the restaurant window Arthur could see his neighbour Bertie hit a straight ball on to a distant fairway and felt reassured to be on familiar ground with familiar sights.

"Shame you're going to have to leave all this," Gordon offered. "Any sign of the house sale going through?"

"One substantial nibble."

"Will you stay in the area?"

"Depends. Depends on what happens over my daughter."

They ordered their food before diving headfirst into the topic they both dreaded.

Arthur drew breath up strenuously through his nose. "Thing is, I've always regarded you as a level-headed, decent kind of bloke."

"Which I am. I hope."

"In which case, why are you leading my girl astray?"

"Let's take this bit easy. You're not on some high-toned plateau, you know, old son, above the rest of us. Your own marriage broke up — "

"Not my doing."

"I wouldn't know the ins and outs, but there's always faults on both sides. I own to my own. But when a marriage is over, it's over. You can't go on living in a grave. I have to come clean with you and tell you that I couldn't resist Tracy. I should have waited; in fact, we both tried to keep away from each other, but it was just asking too much. I love that girl, Arthur, and all I'm asking is a chance to sort out my affairs and marry her. I never see me wanting any other woman."

"You can spare me the Mills and Boon. *I've* hardly had a chance to get to know her. You know the circumstances of her life. When I saw her for the first time I looked at a mirror image of myself. Gender didn't come into it. She's the best thing that's ever happened to me and you're going to take her away from me. Think what you're doing to her! Give her time. She needs it, I need it. And there's an end to it."

Gordon sipped his glass of wine.

"Let me tell you what I think. Will you listen? I think losing your job the way you did tipped you off balance. As it would do us all, I'll give you that. And I think you need work to get the balance of your life right again. Arthur, I'm willing to take you on in a senior capacity. Let's get you doing what you do best, going out there and drumming up business. I'll tell you what I used to think: I used to think integrity stepped through the door when you did. I was ready to do business before you as much as opened your mouth. Do you know what that's worth? If you could can it, you'd be a rich man! I'll tell you something else. Harry Grant is thinking early retirement. He's had a heart scare and his wife wants him to grow taters down in Wales. He goes, we're talking partnership. You *could* be a partner, eventually. Why not? What's wrong with a family firm?"

He stopped. Arthur was shifting about in his chair.

"I'm not hearing you," he said. "Not till you start hearing me. I want to make a home for my daughter. I want her to myself for a while. I want her to take some kind of training. I want her to think about her future."

"Arthur, *listen*. For Christ's sake, *listen*. I'm offering *you* a golden opportunity. What chance do you think you'll have if you go looking for a job on the open market? Do you read the papers? Unemployment is structured into the economy. Nobody has job security any more. We're talking short-term contracts, we're talking portfolios, odds and bobs of work picked up all over the place. Re-train? What for? Soon as you do, that market has gone." He shook his head in exasperation. "I wouldn't do this for just anybody. I am doing it for Tracy's father, because Tracy is the most important thing in my life."

"In other words, you're buying me off."

Gordon was pressed to the edge of his patience. He said exasperatedly, "I'm making you an offer you'd be daft to refuse."

"You're asking me to put my daughter's future in hock for the sake of a job. Well, I want work, but not that badly. I'll go out and find my own job, thank you very much."

"Not if you go on drinking as you're doing." Gordon spoke evenly, his gaze demanding that Arthur look back at him. Arthur was the first to look away.

"I can knock it on the head. Whenever I want to."

"Well, I hope for Tracy's sake you do. How can you look out for her when you're half-sozzled most of the time?"

"What gives you the right to speak to me like this?"

"Because we've known each other quite a long time. Because as an operator you have my respect. Because, as I've already told you, you're Tracy's father. Look, Arthur, I'm not trying to put your life out of joint. Why can't we both look out for Tracy? When she and I are married, you can see her as often as you like. She's very protective of you. It's one of her many nice qualities. If you and I don't get along, think what it's going to do to her."

"You should have thought of that before you got involved. You were old enough to know better."

He had touched a raw nerve. Gordon signalled the waiter ungraciously for the bill. "I think I've had enough of this," he said grimly. "Maybe we'd better leave it at that."

Arthur said in a low, menacing way, "Before you go, you'll listen to me. You've had your say, now I'll have mine. Get Tracy to come back home. Show her where her responsibilities lie. To me and herself for the time being."

"You're making your daughter very unhappy."

"And you're offering her a bed of roses, I suppose."

Gordon paid the bill. "If you come to your senses, give me a ring."

"I will. When hell freezes over."

37

GINNIE CARTER thought she had found the right shop at last. In Wilhowbry. On a busy corner and with a short lease. And now the fun began. Buying the stock. Dougie began to see another side to her: the glam, business-woman side, going off to fashion shows, poring over glossy magazines.

"You can't get over the transition from country mouse to city slicker, can you?" she teased him. But inwardly she worried that she might be turning into the kind of woman Dougie had no time for: the brittle, hard-headed sort who would give no thought to what went on in the likes of Croatia. To reassure both him and herself, she said they should both take another truck out to the refugee camps during his summer holidays.

"Do you really mean that?" he demanded.

"You want to go, don't you?"

"I will go," he said positively. "But I

think you'll have enough on hand, with the shop."

"You think I'll chicken out, don't you?" She was almost shouting at him, flush-faced. "I'll have a shop manager by then: I'll be up and running. You think I've forgotten those little faces in those terrible cots? I think about them every night before I go to sleep. I almost see them as our babies, Dougie, the ones God has made you and I responsible for." She was weeping now and he went and put comforting arms about her.

"OK. We'll both go."

She mopped her eyes. "It seems so little."

"My school kids don't think that. They still want to help too. Keeping the lines of compassion open — that's no small thing, Ginnie. I really don't regard it as such."

"I'll meet influential women through the shop, you know. I'll be able to network like mad. I've got an autumn fashion show in mind, all proceeds to our camp, our babies."

They were both quiet over the evening meal, tussling with their memories of the camp. The stench, the cold, the hunger, the dying babies. At length Dougie said, "I know what's in your mind, Ginnie. That we've kind of caved in. That nobody, including us, does enough. But what is enough?"

"Enough is all of you. Giving all of you. But I can't do it, Dougie. I can go and help but I have to come away again before it gets too much. I want my own life. That's the truth."

"Same here," he said relievedly. "I'm no hero either. One of the Henry plays from Shakespeare has a phrase — 'a warrior for the working day'. That's me. A commonplace kind of warrior. No glory attached." He looked down at her, solemn and wistful. "But that's how it goes. Little you. Little me."

She felt better when the Croatia decision had been made. The death of Frank O'Connor, last time out, never ceased to haunt her thoughts and going out again seemed a kind of restitution for the waste of a good life. She wanted a moral dimension in her life. She wasn't good at explaining it but it was what made her give up everything to look after her mother until it all got too much.

Being good, doing good, had such a sickly ring to it these days. People were suspicious of motives. But she wasn't prepared to give up on it entirely. She saw her attitude like one of the old, lop-sided trucks in the last convoy: getting stuck in ruts, falling into ditches, losing part of its freight to theft and carelessness. All you could say was that it kept going.

The shop was looking good. She decided to dress the windows with the useful little suits that were coming back into women's lives, the skirt lengths everything from very short to ankle length and against their formal intent she set a frivolity of blouses, tops, waistcoats, scarves and costume jewellery and the good leather handbags her clients insisted upon.

Inside, she had floaty dresses, long floral skirts and the two-pieces that were always in demand for weddings. Looking at the latter she was drawn to one that was tea-coloured lace over satin. The skirt was discreetly knee-length, the jacket nipped at the waist and with a little stand-up collar. The pocket flaps were set

at an angle and satin edged, the buttons
— dozens of them — tiny and satin
covered. When there was nobody around
she tried it on. As she had suspected,
it fitted her perfectly. She saw it with
matching shoes and tights and a hat
with a deep crown, turned-back brim
and maybe pale blue flowers.

To set it off, what it needed, of course,
was a bouquet. Something dainty and
minimal. What she was looking at was
a wedding dress. Her head spun as she
turned to look at the back view. So,
was it the time? Was it no accident, the
perfect wedding suit awaiting her on the
stand? She had ordered it, after all.

Dougie was coming to pick her up. She
decided she would keep the outfit on till
he arrived and see what he thought about
it. She acknowledged she was still scared
somewhere inside: marriage would ask a
lot of her. But something in her was
urging her to give, not to be restrained
in what she felt for Dougie. She was
more used to keeping herself in reserve,
she had not given emotionally for a very
long time before Dougie, not even to her
mother.

He knew what she had in mind as soon as she opened the door to him.

"What's this?" he demanded. "Christmas?"

She twirled ahead of him, eyes alight with pleasure. Dougie amazed was a disarming sight. So much so she had no option but to hug him, to let him hug her back and then hug him again. If Sydney made his usual batwinged subliminal appearance from her unconscious, she knew he no longer mattered. She would dance on his memory at her wedding. Stamp on him with her tea-coloured satin shoes.

* * *

Helen Macreevy thought long and hard in her ruminative way before approaching Dr Meera Singh about contributing clothes, goods or money for the Croatia project. Ginnie had stated categorically she couldn't do it: not go up cold to someone she hadn't met and put the bite on her. Helen had met Dr Singh, Ginnie argued, she really ought to go.

"If she's a Muslim, she'll want to help, surely," Ginnie argued uncertainly.

"But she may be Hindu."

"She'll still want to help starving babies, surely."

Meera Singh's face as she answered Helen's ring was not exactly welcoming. Maybe that was understandable, Helen thought, her own face beginning to flush. There had not exactly been a neighbourhood rush to welcome Dr Singh into the sisterhood of coffee mornings and charity committees. Excuses in the main had been on the lame side, on the lines of let them settle in first. But she herself should have done more. Guilt made her voice sound high and artificial.

"Our neighbours Dougie Walker and Ginnie Carter are taking a truckload of supplies out to Croatia. We wondered if you would like to contribute. We're giving things like warm clothes, toiletries, tinned goods, maybe a few sweets and toys for the children."

"Come in," said Meera Singh, after a slight discomfiting pause. "What about dressings, disinfectant, that sort of thing? Soap, maybe."

"Oh, wonderful," said Helen relievedly. She passed a large brass statuette of the little elephant god, Ganesh, in the hall and sniffed something delicious and spicy coming from the kitchen.

"Mother is busy in there," said Meera. "I won't spring you on her. She likes to be forewarned of visitors." She led the way instead into a sumptuous sitting-room full of hot colour, varied textures and unusual ornaments. In her elegant red and green sari she looked like some full-blown exotic flower herself, Helen decided. But despite the warmth of the background, what she was getting from Dr Singh was not welcoming vibes. Rather, constraint and even a certain chilliness. Helen began to regret she had come. Still, it did not do to be too thin-skinned when you were doing charitable tasks. You could ask for others what you would not dream of asking for yourself.

"They've been before, Dougie and Ginnie, to Croatia, I mean. Ginnie still has nightmares about what she saw. An aid worker killed by a sniper's bullet. And the children, the babies . . . she said it was indescribable."

There was no response. She looked and to her horror saw two fat round tears emerge from Meera Singh's rather beautiful dark eyes and meander, almost caressingly, down her cheeks.

"Whatever is the matter? Is it something I've said? Oh, look, I never meant to upset you! I'll go — I'll come back." Helen scarcely knew what she was saying but Dr Singh lifted an arm and dashed the tears away almost imperiously.

"Don't go. I do want to help. Very much. It's just — " She looked away, turning her handsome profile towards the window, fighting for composure. "It's just that this morning my youngest son has gone away to boarding-school and I am finding the house so very empty without all of them. They've all gone now, you see, every last one. I have my work and I have their grandmother but it is not the same." She smiled at last, a watery, wavery smile. "I am so sorry. I suppose it will pass. I just feel — well, lonely and more than a little redundant."

"Oh, gosh," said Helen warmly. She rose from the chair she was in and joined Meera on the large flowered settee, patting her hand. "Oh, I do understand. Mine are away, too, you see. All over the place. I'm very proud of them but I wish — " She stopped and Meera Singh's free hand came over and squeezed hers. Helen felt emotion welling up in her, welling and welling till it seemed all the words were going to be stopped up in her throat. But she felt Meera give their joined hands a little shake. "I'll get tea, shall I?" said Meera, "and we can have a weep on each other's shoulders. Metaphorically speaking." She gave a somewhat shamefaced smile.

"I should have come round sooner," said Helen. "But I've been so worried about our Elizabeth — "

38

IDA and Tracy stood close together in the airport lounge. Closer than need be. Huddled, as though seeking some simple animal warmth from each other. Ida's eyes were dark with the tears she was willing herself not to shed.

"I can't leave Norman any longer. You understand? He doesn't know how to use the washing-machine."

"Then teach him," said Tracy. "He might turn out to have a talent for it." She grinned at her mother, willing her to lighten up. She didn't want her crossing the Atlantic with that sad, lugubrious face on her. She didn't, when it came down to it, want her to go at all. Her mother had suddenly become too vulnerable, too ready to show signs of middle age, too uncertain.

"Tell Norman from me he's to be good to you," she said. "And don't worry. It'll work out here."

"Not with your dad it won't. Will

you not go and see him, Tracy? Just once more? Before he leaves Pinkmount Drive?"

Tracy's face took on that stubborn, immutable expression Ida knew only too well. The look that said she would pursue a certain course of action, come what may. Ida's late father had identified it as perhaps the one family trait that superseded all others. "Always marching towards the sound of the guns." Never mind the danger. People like Tracy refused to see it was even there. She was going to marry Gordon. That was it. A measure of reluctant admiration and respect eased Ida's going, made her squeeze Tracy's arm till it hurt.

They had said all that was to be said, after all. There came a point where you could no longer influence or dominate your children, only let them know you would never cease to care about them. When the time came for Ida to board her plane, they held each other close. Ida patted her child's back and watched as she walked away, accumulating admiring glances in her brief skirt, black tights and stylish shoes, bobbed hair swaying like silk in a breeze.

When Tracy and Gordon went for a meal together that night neither was inclined to say very much. Tracy toyed with her Thai chicken and Gordon pushed his peppered steak away half-eaten. At length, over the coffee, he said desperately, "Maybe what your father says is right. Maybe I've no right to put you through all this."

"What do you mean?"

"You're missing your mum, aren't you? You don't like being at odds with her."

"I never said that."

"It's obvious. Look at you, you've eaten nothing."

"I'm not hungry."

"What is it, then? You're not still brooding about what Melanie said? Melanie was well out of order. But I've spoken to her. I've told her she can have the house. And the Range Rover. It's surprising how that has calmed her down."

"Mum wanted me to try and patch it up with Dad."

His face hardened. "I knew it. Your

mother had one last go at you, didn't she?"

"Not to go back and stay with him. Just patch things up."

"You know he won't wear it. I've tried to get him to see reason. You go back and stay with him, we've had it, haven't we?" He rubbed his temple with his thumb, a habit he had when distracted. "He's made it clear. It's a direct choice between him and me, hard as it is for you, Tracy. What is it to be?"

"You know what I've decided." But it came out sullenly somehow. Her face had reverted to that of an alienated teenager.

In his fear he became blustering. "I haven't forced you to love me, have I, Tracy? What happened just happened, didn't it? And I've done all I could to get your dad to see reason. I've offered him work. I would never willingly come between a man and his daughter. I do try to be Joe Do-as-you-would-be-done-by."

As her expression barely changed, in fact if anything became more sulky and intransigent, he said in a hard voice, "Well, go back to him then. We'll kid ourselves none of this ever happened."

"He is my dad."

"Nobody's disputing that."

"And I didn't have him around for a long time."

He imprisoned her right hand that had been toying with a spoon. "I understand. I do understand. But what move has he made towards us, Tracy? He really has it in for me." He could feel no response in the cold, still fingers that lay between his palms and he put them away from him with a sudden spurt of anger. "Do you want me to walk out of here, then? Is that it? Because I will. If you want me to. And I won't look back."

At last it seemed he had got through. She said in a frightened voice, "Let's go somewhere else."

"Where?"

"Anywhere. In the car. Anywhere."

He drove to the wood that lay off the road on the way to the pub where they had had their first meetings. He turned off the engine and sat back in his seat, his face grim.

"You made up your mind, then? You're going back to your dad?"

"The house is sold. He'll be moving into somewhere much smaller." She turned to face him with her piercing honest gaze, that look of transparent candour that had so enslaved him from the start. "He's going to be lost, Gordon. No Sylvia. No me. No job."

"He brought it all on himself."

She said with difficulty, "He wanted to make things up to me. He knew where he'd gone wrong. He wasn't a bad father, you know. All he wanted was to guide me, help me get a basis for my future. Maybe I should. Get some skills, some education."

"You could do that with me."

She touched his shoulder almost skittishly. "Look what happened with Melanie. You didn't like what she did."

"She went over the top. She jettisoned our home life, our emotional life. You wouldn't do that. You've too much common sense."

She said, with a huge uncontrollable sob rising in her throat, "I can't ever leave you. I love you too much."

He pulled her into his arms. Their lips met, at first to reassure, then to state the ineluctable essence of their being together, then to call up past bliss and finally to repeat all that had gone before. He opened the car door, urging they should go into the back and there they battled for closeness almost like opposing armies, falling back under the onslaught of passion only to advance again for more.

They hurled endearments like lances meant to pierce the heart, they tore at clothes like the savage dogs of war, they broke the truce of quiescence with fierce forays, body to body. Until, like armies falling away into the dusk after battle, they lay in the sweat of ardour and endeavour listening to the late call of birds, the fading notes of day, scarcely knowing if they would rise to fight another day.

"O my America," he said.

"What does it mean? I don't know what it means."

"I can teach you that," he promised. "I can teach you about poetry, about music."

"What can I teach you?" she teased, nipping his cheek with her teeth. "Only

408

about love. That goes on forever."

"Teach me," he implored solemnly. "I'm signed up. Sewn up. Committed."

They did not go to the pub afterwards. They were worn out with passion and argument, too tired even to drink.

And despite everything they were back to the question that never went away: should she see her father again? It wouldn't go away because the silken ties of blood and family never dissolved, could never be entirely shaken off.

Before he dropped her off at her digs, he said with a mouth that felt it had come straight from the dentist, "Well, go and see him then. There will be no peace till you do."

"Why are you scared?" she demanded.

"I just am," he answered and would not meet her eyes.

★ ★ ★

"Daddy, it's me." The shiver in her voice reverberated down the telephone wires. "Can I come and see you?"

Silence. Then, "You picked your time. I'm moving out."

"Today?"

"Aye. This very day. As I say, you've picked your time."

"I could come and help."

"How?"

"Make tea for the men."

"Doesn't seem worth it," he said disdainfully.

"I will come," she said decisively. "I want to see you, Dad. See you're all right."

"I'm all right." The voice rougher. "Come if you like. That's your style these days, isn't it?"

The men had emptied the top rooms and were burrowing purposefully into the lower ones. Some of the furniture had been sold, some was going south to the new flat which Sylvia and Conrad had leased and the remainder to a two-bedroomed semi in a street off the main shopping thoroughfare in Wilhowbry, which would be Arthur's new home. Arthur suggested that if Tracy really wanted to be useful, she should go on ahead to the new place to supervise the unloading there and he would come along when the big house was finally emptied and he had turned the key on his past. He was being reasonably nice to her, seemed pleased to see her and she wanted to do all she could for him, to be daughterly and caring and reparative. The situation, though, was undercut by all the rows and bitterness that had gone before and even as she worked she could feel a kind of subliminal trembling all through her being, as though she were up for some kind of test or judgement and did not know the outcome.

The street of the new house must be one of the most modest in all of prosperous Wilhowbry, she thought, the terraced houses and semis jammed close together, the kerb lined bumper to bumper with dusty cars for which there were no garages. Some houses were better cared for than others and Tracy felt a sharp pang of disappointment to note that her father's was shabbier than nearly all of them, its windows still bearing the tatty, over-patterned nets of the previous owner. The first thing she did was to take them down. Then she made sure the removal men laid the carpet her father had indicated was for the sitting-room and that with a sofa, two chairs and a coffee table this would provide some kind of comfort while the rest was put in order. After providing the movers with yet more tea (what kind of bladders did they have?) she turned her attention to the larger of the two bedrooms, making up the bed, putting up curtains which, though overlong, would give some privacy. Her wish to please and impress her father made her tireless. By the time he had arrived she had even been to a neighbourhood shop and had a salad with cold ham ready on the kitchen table. He did not, however, commend her, merely sat down and ate in automatic fashion, after which he tinkered with the television in order to get the six o'clock news. After that they lay back, boneless, and watched more television. She said she would stay the night, sleep on the sofa and help him further in the morning.

39

SHE wanted to say to him, 'This house can never be yours'. It was too shabby, too intransigently small, its cheap walls flaking and its floors throwing up traps of uneven wood and lino. The kitchen was especially depressing, with gaps between the gimcrack wall units, faulty taps, a chipped sink. Tracy felt hot tears of anger and resentment. After the comfort and elegance of Pinkmount Drive it seemed a dreadful ignominy. The council house back home in Scotland had known austerity, but her mother and grandmother had kept it clean, sharp, decent, the best of its kind. It was the difference, she perceived, between pride and desperation. This was a desperate hole. Why had her father ever bought it?

She tried to get the kitchen as straight as it would go, arranging storage jars, cleaning tiles behind the cooker, even putting some flowers at the window. But when her father came in to join her for coffee, she said, "What made you pick it?" indicating the kitchen's inadequacies with a sweep of her arm.

"I didn't pick it." He was wearing the same shirt as yesterday, grubby from removal grime. "I just took the first place the estate agent offered at my price. What does it matter? It's a roof." He stirred his drink with enormous concentration. "What matters is: are you coming here to stay with me? You could soon smarten it up. Women are good at that sort of thing."

"You know I'm not, Dad. Gordon and me are getting married just as soon as the divorce comes through. I'll stay till then, if you like. I'll help you all I can."

"That's not the deal. You either go to him or you stay with me. Period. You know I want you to get a life of your own before you marry anyone." He threw down his spoon. "What do you know about anything? You might look grown-up and sophisticated, but you're as green as grass."

"I know what I want." His image

shimmered at her through a haze of tears.

"And that's what?"

"Someone to love me."

"Your parents love you. You're not saying Ida and me don't care about you?"

"Someone for me. Someone I choose."

"Ach." He almost spat the sound. "He tried to buy me off with the offer of a job. I listened to all his blarney about what he felt for you. A grown man going on like a love-sick calf. He's promising you everything now but wait, just wait. Gordon Pershor puts work first, last and foremost. You'll end up in a big, posh house counting the delphiniums."

"Is that what you did to Sylvia?" she said.

He didn't answer her. She saw his jaw, the firm, square Blaney jaw that she had inherited, clamp round the sides of his mouth, pulling the contours into the very set of disillusion, negativity and worse. She felt a cold rush of pity, a flash of insight lighting like neon in her brain: he couldn't, wouldn't be reached. Things had gone too far. If she stayed he would twist her too, make her say cruel things she shouldn't. She scraped back her chair.

"I'm sorry," she said awkwardly. "I shouldn't have said that. Daddy, I think for both our sakes I have to go."

He looked at her and said, almost mildly, "Aye, maybe so. And for the record, yes, it *is* what I did to Sylvia, so let it be a warning to you."

"I'll ring you."

"You do that. Just don't bring him round here. He won't be welcome."

★ ★ ★

He had said to Gordon Pershor that he would find a job. Any job. So he went down to the job centre and they were there, the miserably paid, the part-time, the lowly opportunities in the service industries. Jobs. There was one in a timber yard. He took it. On the first morning they put a broom in his hand and asked him to sweep up the yard.

It wasn't so bad. He liked the smell of timber, he enjoyed keeping a tally of the ranks of stacked wood, cutting off lengths for DIY shops and the amateurs who made their own cupboards and shelves. He wore a brown overall and kept a series of pens in the top pocket — they had to be at the ready for swift calculations.

The others didn't bother him. They were men who had been hemmed in all their lives by narrow expectations, in work that gave them security without anything left over for fun. They were sticklers about seniority, about order, about keeping the yard tidy, mean and humourless to a man. He became like them, folding the greaseproof papers from his midday sandwich into a neat square before putting them in the bin, watching the clock, not leaving a minute before or after 5.30.

At home he had the car. It amused him to have the very old Standard that nevertheless started on the button no matter how cold the morning. He tinkered with it endlessly, tuning up the engine, cleaning the chrome, waxing and polishing the bodywork. It still looked what it was, an old banger, but he felt an affection for it he had never known towards the company cars he had previously driven.

Tracy rang and said she didn't suppose he would come to the wedding. He said she was right in her supposition but on The Day he thought of her and the time he had gone to Scotland and come face to face with this bright-faced creature in his own image.

His hatred for Gordon Pershor was deep and unshakeable. He saw him as a usurper. He would not listen to the crystal note of bliss in Tracy's voice. What had the first flush of sexual happiness to do with anything? Life came up with more and more posers, got more and more complex and difficult and he had wanted Tracy to become impregnable. He had wanted to teach her to drive. He had wanted to take her to the Highlands to find out all about his mother's clan, the Macphersons. He had wanted to take her on a fly-and-drive holiday, teach her about cricket. In moments of truth he saw he had wanted to keep her in a kind of semi-childhood, so that he could go back and recover for both of them what they had missed.

Anyway, she was gone. He did not

even allow her to visit in case her happiness broke him down, made self-recognition of what he had become too much to bear. But she telephoned and remembered his birthday. She was his as he had first seen her, with her big unselfconscious smile and her inimitable way, with its Scots inflexion, of denoting his most meaningful role: Daddy.

Sylvia he barely thought of as a separate entity, more as part of that golden era in his life when he had been able to afford it all, when he had made speeches at fat dinners and rubbed shoulders with what he had then thought of as the great and good. The recession had brought a number of them down, sometimes in quite spectacular fashion. By degrees he allowed back the memory of that day, the day he had been called in and told his services would no longer be required. Probably, all told, the bitterest day of his life. Had no one ever thought of setting up a Post-Redundancy Trauma Unit? Because he did not know anyone to whom it had happened who had not reeled from the experience as though hit by a thunderbolt or been altered like a face in a distorting mirror. The paint-stripper they sold at the yard had nothing on it. The process was just as blistering.

This was the way the world changed, on the edge of the great millennium. He doubted if even the politicians and academics knew how things would shake down after the snowstorm settled in the little glass ball. Class, status, steady jobs, full-time jobs, the pecking order, would they all go? And how would society work if there was no one to look up to and no one on whom to look down?

One free Saturday he took the old car out and drove along Pinkmount Drive, thinking that maybe it held the answer. Once it had seemed the centre of the world. Middle class. Middle England. Tolerant, dutiful and blinkered. And what if, as Sylvia was fond of quoting, for she had loved the Irish poet Yeats, the centre could not hold? Did things then fall apart? Would 'mere anarchy' be loosed upon the world? Was it already there?

He stopped the car at the top end of the drive, where he could see the golf club, of which he was no longer a member, and a gaggle of plus-two'd sportsmen set out for the Saturday afternoon competition. Would old Bertie Macreevy be among them? He was fond of his old neighbour, seeing his long battle against the state of retirement as something heroic, or at least semi-heroic. With no more real battles to fight, he'd taken the struggle to the bunkers and putting greens. With a smile, he remembered how Bertie had made him laugh the day before his court appearance.

As though converging in his line of thought, a Porsche driven by a woman in a sari went past, with Helen Macreevy in animated chatter by the driver's side. He thought Helen caught sight of him, her head tilting and jaw dropping as the big car moved out of sight.

He'd heard Ginnie and Dougie had got married and the new gown shop was doing well. Mavis Higgison was clinging on to her mansion but it had borne a forlorn look as he'd driven past.

He had been happy here, but it had been an unthinking, unexamined happiness. A kind of neutrality. Sylvia had said in one of her less kind moments that he was emotionally illiterate. Not now. He knew the book from A to Z.

He switched on the engine, let in the clutch and drove back down the avenue fast, so the houses merged in a kind of blur. No answer here. He was still in free fall and who knew where he would land?

THE END

TO FIGHT THE WILD
Rod Ansell and Rachel Percy

Lost in uncharted Australian bush, Rod Ansell survived by hunting and trapping wild animals, improvising shelter and using all the bushman's skills he knew.

COROMANDEL
Pat Barr

India in the 1830s is a hot, uncomfortable place, where the East India Company still rules. Amelia and her new husband find themselves caught up in the animosities which seethe between the old order and the new.

THE SMALL PARTY
Lillian Beckwith

A frightening journey to safety begins for Ruth and her small party as their island is caught up in the dangers of armed insurrection.

THE WILDERNESS WALK
Sheila Bishop

Stifling unpleasant memories of a misbegotten romance in Cleave with Lord Francis Aubrey, Lavinia goes on holiday there with her sister. The two women are thrust into a romantic intrigue involving none other than Lord Francis.

THE RELUCTANT GUEST
Rosalind Brett

Ann Calvert went to spend a month on a South African farm with Theo Borland and his sister. They both proved to be different from her first idea of them, and there was Storr Peterson — the most disturbing man she had ever met.

ONE ENCHANTED SUMMER
Anne Tedlock Brooks

A tale of mystery and romance and a girl who found both during one enchanted summer.

CLOUD OVER MALVERTON
Nancy Buckingham

Dulcie soon realises that something is seriously wrong at Malverton, and when violence strikes she is horrified to find herself under suspicion of murder.

AFTER THOUGHTS
Max Bygraves

The Cockney entertainer tells stories of his East End childhood, of his RAF days, and his post-war showbusiness successes and friendships with fellow comedians.

MOONLIGHT
AND MARCH ROSES
D. Y. Cameron

Lynn's search to trace a missing girl takes her to Spain, where she meets Clive Hendon. While untangling the situation, she untangles her emotions and decides on her own future.

NURSE ALICE IN LOVE
Theresa Charles

Accepting the post of nurse to little Fernie Sherrod, Alice Everton could not guess at the romance, suspense and danger which lay ahead at the Sherrod's isolated estate.

POIROT INVESTIGATES
Agatha Christie

Two things bind these eleven stories together — the brilliance and uncanny skill of the diminutive Belgian detective, and the stupidity of his Watson-like partner, Captain Hastings.

LET LOOSE THE TIGERS
Josephine Cox

Queenie promised to find the long-lost son of the frail, elderly murderess, Hannah Jason. But her enquiries threatened to unlock the cage where crucial secrets had long been held captive.